IMP(the)OSSIBILITY T(of)OMORROW

D1057149

IMPOSSIBILITY the

TOMORROW of

AVERY WILLIAMS

SIMON & SCHUSTER BFYR

New York London Toronto Sydney New Delhi

SIMON & SCHUSTER BFYR

An imprint of Simon & Schuster Children's Publishing Division
1230 Avenue of the Americas, New York, New York 10020
For information about special discounts for bulk purchases, please contact Simon &
Schuster Special Sales at 1-866-506-1949 or business@simonandschuster.com.
The Simon & Schuster Speakers Bureau can bring authors to your live event.
For more information or to book an event, contact the Simon & Schuster Speakers
Bureau at 1-866-248-3049 or visit our website at www.simonspeakers.com

alloy**entertainment**
Produced by Alloy Entertainment
151 West 26th Street, New York, NY 10001
Also available in a SIMON & SCHUSTER BFYR hardcover edition

Book design by Liz Drezner
The text for this book is set in Janson.
Manufactured in the United States of America
First SIMON & SCHUSTER BFYR paperback edition June 2014
2 4 6 8 10 9 7 5 3 1
The Library of Congress has cataloged the hardcover edition as follows:
Williams, Avery, 1977–
The impossibility of tomorrow / Avery Williams.
p. cm.
Summary: Seraphina enjoys a life free from her controlling ex-boyfriend and purses
a relationship with Noah, who delivers a message from Seraphina's ex that threatens
to expose her secret and reveals frightening truths about her new friends.
ISBN: 978-1-4424-4319-8 (hc)
1. Alchemy—Juvenile fiction. 2. Immortality—Juvenile fiction.
[Fic]—dc23
2013951943
ISBN 978-1-4424-4320-4 (pbk)
ISBN 978-1-4424-4321-1 (eBook)

FOR VENDETTA LUNA,

escape artist, tiny ghost, adventurer, and friend

ONE

In 1812, there was an earthquake in the unlikely location of New Madrid, Missouri. It was so violent and ruptured the ground with such force that the Mississippi River temporarily ran backward. Cyrus and I were living in Manhattan at the time, and I remember what he said to me as we strolled through the market: "It takes an earthquake to alter the course of a river. What does it take to change the course of a life?"

I wish I didn't know how easily it is done. I wish I didn't know that sometimes, a life pivots from its intended path in the wake of the tiniest thing.

Sometimes all it takes is one word.

Alchemy.

It can be uttered by a platinum-haired boy as he pulls out a vial of potion dangling on a silver chain. Or delivered the modern way, electronically, the brightly backlit screen of a cell phone belying the dark message it displays.

I sink to my knees on the musty, stained carpet of Cyrus's motel room. Kailey Morgan's iPhone lies in front of me, unharmed from when I dropped it on the carpet. I want to smash that stupid phone. But I don't. I pick it up, coaxing it back to life with trembling fingers, and stare blankly at the Words with Friends screen, as the last droplets of hope evaporate from my soul.

It's still there. *Alchemy.* The word was played on Noah Vander's phone. It must have been typed with Noah's fingers. But it couldn't have come from Noah. Only one person in Berkeley knows what that word truly means.

Cyrus.

My longest companion, my greatest enemy, who would cage me like a bird. Who used alchemy to make me what I am now: an Incarnate, a wandering soul who takes up residence in human bodies. When I ran away from the coven several weeks ago, it was with one vow in my heart: that I would never again take another life. I was ready to die. I only took sixteen-year-old Kailey Morgan's body by mistake, when her car crashed right in front of me, a fiery display of gasoline and cracked glass.

I look upward, at the bare bulb that illuminates the motel room, suddenly feeling exposed. I shove the phone in my pocket and dart to the light switch, flipping it off. The room disappears into a velvety, choking darkness. I blink, waiting for my eyes to adjust.

I don't think Cyrus will kill me for leaving him. In his own sick, twisted way, he loves me too much for that. But one way or another, he'll make me pay. He's already made me pay by taking Noah.

A volcano of pain erupts in my heart. A sob rises from deep inside me as I picture Noah's beautiful face, his strong jaw, his smiling lapis-lazuli eyes as he holds up his camera, his hand pushing his reckless crow-colored hair out of the way. The next time I see him, his face will be transformed by Cyrus's soul, a hideous change that will be invisible to everyone except me. The thought of Cyrus inside of Noah's body, of Noah's soul shoved out into an uncaring foggy night, is almost unbearable.

A loud peal of laughter sounds from outside the room, from the direction of the parking lot, followed by a heavy footstep on the stair. My heart starts to thud. Whoever's making those footfalls is big—much bigger than me. And suddenly I realize that the message on Kailey's phone means so much more than Noah's death.

It means Cyrus knows who I am. And even worse, *where* I am. He's probably right outside, waiting for me to emerge.

The image of the rabbits we dissected in Cyrus's biology class flits through my mind. *A rabbit is a prey animal*, he'd said while posing as a substitute teacher named Mr. Shaw. *And its best chance at survival is to outrun its hunter. Sometimes escape is the best defense, better than any teeth or claws.*

But I have been running for way too long. I have lost this game, and it's time to face him. My pulse hammers in my ears as I turn the knob and open the door. A blast of damp air meets me.

But the man on the stairs isn't Cyrus. He's tall and thin, with deep brown skin and a neatly trimmed goatee. He's carrying a woman, whose head is tipped back. She's giggling softly.

He looks up at me. "Well, hello there," he says, somewhat gallantly, though he's slurring his words. The woman laughs louder.

"Put me down," she demands. "I'm too heavy for you."

"Yeah, right," he answers, shifting her weight. "You're drunk, baby. You'll fall down these stairs." He leans over and kisses her cheek.

"We just got married!" the woman exclaims to me, punctuating her statement with a small hiccup. "We're a family now!"

At the word *family*, a coldness that has nothing to do with the night's mist settles upon me. A slow realization, an icy chill that hisses as it laps in my veins. It's not just Noah who was in danger. And not just me, either.

Kailey's family, who I've come to love, is utterly defenseless against Cyrus. Her mother, her father. Her brother Bryan, who I think of as my own. Cyrus could be at their house, right now.

I squeeze past the couple on the stairs and sprint to the Dumpster, where I'd stashed Bryan's bike earlier. The woman calls after me. "Hey! Aren't you going to congratulate us?"

"Congratulations!" I call, tears pooling in my eyes as I hoist myself onto the bike. "Hold on tight to each other. While you can," I add under my breath. All my time on Earth has shown me that love is a rare and fleeting thing.

TWO

The road looks flat, but the burning in my legs and my ragged breath tell me it's uphill. I pedal faster, away from Cyrus's motel room, squinting as the cold, damp air blasts my eyes, coaxing tears from their corners.

I throw the bike into its highest gear and swerve to avoid a pile of crushed glass from a car's shattered window. I gulp air, ignoring the pain in my exhausted muscles as I steer into the center of the lane.

I coast through a red light without bothering to look for cars. There's no one else out at 4 A.M. on a Friday in

November. No one to witness the immortal disguised as a young girl pedaling furiously along the road that leads back to the Morgans.

Cyrus wouldn't hesitate to kill Kailey's family in order to punish me—and to give me a warning never to run away from him again. I can picture him now: his ice-blue eyes, his falsely angelic face. *See what happens when you disobey me, Sera?* he'd say. *People die. Innocent people. And I know how much you hate that.*

The others in our coven—Jared, Sébastien, Charlotte, and Amelia—wanted what Cyrus offered. Perhaps this is why they never felt guilty for what they did, why they only laughed when I described us as monsters. Because that's what I think I am—a monster, a predator, a killer. Whenever I said those words to Cyrus, he just smiled, like he enjoyed it. He must have loved taking Noah's body.

I bite my lip to keep from crying. *Oh, Noah*, I think, blinking back tears. *I am so sorry.*

The boy I love is dead. But the Morgans might be alive. There's a chance I can save them, and I cling to that thought. I won't be able to beat Cyrus in a physical fight, but I can placate him by leaving with him—and take him far away from Kailey's family.

North Berkeley flies by as I near the Morgans'

neighborhood, a blur of restaurants and vintage houses presided over by redwood trees and Japanese maples. My legs have finally, mercifully, gone numb from the exertion.

I wish I could say the same for my heart.

I turn off Shattuck and enter a leafy expanse, coming to a stop in front of the Morgans' house, a Craftsman bungalow with an unwieldy, storybook garden. My heart slams in my chest. But Cyrus, wearing Noah's body, isn't outside waiting for me as I had expected.

For a moment I just stand there. It feels as though I'm watching myself from outside my body: a small, solitary figure in the middle of an empty, lonely road. The silence is as thick as the fog, and in the early morning gloom, I feel obvious. A beacon. Hunted. But no, I remind myself. I'm the hunter now. I wish I really believed that.

Dismounting from Bryan's bike, I tug it over the root-broken sidewalk and leave it inside the Morgans' chipped picket fence. Across the street, Mr. Vander's Lexus is parked at the curb. It looks fairly new but is marred with dents and scratches, missing a side mirror. Noah's father is a drinker. Noah's bedroom window is dark, just like the rest of his house. Keeping to the shadows, I watch, looking for the smallest movement, the tiniest shift in the curtain that will reveal Cyrus's presence. But there's nothing.

I turn and walk up the Morgans' slick wooden steps,

adrenaline coursing through my veins. When I try the doorknob, it opens easily. I suck in my breath. Did I leave it unlocked? I left in such a hurry that I can't remember.

My scalp prickles as I step into the foyer. I pause, allowing my eyes to adjust to the darkness, dreading the unspeakable carnage I fear I will see. But surprisingly, nothing is out of place. Mrs. Morgan's leather purse hangs from a large brass hook, and several colorful umbrellas are folded into a wrought-iron stand. In the living room, two pillow-laden velvet couches slump on faded Persian rugs. The refrigerator hums in the kitchen, and I can hear the faint sound of Mrs. Morgan snoring from the hallway that leads to the master bedroom.

I move softly in the opposite direction. Bryan's door is open a crack, and relief settles over me at the sight of him, tangled up in his sheets, his chest rising and falling with reassuring regularity.

At least I don't have their lives on my hands. Yet.

Cyrus will come for me before the night is over to take me back to the coven. He'll force me to switch bodies and keep me on a closer leash than ever. I won't go down without a fight, though. I have no illusions—I'll probably fail. He's stronger than me, more ruthless, and altogether more deadly.

But I need to try.

I tiptoe through the living room and stumble into a stool at the kitchen counter, wincing as it hits the floor with a loud crash. For a long, panicked moment, I wait for the Morgans to stir or for Cyrus to leap out from behind the curtains to grab me. But when no one emerges from the darkness, I grab a knife from the wooden block in the kitchen, then pad back down the hallway.

The shadows are long and the hardwood floor groans under my weight, no matter how lightly I try to step. I hear a noise from the bathroom and cock my head, holding my breath. But it's just the water that always drips from the old faucet. In Kailey's room, I look around quickly, expecting Cyrus to be sitting under her window or sprawled out on her bed. But it's empty. I latch her door and the window. Flimsy locks, both of them. They won't stop Cyrus. But they'll buy me precious seconds.

I crawl onto Kailey's bed, my hand wrapped tightly around the knife, and lean against the wall. I'm ready.

Let him come.

THREE

There's a loud bang on the door to Kailey's room.

"Kailey—is your door *locked*? Are you okay?" Mrs. Morgan's voice is stressed.

I blink my bleary eyes, trying to understand what's happening. My neck is painfully stiff, and I'm still gripping the knife. I must have fallen asleep.

"Can you hear me? You're going to be late for school," she calls. "Open this door!"

I try to speak, but my throat is dry. "I'm . . . I'm up. Just a second." I unwrap my fingers from the knife's handle, ignoring the stabbing pain that courses through my hand.

After hiding it underneath Kailey's pillow, I open the door.

Mrs. Morgan is ready for work in crisp wool trousers and a green blouse that matches her eyes. Her wheat-blond hair is pulled back in a low ponytail. Concern flickers across her face as she takes in my appearance. I'm fully dressed in yesterday's jeans and sweater; I even have sneakers on.

"Did you sleep in your clothes?" she asks, narrowing her eyes. "What's going on in here? Why did you lock the door?"

"I fell asleep reading," I lie. "And what's wrong with a little privacy?" I try to approximate a casual teenage surliness.

"Okay, Miss Cranky. There's nothing wrong with privacy—you just had me worried." She frowns. "It's not like you to lock the door. You'd better get ready for school. Bryan had an early practice, but Noah will be here any minute to pick you up." She closes the door with an exaggerated flourish.

I'm numb—and confused. Why am I still here? Why didn't Cyrus come for me?

In a fog, I drag a brush through my chin-length dark blond hair, wincing as it pulls at the tangles. Noah and I ate Thai takeout on the beach last night, and salt and sand are crusted in my hair. I finally give up, pinning it back with barrettes that I find on Kailey's vanity.

I pull on gray cords and a black button-up shirt in slow

motion. Glancing dully at the getaway bag I packed just last night, I take out my few belongings and place them in Kailey's backpack. My hands hit something solid and heavy—the bottle of Kailey's jasmine perfume, the scent so indefinably her.

The room swims, and I collapse at Kailey's desk. Her room is colorful with its peacock's palette, its evergreens and violets, as colorful as I imagine her personality was. And here I sit, a drab grayness, an absence, sucking the life out of the jewel-toned walls just as I sucked the life out of Kailey's body the night she died in Jack London Square. I feel so empty. A husk. A body without a soul inside.

When the dizziness subsides, my eyes focus on one of Kailey's paintings. A vaguely familiar girl with shaggy brown hair stands on top of a cathedral, balanced between two sides of a roof that pitch steeply away. She has a guitar strapped to her back like a quiver of arrows. From the lift of her hair and the sway of her feather earrings, it's clear that the wind is blowing, but she looks so surefooted. In the sky above her floats another girl with blond hair and wings that glint in the setting sun's light.

"Kailey! Noah's here!" Mrs. Morgan calls from down the hall.

Game time.

The kitchen knife is too unwieldy to hide in my bag, so I

rummage through Kailey's desk for the Swiss army knife I saw there last week. It's pathetic, but it's something.

My resolve has not changed. Cyrus has come to drive me back to San Francisco, where he'll lock me in our condo for as long as it takes to break me, to make me his again. But with any luck, we won't make it farther than the Bay Bridge. I will attack him the first chance I get.

In the kitchen, Mrs. Morgan is murmuring to the boy she thinks is Noah. He's wearing an argyle sweater that I've never seen before, and his hair is neater than usual. I try to lock my grief in a glass box deep inside me. But looking at Not-Noah—at his broad shoulders, the hands I held just yesterday, the lips I kissed—creates hairline fractures in its walls. Even now I find him beautiful. I grit my teeth and ignore the way my stupid heart tugs at the sight of him. *It isn't Noah*, I remind myself.

"Hey, guys," I say carefully.

Mrs. Morgan looks up. "We were just talking about that teacher who was killed last night. It's all over the news. Awful, absolutely awful."

His eyes are as bloodshot as mine. "I couldn't sleep. I kept thinking about Mr. Shaw."

"Yes. Poor Mr. Shaw." There is just the slightest hint of bitterness in my voice. Mrs. Morgan would never detect it. But Cyrus does, and his jaw tightens.

He picks up his backpack and tilts his head toward the front door. "We should go."

My heart starts to pound, and I hug Mrs. Morgan tightly. "Bye, Mom. Love you."

"Be careful out there," she says into my hair as she kisses the side of my head. "It's a dangerous world."

"I know." I hold on to her as long as I can, knowing this is likely the last time I will see her.

I'm grateful to Cyrus, at least, for not breaking into the Morgans' house last night. For not causing a scene or punishing them, too. By pretending to be a boy picking up his girlfriend for school, Noah Vander and Kailey Morgan can simply disappear. It's tragic for their families, but it's better than the bloody scene I'd imagined. And with Kailey's mysterious past and Noah's unhappy home life, they will likely be labeled runaway lovers.

My throat grows thick, but I swallow hard. I need to stay numb. The only emotion I can allow is my hatred. Hate keeps me strong. Hate will let me exact revenge.

Outside, the sun strains to break through the clouds, the rays too bright for my sleep-deprived eyes. I squint at Noah's car and touch my pocket, feeling the outline of the knife.

Cyrus's hand is at the small of my back, urging me forward. I glance at him, but he's looking everywhere but at me—at the rippling sky, at the shocking orange blur of California poppies that shiver in the Morgans' garden. Entering a new body is intoxicating for Incarnates. Colors are more vivid, the breeze is delicious, and the body thrums with a vitality that most humans will never know.

I hope that the beauty of the world will distract him as he drives. I only need him to falter briefly. Then I will strike.

Cyrus opens the car door for me, playing the part of the perfect gentleman, but I feel like I'm climbing into a hearse. The VW that I used to look forward to riding in is suddenly stifling, claustrophobic.

As he pulls away from the curb, I watch out the window. The hundred-year-old houses slide by, the sky half cloudy, half clear. I want to remember every detail—the young bearded father with a baby strapped to his chest, the UC Berkeley students with their messenger bags, the old man who sweeps the sidewalk outside the organic cheese shop. I feel tears in my eyes as I realize how much I'll miss this neighborhood, this life. My Noah.

Silence reigns until I can no longer stand it. I reach forward and turn on the radio.

"—and police have no new information on the death of Jason Shaw, a popular substitute biology teacher at Berkeley High. Bereaved students have already started an online memorial . . . ," a newscaster intones. I snap the radio off.

Cyrus shakes his head. "It's so odd. Everyone is mourning Mr. Shaw, but no one even knows who he really was or that he came to Berkeley to find his true love," he murmurs, smoothly changing lanes to avoid a bicyclist. "They met when they were just kids—she was fourteen, and he was a couple of years older. It was at a masquerade party."

I close my eyes, remembering that night, almost able to smell the pomegranate wine, the smoky torches, the roses' heady perfume. I can recall every detail—the way my mask made it difficult to see, the cool air pouring over my face when Cyrus asked me to remove it.

"He knew that night that he had to be with her, always. That it was meant to be. They ended up running away together. They left their homes, their families, everything. But it didn't matter. They had each other."

Oh, it mattered. I remember sobbing like the child I was when I realized I could never return to my parents. They thought I was dead, and I couldn't even comfort them while they quietly wept at my funeral. I feel my throat grow thick, and I wonder why he is telling me this, why he's making our life into some sort of dark fairy tale.

"They traveled the world together until one night, she left him. He didn't understand why."

It's a parable, I realize. A lesson. He's treating our life like a story because he doesn't know how to speak to me directly. He's telling me how badly I hurt him, how much he loves me.

He brings the car to a stop at a red light. "He was sure she came to Berkeley. He came here to find her."

I wrap my fingers around the knife in my pocket, pulling it out with a jerk. Fury makes my fingers tremble. I drop my hand down between the passenger seat and the door so he won't see.

The light turns green, and to my surprise, he doesn't turn right, toward the freeway. As I watch him, trying to figure out his plan, I slide the blade open in my right hand. I run one finger along its edge, never looking away from him.

"How does the story end?" I whisper.

He guns the engine. "How do you think?"

I am shaking. I am shaking so hard that I drop the knife. My heart sinks—I've lost my chance.

But then he makes a sharp left, and I realize where he's taking us.

Berkeley High.

He jerks the car into an open spot, yanks the keys out of the ignition, and sits quietly. He won't look at me. The sun has finally won its battle with the fog, and I stare at the motes of dust that twist in the air and settle on the faded dash. All around us, kids stream into school. I can see them laughing, but it's like watching TV with the sound turned off.

I fight the urge to throw open the car door and run. I wouldn't make it ten feet.

"Why are we here? At school?" I ask, my pulse wild, my breath rapid. Anything is better than this suspense, this not knowing what comes next.

He leans back in his seat and drapes his wrists over the steering wheel, tucking his chin to his chest. "It does feel a bit ridiculous, doesn't it?"

"To say the least."

"Today is a day to be with friends." His voice is rough. It drags over my heart like wheels on gravel. He meets my gaze. "You never know—it could be the last time you'll see them."

Finally, I understand. He's going to give me one day to say good-bye. Perhaps he's remembering how devastated I was to leave my mortal family with no farewells. He's trying to be kind. But what can I even say to my friends here? What can I say to Leyla, to Bryan? Nothing.

And I can't say good-bye to the person who matters most. I picture Noah, the last time I saw him. Only last night, walking away from me on the Golden Gate Bridge, disappearing into fog. If only I could touch him one more time. It's not till I taste salt that I realize I'm crying.

The boy who looks like Noah strokes my hair. He finds my hand and squeezes it so hard I feel my bones sliding against each other. I want to pull back, but I force myself not to move. I pretend I am a statue. A statue doesn't care what happens to it. A statue doesn't flinch.

I know he wants me to forgive him. Killing Noah wasn't enough for Cyrus. He still thinks, after everything that's happened, that I will love him. He wants me on my knees, crawling back to his familiar crushing embrace.

FOUR

"Come on, Kailey," Madison Cortez pleads in our art class. "You're the best artist I know. It can be whatever you want—I don't know, ice fairies? Snow queens? Deer? You love antlers." She fixes me with her brown eyes, shining beneath the heavy line of her blunt chestnut bangs.

I force a laugh, despite the hollowness I feel, knowing my time here is quickly ticking away. I can only hold on to the fact that with me gone, my friends will be safe. "I'm just *busy*. I have a job and—"

"And Noah. I know. Hey, why don't you paint Noah for

the mural? Two birds, one stone. Make him into a snow-man, whatever."

The mention of Noah makes me want to scream. Cyrus has barely left my side today, appearing outside each of my classes to escort me to the next one. He stopped short of actually grabbing my elbow to steer me along, but his meaning is clear. *Don't even think about running, Sera.* Not that I plan to. I have nowhere to go, no one to run to.

Madison snaps her fingers. "Kailey? Hello? The mural for the dance? Will you do it? Please say yes. I need to cross it off my list."

This has been going on for the entire class. Normally art is quiet, but the whole classroom has been abuzz, unsettled and loud. Madison is fixated on the dance, but I know what everyone else is talking about: Mr. Shaw's death. When I got to my biology classroom this morning, there was a make-shift shrine set up outside the door: candles, flowers, and science books laid out in mourning for Mr. Shaw. It made me sick. Cyrus, who has murdered hundreds of humans, being grieved? When he's not even dead? All day, my rage has been growing, glowing in my belly like a hot coal.

"I'll be your best friend . . . ," Madison tries.

I was taken aback to hear that Madison is the chair of the winter dance committee, given her rock-'n'-roll bad-girl vibe. I would have pegged her for one of the kids who smoke pot in the parking lot and wouldn't be caught dead at a school dance. But I guess even after six hundred years, people can surprise me.

The other girl who shares our table speaks up shyly. "She's right, Kailey. You should do the mural. It would be good for your soul to honor the solstice." I don't know if I've ever heard her speak before, and I struggle to remember her name. Enid? Erica?

She watches me for a few seconds, her eyes outlined in a thick stroke of silver eyeliner that stands out from her dark skin. It mimics the shape of the vintage cat-eye glasses that constantly slip down her nose. She's wearing neon-blue high-waisted bell-bottoms and a T-shirt that reads I ♥ without the initials of any city that would traditionally follow. Metallic gold clogs peek out from the hem of her pants.

She's bent over a piece of leather that she's painstakingly engraving with a blade and an awl. I watch what she's doing for a bit, until her thick curtain of braids falls in the way. She's got yarn and ribbons and feathers braided into her hair. I wonder how she washes it.

Madison sighs, running her fingers through her shaggy brown hair. "Does this mean you'll do it? The mural?"

"I'll . . . consider it," I deflect. I'll either be dead or back with the coven by the time the dance rolls around. But even if, by some miracle, I *am* in Berkeley on December first, I wouldn't want to do it for one small, yet significant reason: I can't draw. A fact I've only been able to hide thanks to a long ceramics unit.

"Class, may I have your attention?" We're interrupted by Mrs. Swan. She stands at the front of the studio with hands clasped, next to a boy I haven't seen before. He's wearing a vintage-looking vest over his white button-up shirt, closed with cuff links at the wrists, and striped wool trousers that remind me of the 1930s.

Mrs. Swan smiles, tucking a lock of long gray hair behind her ear and smoothing her ankle-length skirt around her hips. "Please welcome Reed Sawyer to our midst. He joins us from Sonoma, where he worked on his family's vineyard." She beams, and the class makes a collective rustling sound.

The boy is good-looking, though not my type. He's got very short brown hair that looks freshly attended to with clippers, and he turns a fedora over and over in his hands. I wouldn't call myself an expert on high-school fashion, but he looks like he's wearing a costume.

Mrs. Swan deposits Reed at our table before disappearing in a cloud of her tuberose perfume. He catches my eye and smiles, revealing large white teeth.

"Hey," he says, sitting on the stool across from me. "I'm Reed."

"I'm Kailey," I answer listlessly. It feels so pointless to meet a new person when I'm about to disappear.

"Kailey, huh?" He gazes at me for a second, then smiles. Two deep dimples appear in his tanned cheeks, darkened with a fledgling beard. "You look familiar. Have we met before?"

"I don't think so," I say, though I suppose he could have met Kailey.

"Have you ever spent time in Sonoma?" he presses.

"Nope." *Not in this body, at least.*

"Maybe you know each other from a past life," Enid-or-Erica says in her musical voice as she looks up from her project. "Way more common than you'd think." She offers her hand to Reed. Her long fingers are covered with at least six silver rings.

"I'm Echo," she tells him. Ah, so that's her name. Like the nymph.

"I'm Echo," he responds.

She throws her head back and laughs, the sound like a carillon of bells. "You know," she says, looking at him more closely, "I haven't actually heard that one before."

"Probably because people have no idea who Echo is," he replies. "No one studies Greek mythology anymore."

Echo smiles, looking pleased, and Madison introduces herself as well. Her lips have somehow acquired a coat of cherry-red lipstick that looks like fresh blood against her pale complexion.

"It must be kind of a weird day to be starting here," she says apologetically, batting her eyelashes, which are coated with several layers of black mascara. "You know, with Mr. Shaw . . ."

Reed flinches, looking down at our table. "Yeah," he admits. "My parents are freaking out. People don't get murdered in Sonoma. Like, ever. They were ready to pack up and leave when they watched the news this morning."

"We definitely need some healing energy," Echo says. "I brought some sage to burn at lunch," she adds, patting her canvas backpack.

"And as we all know, sage fixes *everything*," Madison says drily.

Reed ignores Madison and smiles at Echo. "It's not a bad idea. Herbs are more powerful than people think."

"*I* think we ought to get back to discussing real issues," Madison sniffs. "Like the mural Kailey should be painting for the school dance."

Damn, the girl is persistent.

The rational piece of me realizes she's just dealing with Mr. Shaw's death in her own way, but I'm losing patience with her. My entire life is falling apart, crumbling like an old bridge over choppy waters, and I can't keep pretending everything's fine.

But before I have to answer, the bell rings, and I scoop up my sketchbook and my backpack. "I guess we'll have to continue this conversation later," I say, darting for the door.

Cyrus is already outside. He is leaning against a wall of lockers, arms folded over his chest. Even though I know it's Cyrus, the sight of Noah's body brings me, as usual, a fluttery feeling. I walk toward him slowly, wanting to bask in the illusion, wanting to pretend that it's really Noah. That last night never happened.

"Everyone's eating outside," he says. "Since it's such a beautiful day." But then he smiles—Noah's smile—and leans close to me. Close, closer. His hands are in my hair, his hands are under my chin. And then his lips—Noah's lips— are on mine, kissing me. I kiss him back. I am dizzy, flames licking the side of my body. His passion is real. Mine is too, but it's misplaced. It's almost like kissing Noah. Almost isn't enough.

I force myself to pull away. It's nearly impossible, but I do. I shove the fire down, inside the extinct volcano of my heart. What if Noah's soul is nearby, watching this? Seeing his body being used as a puppet? Seeing that puppet kiss the girl he loved—the girl who got him killed? Or is Noah's soul long gone to some other dimension, some peaceful realm far away from here, where everything is starlit and joyful

27

and earthly problems have lost their significance? I cannot pretend to know.

That's the thing about Incarnates. We know everything about being alive and nothing about death—except how to cause it, over and over and over again.

FIVE

The wind has picked up, warm and dry, the kind of wind that means fire danger for California, no matter how much rain has fallen recently. In the south they call them Santa Anas—up here it's the Diablo wind, picking up ferocity as it screams through narrow canyons to the ocean. Saint or devil, the result is the same. The whole state is tinder.

It seems like the entire student body is outside for lunch, taking advantage of the sun. The oak tree we're standing under shakes, and small dried leaves fall around us like little dead wings. I am surrounded by Kailey's friends—*my* friends now, though I feel a tinge of guilt for thinking of them that way.

The atmosphere is misleadingly festive as we watch a group of students play an acoustic version of "Amazing Grace" in memory of Mr. Shaw. The song is uplifting, and I love the soft jangle of banjo and violin, but I hate that they're playing it for Cyrus.

I recognize the band members from the party in Montclair that Bryan brought me to just days after I became Kailey. The girl with blond dreadlocks isn't playing the accordion this time—she sits with a conga drum clutched between her knees, her flowing mauve dress the same color as the fake flowers she has pinned in her hair. The boy with the violin is wearing the same crumpled cowboy hat he had on at the party, a shock of golden hair peeking out at his tanned neck. His eyes are trained on the banjo player's fingertips as they move up and down the metal strings.

They've drawn quite a crowd. As I watch the violinist, I smile in spite of myself, remembering how I borrowed his instrument at the party, how I gave myself over to the music. I loved that night. A bonfire, and redwood trees creaking in the wind. Bryan helping me sneak out of the Morgans' house. The first time I felt comfortable with Kailey's friends. Noah, standing in the kitchen, giving me a smile that made my pulse race . . .

Stop it, I remind myself. *Don't think about him.* I swallow hard.

When the song ends, a low murmur of voices ripples

through the crowd, rising above the muted applause. Like in art class, Mr. Shaw's name is on everyone's lips.

"I just can't believe he's gone. It doesn't feel real," Leyla Clark, Kailey's best friend, murmurs next to me.

It's not, I want to tell her, but I bite my lip. The boy who looks just like Noah is on my other side, his fingers firmly laced through mine.

Leyla's dressed in purple down to her scuffed lavender high-tops. A knit cap is tugged low over her ears, and her dark, magenta-streaked hair spills out the bottom. The wind keeps blowing into her mouth, where it sticks to her grape-scented lip gloss. On the other side of her is Bryan in his letterman jacket, his sandy blond hair gelled into spiky submission and immune to the wind. She shifts, leaning into him as he puts his arm around her shoulder.

"I heard he was trying to buy drugs," says Chantal Nixon, who is, as usual, perfectly composed and ladylike in a headband and blazer.

Leyla scoffs. "No way. He was a teacher. He just got mugged. It can happen to anyone."

"Remind me to stay out of Oakland," sniffs Nicole Harrison, who wanders up to the group with Madison in tow. Nicole looks uncharacteristically chaste in a black turtleneck under a cable-knit sweater. She doesn't have on any makeup, and her red, puffy eyes suggest she's been crying.

"Don't be such a priss, Nicole," Chantal retorts, which is odd coming from a girl wearing pearls. "Lake Merritt isn't exactly the 'hood. There are worse neighborhoods in Berkeley."

"It's so awful that he fell into the lake after he was shot. I heard they haven't found the body yet." Madison's voice is dull, her face half swallowed by giant sunglasses. Her dark hair sweeps behind her in feathered tangles, and the sun glints off the small diamond stud below her lip. Her hands shake as she fiddles with a lighter. She's much more somber than she was in art. Her best friend, Piper Lindstrom, isn't here and won't be for weeks, maybe months—according to a text she sent Madison, she has mono. Without Piper to gossip with, new boys to charm, or dance business to occupy herself, I suppose Madison has no choice but to face death, just like the rest of us.

Cyrus tightens his grip on my hand. "The police are still looking?" he asks. "For the body?"

Madison nods. "They're going to dredge the lake."

Bryan's brows knit together. "Seriously? Lake Merritt isn't even ten feet deep. It's not like the muggers pushed him off the Golden Gate Bridge."

"Maybe someone moved the body," Cyrus says. "Or maybe the detectives working the case are completely incompetent."

Or maybe the body is nothing but dust, I think pointedly.

"There's going to be a candlelight vigil," says Leyla. "We should go."

"I'm in," Nicole offers, pushing her shiny curtain of brown hair back from her freckled cheeks. "I heard he didn't have any family. There might not even be a funeral."

Cyrus catches my eye, shooting me an unreadable expression. "If only he had found Seraphina," he murmurs.

I stiffen, a spark of rage shooting through me. He's playing with me, gloating.

"Who?" Leyla asks.

Cyrus's eyes glisten in a perfect replica of human emotion. "No one."

I refuse to indulge Cyrus. I keep my mouth tightly shut as the band strikes up another song. They're covering my favorite Beatles tune, "Blackbird," about a bird who learns to fly, broken wings be damned. I concentrate on the music, letting it momentarily stanch my anger.

What am I going to do? I can't run, obviously. I don't have the advantage of being in disguise anymore, and the only way I will switch bodies again is by force. I need to think of a plan more foolproof than my Swiss army knife, but nothing comes, and Cyrus's firm grip on my hand makes it impossible to think clearly.

The smell of sage cuts through the air, and I see Echo

33

holding the promised smudge stick, sweet herbal smoke greedily snatched by the wind. It reminds me of the warehouse raves Cyrus dragged me to in the 1990s, electronic music pushing baggy-pants-wearing dancers into a delirious trance. Techno was Cyrus's passion, not mine, but I've always loved to dance, to forget myself in the rhythm and the crowd.

A chorus of applause erupts as the band finishes the song. I rip my hand away from Cyrus's grasp to clap loudly, and the boy with the violin catches my eye, a sunny grin spreading across his face. His ice-blue eyes crinkle at the corners, and he tips his hat at me. I feel a blush rise in my cheeks, and I steal a glance at Cyrus. I don't want this violinist paying any attention to me—Cyrus's jealousy has proved deadly before.

"Nice," says Cyrus warmly, summoning his immortal charm. He's not mad, I realize. Why would he be? He won, after all. He's captured me.

"Thanks." The boy's eyes flick between Echo and Leyla as they drift away across the quad; the music over, the crowd has begun to disperse.

"'Blackbird' is one of my favorite songs," I say tentatively to the violinist.

"It's a classic," violin-boy says, his eyes bright. "It's nice to meet another Beatles fan."

"Oh, we met before," I correct him. "At Dawson's party in Montclair. I borrowed your violin."

He cocks his head.

"Are you guys talking about the party in the hills?" The tiny girl with the blond dreadlocks sets her conga drum down on the grass and throws an arm around her bandmate's shoulders. "Because Eli here was high as a kite that night. Seriously, he almost fell into the canyon. Don't believe anything he says about that party."

Eli chuckles, holding up his hands. "In that case, I plead the Fifth." But I barely hear him.

Almost fell into the canyon. The phrase ricochets through my mind. An idea takes hold suddenly, and I know how I'm going to kill Cyrus. Well, perhaps that's too optimistic.

I know how I'm going to *try.*

I reach for Cyrus's hand. I tug on it, and he gives me his full attention.

I gaze into his deep blue eyes, making my face into a contrite mask, lifting my lips in a veneer of love and obedience. "I have an idea," I say, ignoring the nervy ball of dread that sits in my stomach. "Let's go hiking tonight in Tilden Park. Before we go home." The word *home* feels false in my mouth. The coven's San Francisco condo will *never* be my home. As long as Cyrus is there, it can only be my prison. "Just you and me," I add.

He looks at me for a long moment while my heartbeat thuds down to my toes. But he pulls me close, wrapping his arms around me. "That would be really great," he murmurs into my hair.

A flock of birds lands on the concrete, then takes off, one by one, dipping and swooping in the air, aloft on invisible streams. And free, like I could be if I succeed.

"Not right after school, though." I make my voice confident, breezy. "I have a few things to take care of first." I need it to be dark when we set out on the path. I don't want any witnesses to what I intend to do.

I pull away and smile at him. "That's allowed, right?"

"I suppose so," he says, cupping my cheek with his warm hand. Behind us, Eli's band launches into another song, a traditional ballad that reminds me of something my mother used to sing, a mournful tale of love and loss.

I turn away from Cyrus and set my lips grimly, watching Eli's fingers dance over his violin strings. Cyrus agreed readily—perhaps *too* readily—to my plan. Perhaps he has no intention of taking me back to San Francisco, and I have just set the scene for my own murder.

I can't think like that. I've been losing to Cyrus for centuries, but this has to be the one game I win.

You're a killer, Sera. That's what Cyrus always says. *Now act like it.*

SIX

I can't stop staring at the girl's hair. She sits with her back to me, headphone wires trailing from her ears, plugged into a sleek laptop. She has no idea I'm here, hunched low in the library's poetry section, but I've been watching her for close to an hour, the minutes ticking by far too quickly. When I leave here, I will meet Cyrus, and I am scared. No—*terrified.*

The girl's hair is wavy, rippling down the back of her faded green sweatshirt, and veers between auburn and scarlet and brilliant persimmon, depending on the angle of her head beneath the fluorescent lights.

From behind, she looks exactly like Charlotte, my best friend for two hundred years. But then she twists and bends to her side, pushing down her knee sock to scratch at a mosquito bite on her pale ankle. Her profile is nothing like Charlotte's—her nose is strong, rather than pert, and she's missing Charlotte's light smattering of freckles.

The illusion broken, I glance at the clock that rests on a sagging shelf of reference books—4:25 P.M.

Reluctantly, I leave the safety of the library and make my way outside. The wind shows no signs of stopping. It lifts my hair, whipping it harshly around my face. The gusts are warm and dry, but the weather reminds me of *le mistral*, a freezing wind that rages across the south of France. In 1349, right after he made me into an Incarnate, Cyrus and I fled to Les Baux-de-Provence. *Le mistral* was in full force, ripping tiles from the roofs of houses. Local legend said it brought ill spirits and bad tempers, but I loved it. I loved the way it threw my long, dark hair above me like a banner. The way it blew away memories of my childhood in foggy London, of my mother and father. Losing them was too painful to think about, but the wind scrubbed me clean.

Oh, California wind, please do the same.

I reach our meeting place, the gnarled oak tree now backlit in the rapidly setting sun. Cyrus sits with his back against the trunk, his knees pulled up to his chest, poring over a thick text. My heart is pounding, but I force my face to remain impassive, to pretend that this is a normal afternoon. To pretend that this isn't the afternoon when either Cyrus or I—or both of us—will die.

"Hi there," I say, a sweet smile on my face.

He looks up, surprised, acting as though he wasn't aware that I was standing in front of him. His expression is a lie, just like mine.

"Are you ready?" he asks, his eyes steady and flecked with gold in the dying sunlight. Static electricity bridges the air between us.

"As ready as I'll ever be," I say.

He stands, swinging his backpack over one shoulder. I am struck by how tall he is, how hard he will be to overpower.

We walk toward the parking lot, arms brushing. I wish I could put some distance between us, but he has to believe I've forgiven him. If I am to avenge Noah, if I am to save those whose bodies Cyrus would eventually steal, I have to play this exactly right.

There are only two cars left in the lot: Noah's, and an Oakland police cruiser a couple of spaces away. A man sits inside the police car, leafing through a notebook.

He rolls down the window. "Excuse me," he calls. His gravelly, world-weary voice is a contrast to his youthful face.

He's got a shaved, tan head and a dimple in the middle of his chin. Mirrored sunglasses hide his eyes. "Do you two go to school here?" His lower jaw works on a piece of gum.

Cyrus turns to me and raises his eyebrows. "Yes," he answers the cop.

The officer rolls up his window and climbs out of the car. He's holding his notebook open to a page that is, I notice, covered in coffee stains and surprisingly elegant, cursive handwriting. "I'm Officer Spaulding," he announces, walking closer to us. I can smell the spearmint from his gum. "I'm investigating the murder of a teacher here—Mr. Shaw—did you know him?"

The hairs on my arms stand on end. Cyrus's posture straightens, and he fixes his eyes on the cop. "Yes," he answers. "He was our biology teacher. Are there any developments in the investigation?"

Officer Spaulding takes off his sunglasses. His eyes are a light green color that I can only describe as feline. "I can't answer that," he says, "but there were some *irregularities*, let's say." He smiles, revealing very white, very straight teeth.

"What kind of irregularities?" Cyrus presses, narrowing his eyes. He must be worried that he made a mistake, left behind some pieces of evidence that won't add up. Officer Spaulding doesn't reply. Instead, he looks at me. "How about you? Did you know Mr. Shaw?" He reaches up to his head, as though to push back a mane of hair that's no longer there, and awkwardly pats the back of his neck.

"Yes," I answer quietly. "He was the biology teacher, like Noah said." It feels absurd to use Noah's name.

"And did you ever notice anything strange about his behavior? The way he interacted with female students, for example?" The cop narrows his eyes, studying my face.

Does this mean that the police found Cyrus's yearbook? The one with X's through the faces of the female students he had ruled out as being me? What other evidence might they have?

"Absolutely not," answers Cyrus. "What are you trying to imply?" He sounds angry. He nods his head to me, reminding me to stay in line. "Did Mr. Shaw ever act weird around you?"

"N-n-no," I stutter. "Of course not. He was a great teacher. I can't believe he's dead."

"Sorry, kids. I've got to follow up on every lead. It's my job." Officer Spaulding tucks his pen behind his ear, where it perches precariously. He smiles again, no longer chewing his gum. I wonder if he swallowed it. "Thanks for your time. Please give me a call if you remember anything—anything at all—about Mr. Shaw. Especially," he adds, looking at me, "if your girlfriends have anything they want to say."

I shiver and take the business card he's holding out. I wish I could tell him that Mr. Shaw was nothing but a mirage. That the man who "killed" him is standing right in front of his squad car. And that if I succeed, that killer will finally, *finally* meet his own end at the base of the canyon in Tilden Park.

SEVEN

"I got you something," Cyrus says when we reach the trail-head, and holds out his hand. He is smiling shyly, as though we're any human couple on a date.

It's only five in the afternoon, but darkness has fallen quickly, like a curtain on a stage. The first cold needles of starlight shine above us, piercing the faded azure sky. I was on edge the entire drive to the park, the road winding around the Berkeley Hills. Cyrus drove fast, taking the turns with practiced speed.

I force myself to smile, to say, "What is it?"

He opens his palm and reveals a necklace on a silver

chain, pooled in the center of his hand. He holds it up so I can see the small birdcage charm that hangs from it, complete with a tiny bird inside. It glints in the light of the full moon that rose when I wasn't looking.

A bird, caged in silver. Like me.

It's the silver cord that binds your soul to your body, Cyrus said to me when he made me what I am. *This potion is unraveling it. You'll soon be free.*

Free. Nothing could have been further from the truth.

"I love it," I lie. He gestures for me to turn around, and I oblige, lifting my hair from my neck so he can fasten it. The chain is like ice against my skin.

The wind shakes the eucalyptus trees that grow here, releasing their minty oils into the air. Cyrus wraps his arms around my waist, and I feel heat, the sun of six hundred years' worth of summers.

"Should we walk?" he asks softly. "Don't get me wrong. We can just stand here if you want. I kind of like it." I can't see his face, but I know he's smiling. He tightens his grip on me, but I pull away.

"Let's go," I answer, turning to him, a smile painted on my chapped lips. As I move forward along the path, I have the sensation that I'm leaving one world for another, from a dream to waking life. Two places with different logic, different rules.

44

We set off, and I match the speed of my steps to his. I don't like having him behind me—I don't trust him. *It's been too easy to appease him*, my brain tells me. *He knows what you're going to do*, it says. *He always knows.*

So what if he knows? I argue back, fiddling with the knife in my pocket. *One way or another, this ends today.*

The trail tangles up the hill in front of us, littered with eucalyptus leaves and thick strips of its flammable bark. I hear a rustle in the trees ahead of me. I stop abruptly, a chill raising goose bumps on my arms.

"What's wrong?" he asks.

"Didn't you hear that?"

"No," he replies, cocks his head, listens. "There's no one else here—the parking lot was completely empty."

"Are you sure?" I say. I don't need any heroic witnesses trying to save the life of someone who should have died centuries ago.

"I'm sure."

We wait, but there's nothing except the breeze working its way through the forest. "Do you want to go back?" he asks, his eyes trained on the trees.

"No, it's okay," I say, setting off again. I walk faster, determination tensing my muscles.

We reach the cliffs, breathing hard. The whole Bay Area is spread out below us in a shimmering sprawl, like a topographic map brought to life. We can see the Golden Gate Bridge, arcing toward the Marin headlands. The cities of Berkeley and Oakland twinkling in the clear air. The Bay Bridge, just a ribbon of light cutting across the choppy blank water.

"It's beautiful," he says, taking my hand.

Below us, the land falls away sharply. I let go of his hand and edge closer. "Come see," I say, only a few feet from the lip of the drop.

"That's okay," he says. "I'll stay right here."

I shrug my shoulders and move closer, closer, till I can see down. The moon bathes the chasm in milky light. There are rocks at the bottom. I close my eyes, just for a second, and picture Noah's body lying at the bottom, twisted and broken.

No, I remind myself. *You won't have to see it. He'll turn to dust as soon as he hits.*

"I want you to come here with me," I say, my voice unwavering.

He waits, then appears to come to a decision. "Okay, but only for a second." And then he's at my side. I watch his profile in the moonlight, half lit and half dark. Like Cyrus himself. Half passionate alchemist, seeker of truth. Half killer.

"Look at San Francisco," I say. "It doesn't seem real. It's a toy town."

"I'd rather look at you," he says. I feel his hand on my cheek. It's rough and warm. I take a shaky breath. "You look so pretty." I feel heat rising to my face and curse myself for being so weak as to blush at a moment like this, when I'm supposed to be an avenger.

"I thought you didn't usually like blondes," I say lightly. His weakness is long, chestnut hair.

"That's idiotic," he says. "I like *you*. Beauty is a fringe benefit."

I take another step toward the cliff, pulling him with me. We are only a foot away from the lip of the canyon. I can do this. I can. I will take the fall with him if need be. We will turn to dust together, two old souls with too much blood on our hands.

"Thank you for coming up here with me," I say, wrapping my arm around his back, trying to find the best position for my hand. I raise my elbow behind his back, for leverage.

"I really needed to get away," he whispers.

I coil the muscles in my legs. But just as I am about to shove, he turns to me. I suck in my breath when I meet his lake-blue eyes. They stop me cold. I'm not sure why at first. They are the color of water when shards of sun hit the bay.

They are *Noah's* eyes.

But this is *Cyrus* . . . isn't it?

I hesitate. I hesitate again. I'm reeling. I'm muffled in

cotton. *Dear God, forgive me if I lose my chance. But I need to be sure.*

"When . . . did your feelings for me change?" I ask.

"You already know that," he answers, stroking my hair.

Doubt creeps into me. It tingles, like I'm waking up from anesthesia.

"Tell me again," I say urgently, grasping for something— for someone—that my brain tells me is gone. But another part of me, maybe the illogical part, isn't so sure.

He laughs. "Okay. Right after your car accident. Something was just . . . different. It started that night that I found you sneaking out of your house."

"And what happened right after that?" I press.

He puts his hand thoughtfully to his chin. "I seem to recall you acting really weird. Kind of like now. And then you went back inside to go to sleep. Wait." His voice grows tense. "Are you having some kind of concussion relapse?"

It's not possible. It's not possible. There's no way Cyrus could know that. "No," I whisper. "The other night—you played a word. On our game."

"Yeah. And you never played your turn."

"Why," I ask slowly, "did you play that word?"

"Because I had the letters for it, genius." His brows are furrowed, his confusion clear.

"Tell me why," I say.

He sighs. "And because I had just found out about Mr. Shaw. Okay? I know you didn't like him. But he was teaching me stuff before he died. About . . . I don't know, esoteric stuff. He used to talk about alchemy constantly." His voice grows sad.

The wind buffets me, but I am granite. I am listening.

"And I was just sitting there, upset, thinking about him," he continues. "And I don't know why, but I pulled out my phone. I think I was trying to distract myself. And I was staring at my letters—and the word just jumped out at me. *Alchemy.* I mean—it was like a *sign*, like he was *okay*. It was like . . . his ghost was telling me not to worry about him. So I played it. And I felt better."

I am silent. It's him. It's Noah. My Noah.

He steps backward, pulling me with him, away from the edge. Away from a death that happened only in my mind. He envelops me. A bird leaves its cage.

My mouth finds his with windswept urgency, my fingers tangling in his hair. He kisses me back. Hundreds of years have led me here, to this place, to the lip of this canyon, to Noah's lips.

"I'm so sorry," I breathe.

"What for?" he answers.

"For being so crazy today," I say.

"It's a crazy day," he answers. I feel his hands on my

shoulders. I feel his lips on my neck. "But everything's going to be okay. Better than okay," he murmurs.

We stay for a while longer, not speaking. Just being. And when we leave, I almost skip down the trail.

It's only when we reach the parking lot and see the briefest of red flashes—taillights of a car pulling out, their scarlet gleam bouncing off the asphalt and the trees—that a darkness edges against my euphoria.

Even though I'm away from the cliffs, I'm still in danger. I could still fall. I could still lose everything. Because there was no other car there when we arrived. Someone followed us. And if Cyrus isn't Noah, who could he be?

EIGHT

Humans love to hate Monday: back to school, back to work. They groan about it constantly. Of course, it's different for Incarnates. One day feels like an instant to us. It's over almost as soon as I open my eyes.

Except for today. Today I feel phantom eyes boring into my back. I sniff the air hesitantly, expecting to catch a whiff of Cyrus's vetiver soap, but smell only rain.

Noah is alive. I repeated those words to myself over and over all weekend, like some kind of prayer. I whispered them as I sneaked into the antique store where I work, so that I could return the money I stole—I don't need it anymore.

I'm not going to run away like I'd planned to before I found out that "Mr. Shaw" was dead. I kept the thought of Noah curled around me like a blanket while I drove to the Golden Gate Bridge to retrieve Kailey's jacket and ID, which I'd left there as the world's least eloquent suicide note.

I had to go. I can't have any concerned San Francisco policemen knocking on the Morgans' door, wondering why their daughter left her things on the railing.

But now that I'm back at school, surrounded by people, I should feel safe. In movies, the heroine is never threatened when she's in a crowd.

Except that Berkeley High feels more menacing than ever. It's even worse than when Cyrus taught biology. At least then I knew who he was. I knew when to be on guard. Now he could be anyone. Anyone at all.

"Today we're going to talk about an invention that completely changed the way information is shared, that gave common people the power to publish their ideas and spread them throughout the world. Does anyone have any idea what I'm talking about?" Mr. Yee, our history teacher, rubs his hands together expectantly and peers at the class through his Buddy Holly thick-rimmed glasses. No one meets his eyes.

"Madison? Want to take a guess?" He leans on the desk and folds his arms across his chest.

"Um, Twitter?" Madison ventures.

"No—earlier than that."

Madison taps her pencil against her cheek. "MySpace?" she tries.

Mr. Yee sighs. "I'm talking about the printing press. Possibly the most important event in the fifteenth century."

I exhale and lean back. I don't need to listen in history class—I already lived it. I was nearly a hundred when Gutenberg printed his first Bible. Instead I should be coming up with a plan. I *know* Cyrus is alive. I know it somewhere beyond words, beyond logic, beyond proof.

Not two days ago I was convinced that Noah was Cyrus. So certain that I nearly pushed him to his death. So now that Noah has proved to be no one but himself, why am I so sure that Cyrus's soul continues to walk this earth?

My belief is bolstered by nothing but intuition and gut feeling and everything that Cyrus would call "bad science."

I have no proof.

And if I'm wrong, well, I'll go ahead and laugh at myself later. But if I'm right? Then every single person in my life—everyone except for Noah—is a suspect. Even my friends. Leyla, Madison, Chantal, Nicole—even Bryan. Even Kailey's parents. Cyrus could be any one of them. Just as he could be any one of the students in this classroom. Or the teacher.

"Kailey? Can you pay attention, please?"

I shake my head, a furious blush heating up my cheeks. "Sorry, what was that?" I ask.

"I asked what effects you thought Gutenberg's invention may have had throughout Europe." Mr. Yee's normally friendly expression is stern.

I say the first thing that comes to mind. "That assumes he invented the press. And discounts the work of Laurens Coster, who many say was the first to work with movable type."

Mr. Yee raises his eyebrows. "I had no idea you were such an expert."

I feel everyone's eyes on me. *Damn it.* Just what I need—to stand out when my life depends on fitting in.

"Kailey's right," I hear a boy say behind me. I whip my head around to see Reed, a bowler hat on his head and suspenders punctuating his vintage button-up shirt.

"Go on," prods Mr. Yee, amused.

"Well, there was Hadrianus Junius's account—I think it was published in the late fifteen hundreds?—that backs up Kailey's claim." My hair stands on end. "I studied a bit of typography at my old school," Reed continues. "We had an antique printing press. It was really quite—"

The bell signaling the end of class shrieks through whatever Reed was going to say, and I bolt from my chair before it stops ringing. My backpack bangs into several chairs and people as I rush to the door. "Sorry, sorry," I repeat to no one in particular.

The air outside the classroom is damp with mist, courtesy of the rain that's falling softly sideways, making a mockery of the open-aired school's covered walkway. It's the kind of rain that makes me feel silly when I whip out an umbrella but nonetheless soaks my hair and my clothes if I don't.

I shove through the throng, hurrying to meet Noah, the one person in Berkeley I can trust. I'm watching the floor when I collide with another person in the hallway, the force reverberating through my wrists.

"Sorry!" I say, bending down to pick up the textbook I'd been holding and coming face-to-face with a familiar boy. Eli's not wearing his cowboy hat for once, and his ice-blue eyes are more striking without its shadow.

"No harm done," he replies, shifting his violin case and scooping up my book before I can grab it.

"I wasn't looking where I was going," I explain.

"I prefer to think of it as a collision course with destiny," he replies in a deadpan tone. "As if there was such a thing." His eyes crinkle at the corners as he grins.

"Oh, I'm a big believer in destiny," I say.

He fiddles with the zipper on his sweatshirt but doesn't reply.

"Well, I'll see you later," I say, filling the awkward silence.

His bandmate appears at his side, the short dreadlocked girl who plays accordion and drums. "Eli. I've been looking for you everywhere. We have practice."

He furrows his brow. "Sorry, I forgot."

"Hey, Kailey," she says, as she leads him away.

"Hey," I reply, but they're already swallowed up by the crowd.

I find Noah at the end of the hallway, immobile, staring at the memorial shrine for Mr. Shaw outside our biology classroom. His hood is pulled up over his forehead, escaped locks of dark hair coated with droplets that remind me of icy tree branches in New England.

"Hi," I murmur, placing my hand on his arm. His eyes warm when he sees me, and I turn him gently away from the shrine. His sweatshirt juts out below his neck, concealing what I assume to be his camera, safely zipped up to protect it from the weather. I poke the lump.

"Is this your battery pack?" I tease.

"It's my camera. Contrary to popular belief, I'm not a robot." He grins, but I can tell he's making an effort. The shrine, and what it represents, grips him. I take a moment to study the shrine out of the corner of my eye. It's grown since Friday, flowers and handwritten notes and even laboratory beakers huddled against flickering candles.

I forge ahead. "Well, you should get some rain gear for your camera. Maybe one of those miniature cocktail umbrellas."

Noah's laugh sounds actually sincere.

I feel a tap on my shoulder. "Nice escape attempt, Kailey," a throaty female voice says. I turn around. Madison stands before me, holding a clipboard, a pencil tucked behind her ear. She squares her shoulders inside her oversize blazer, sleeves rolled up to her elbows. Her T-shirt is emblazoned with HER DUMB ALLERGIES, which I can only assume is another band I've never heard of.

"Hey, Maddy." Noah nods.

"Sir Noah," she acknowledges. Behind her, I see Reed making his way down the hall. I think again of what he said in class, and a wisp of nervousness curls in the bottom of my stomach.

"Did you want to talk about something?" I ask Madison.

"I thought you'd never ask," she answers, whipping the pencil out from her ear and holding it up to the clipboard. "Ugh, my notes are getting wet," she complains, shoving the clipboard inside her blazer. "I wanted to ask you guys if you'd be on my committee."

"Are you . . . running for office?" I ask, amused.

"Kailey, I'm talking about the winter dance. I'm hiring! Except there's no pay. Just glory. C'mon, will you do it?" She chews on the end of her pencil, lipstick imprinting itself on the eraser.

"Do what?" Reed comes over, followed closely by a beautiful girl. She's tall and willowy, and her sandy blond hair falls just under her chin in a neat bob. She and Reed share the same soft features—and classic fashion sense. She's wearing a dress with pouffed sleeves and a narrow waist, and a tiny feathered hat is pinned to her head. They both look like extras from a 1930s movie.

Madison brightens at the possibility of new recruits. "I was just asking Noah and Kailey if they'd be on the dance committee, which is going to be *awesome*, by the way, especially if you're looking to meet some cool people at school."

Noah whistles. "Look at this saleswoman. You two had better run if you want to avoid Madison's clutches," he says, nodding toward Reed and the girl beside him. "I'm Noah, by the way," he adds, offering his hand.

"Thanks for the warning. I'm Reed. And this is my sister."

"Rebecca Sawyer," she tells us in a formal tone, shaking my hand. Her skin is cool and damp, her handshake limp.

"How do you know Kailey?" Reed asks Noah, who cocks his head.

I jump in. "Noah's my boyfriend."

"Boyfriend?" Reed repeats, a mocking glint in his eye.

"And here I was thinking I was special, since we know each other from a past life and all."

Noah doesn't say anything, but I can see the telltale twitch in his jaw. Madison is rapt, clearly enjoying the drama.

Reed forges on. "What I mean is, you're a lucky guy. Kailey's wonderful. You should have heard her in class just now. Completely schooled the teacher in the history of the printing press."

"Well," I interrupt. "This has been great, but I've got to get home." I turn to Noah. "Can we leave?"

"Wait!" Madison clears her throat. "Can I put you guys down for the committee? It's the kind of thing that looks fantastic on your college application. Plus, we're going to have the dance *anyway*—it may as well be a kick-ass party."

"Okay, I'll do it," Noah relents. "I get the impression you won't take no for an answer."

"Correct," Madison replies. "First meeting's this Thursday after school. Kailey?"

"Sure," I say, hoping she won't ask about the mural again.

Rebecca pipes up. "I'm in too. Is there a theme?"

Madison's brown eyes look worried. "The theme is winter dance—I dunno, I was picturing snowflakes and, like, blue. Everything blue. Maybe silver? Is that dumb?"

Reed hooks his thumbs on his suspenders. "It's kind of ordinary. And you don't seem like an ordinary girl."

Madison blushes, and I silently curse her for falling prey to Reed's flattery.

"We'll think of something great," Rebecca promises her. "I love your blazer, by the way." She sounds completely insincere, but Madison appears to be eating it up.

"You just made my day. All of you. Okay, I see Nicole and Chantal over there—I've got to go recruit them, too." Madison flashes her toothy smile and leaves us, fighting upstream through the hallway to Nicole and Chantal.

"Why do I feel like I just sold my soul to the devil?" Noah muses.

"You don't actually believe in the devil, do you?" Rebecca asks, staring at Noah intently.

He stares back. "It's an expression."

Reed clears his throat. "We were headed to the parking lot. Shall we walk there together?"

"I just realized I left something in my locker," I reply quickly. "See you later?"

"They're charming," Noah says once they're gone, in a tone that suggests the exact opposite.

"They could use some help in the social interaction department," I agree. "But we should cut them some slack. It's hard starting a new school. Not knowing anyone . . ."

"Like you would know. You've lived here forever."

"I just mean I can imagine it."

Noah grins. "You can imagine anything. You think unicorns exist."

"Are you saying they don't?" I bite my lower lip in a pretend pout, and he laughs, pulling me into a hug.

"Of course they do," he assures me. "And speaking of magic, I want to take you out tomorrow night. On a date."

I pull back. "A date, huh? Where are we going?"

"It's a surprise." He looks very satisfied with himself.

"You're supposed to give me a hint," I inform him. "So I'm dressed properly."

He chuckles. "We're not going hiking. I'm taking you out to dinner. Do with that info whatever it is girls do."

"Anything but hiking gear. Check. Clothing that allows for ingestion of food. Clear as mud . . ." But something has caught my eye, and my voices trails off as I realize what I'm seeing.

It's nothing. Just a scrap of paper. So light and small it could have easily been carried away by the wind before I noticed it.

In the center of Mr. Shaw's memorial shrine, tucked among the candles and dying flowers, is a sheet of thick, creamy paper. Its edge is jagged, like it was torn from an artist's sketchbook.

Written on it, in an old-fashioned, classic script, in handwriting so familiar it could be my own: *Love never dies. —C*

NINE

An indistinct buzzing rings in my ears. I feel the blood drain from my face. I can't faint. I *won't* faint.

"Kailey?"

I am frozen. I think of a photograph I saw once, of an apple that was dipped in liquid nitrogen and shot by a bullet. It shattered like glass.

"Are you okay?" Noah's hands are on my shoulders.

I whip my head around. The movement makes me dizzy. The note wasn't there a few minutes ago. I'm sure of it.

Or am I?

The covered walkway is emptier now, sapped of the brief burst of after-school energy. *Think, Sera!*

There's Madison, chattering away about the committee to a politely listening Chantal and a bored-looking Nicole. There are Leyla and Bryan, splashing through puddles, huddled together under her ladybug-print umbrella. There's Echo, adjusting her floppy, canary-yellow hat before she steps into the mist. And at the end of the hallway, his back to me, a man with thick auburn hair moves briskly through the crowd, through the double doors leading inside, and is gone.

"Kailey! You're acting really weird."

I meet Noah's eyes. "I just remembered—I'm supposed to meet with the guidance counselor. I'm already late."

"Okay—"

"Don't wait for me—I'll take the bus," I call behind me as I take off running in the direction the man disappeared. I know it's dangerous, but if it's Cyrus, I have to know—I have to see for myself and hope he does not see me.

I throw open the steel doors, the chipped red surface slippery in my hands, and step inside. I pause. In front of me is a staircase where two students are chatting, a boy and a girl I recognize from my English class. To my left is another hallway.

"Did someone just come through here?" I ask.

The girl looks annoyed. "I'm not the hall monitor," she informs me. The boy just shrugs.

I cock my head. From down the hall, I hear another door slam. The linoleum is slick with tracked-in rain, and I force my steps to be light so my sneakers don't squeak.

I dart past open classrooms, rows of lockers, and a few lingering students. But the man I saw seems to have vanished into the air. When I reach the end of the hall I find another set of double doors, but throwing my shoulder against them results in nothing more than a thud reverberating through my frame. The doors are firmly locked.

Dejected, I return the way I came. When I come to the staircase, I decide to go up, taking the stairs two at a time and earning myself a puzzled glance from Ms. I'm-Not-the-Hall-Monitor. I couldn't care less.

I round the corner at the top of the stairs and find yet another hallway, this one deserted and dim. The school must be trying to save money on the electricity bill. The only light comes from a small window at the end of the hall.

I am more cautious now, my heart skittering in my chest. I walk softly, hugging the right side of the hall, eyes flitting around, willing myself not to miss anything. Not to get caught with my guard down. The air smells strangely like mint.

Mint—not vetiver or cedar. I'm not sure what I'm doing

here, whether I'm hoping to find Cyrus or not. I'm not even armed. I'm ridiculously vulnerable.

My neck prickles. I whirl around, suddenly sure someone's watching me.

In the center of the hallway stands a man, next to a door that I know was closed only moments before.

His police uniform fits snugly, emphasizing his powerful body. "Looking for someone?" he asks, snapping his gum.

Officer Spaulding. The cop who's investigating Mr. Shaw's death.

"Nope," I reply smoothly. "I thought I left a book up here. But then I realized I had it all along. In my backpack."

"In your backpack," he repeats with a smile. "Isn't that funny? You think something's lost, and it was right in front of you the whole time."

"Yes," I agree tentatively. My eyes stray to the gun holstered in his belt.

"Happens all the time in police work. You can't just look at the evidence once—guaranteed there's something you're missing."

A peal of feminine laughter spills out from the open door to his right. Officer Spaulding follows my gaze and nods. "I'm interviewing students, looking for new evidence in the Shaw case."

I relax in spite of myself. The reassuring murmur of voices inside the open classroom floats into the hall. "I don't understand. He was killed by muggers, right? What could you find out here?"

"You never know." He shrugs. "The police need to be sure."

"But didn't the newspaper say there were witnesses?"

He smiles. "Yes, a young man and woman from San Francisco. Not much older than you."

But I know better. The so-called "witnesses" are Jared and Amelia, Cyrus's obedient and loyal servants. I remember when Jared stopped a thief from picking Cyrus's pocket in 1660, aboard the merchant ship taking us to New Amsterdam. When Jared offered with a smug grin to kill the man, Cyrus was delighted. Jared's been doing Cyrus's dirty work ever since. As for Amelia, she's been in love with Cyrus since the day he made her immortal. Not that I care.

"Are they . . . okay?" I press.

He cups his chin. "They're shaken up, sure. Who wouldn't be? They asked us to keep their identities anonymous. For some reason they seem to think the killer has friends who could come after them. But they've been cooperating fully. Helped our sketch artist with drawings of the suspect."

Of course. No doubt Amelia and Jared are enjoying this

performance, sending the cops on a wild goose chase for a killer who doesn't exist.

"Well, I should be going," I say.

"Take care," the officer replies. "I didn't catch your name?"

I'm seized by the urge to lie for some reason, but I know no good can come from that. "Kailey," I answer, which is its own kind of lie.

"Bye, Kailey," he replies.

Downstairs, I hurry past the shrine, ignoring my desire to take the note Cyrus left so that I can study it more later. But for all I know, he's watching the shrine right now. And I can't afford to make any more mistakes.

I squeeze into the girls' bathroom and splash cold water on my face, letting the full force of the day's events wash over me.

Cyrus is alive. My intuition was right. I should feel vindicated, but instead I just feel confused.

I was wrong about Noah and barely avoided making a terrible mistake. This time, I need to be more like Cyrus. I need to be careful, systematic, to rely only on the evidence, regardless of the way my heart might waver in my chest like torn notebook paper in the breeze.

And I need to do it alone.

Jared and Amelia are in San Francisco, playing up

their roles as witnesses, and no doubt keeping the rest of the coven—my best friend Charlotte and sweet, quiet Sébastien—under close watch. I suck in a breath as I remember that when I went to the Golden Gate Bridge this weekend, I was so tempted to go by coven headquarters and see Charlotte. How trapped I would have been.

It's just me against Cyrus. Kailey's friends run through my mind. He could be any of them. And whoever he's become, whoever's body he's taken—that person is already dead.

All I can do is rule them out, one by one. Ask them questions to which only they would know the answers. And hope to hell I don't get caught first.

TEN

The next day after school, Leyla parks her car in front of her favorite thrift store, a place called Aunt Bea's. She's apparently on a mission to find outfits that are "more *Mad Men*, less *Punky Brewster*," as she puts it. This is my chance to prove she's not Cyrus, though I don't really suspect she is— he always said he'd never take a female body again. In the hundreds of years I've known him, he's done it only once, and barely lasted two days before he traded the wool merchant's daughter for a stable boy from a neighboring village. He said he hated how weak her body made him feel.

"But I like your style," I say as we walk inside. My eyes

are drawn to the vintage posters cluttering the walls, but Leyla turns and starts to expertly flip through the racks of dresses. Her hair is pulled back in two high pigtails, shot through with her trademark magenta streaks. It reminds me of streamers on a kid's bicycle.

She sighs. "I'm just getting too old for the whole ragamuffin look."

I have to laugh. I suppose "ragamuffin" is a good description. Today she's sporting a black hoodie over a yellow lace miniskirt with purple-and-black striped tights. Beat-up cowboy boots complete the outfit. I adore it.

"Aha!" She pulls a vintage Chanel sheath dress from the rack. "Look, it's only twenty dollars because it's got a broken zipper. I can totally fix that."

"It's nice," I admit. "But it's a little . . . stuffy."

"I know," she says happily. "I think I'll wear this to *The Nutcracker* tomorrow night—you know my little sister's playing Clara, right? Bryan said your whole family's going."

I don't say anything. No one has mentioned this to me; it must have been planned for a while. Since Kailey was still alive.

Leyla is too enamored with the dress to notice my silence. "I'll have to get, like, *pumps* to go with it," she muses. "Ladylike shoes."

If this is Cyrus, he's a far better actor than I give him credit for.

"Does this have something to do with Bryan?" I ask. I know the two of them went out on Saturday night, and judging from the goofy grin that Bryan hasn't been able to suppress ever since, I'd say it went well.

"Ha. No. I don't think the subtleties of fashion are really his thing. You know that girls dress up to impress other girls, right?" She meanders over to a jewelry display and fingers a strand of pearls. "Too much?" she asks. "Too much," she answers before I can reply.

"Okay, then, what girl inspired this Leyla makeover show?" I trail behind her as she digs through a pile of high heels. I recognize a pair of Dior strappy sandals that I used to own back in New York in the forties.

"Rebecca Sawyer—you know, the new girl with the hot brother? Just moved here from Sonoma? Their family has a winery up there."

"I met her yesterday. She's a bit . . . different," I say cautiously.

"That's what I like about her," Leyla replies. "She wears, like, *capelets*. And pencil skirts. And a freaking awesome pink tweed suit. If I saw her on the street, I never would've thought she was in high school."

"But doesn't that seem, I don't know, pretentious? Like she's trying to be someone she's not?" So far Rebecca and her brother have failed to impress me. Not to mention that they arrived at school the day after Mr. Shaw "died." I can't help feeling on edge when they're around.

Leyla shrugs. "She's a little awkward, I'll give you that. But at least she's being *real*. People who always fit in perfectly and always know just what to say are usually the ones hiding something."

"Interesting theory."

"Reverse-reverse-reverse psychology," she declares, arching an eyebrow. I giggle as she adds a lavender crepe dress to the pile on her arm. "Anyway," she continues, "I invited Rebecca to go with us to the party on Treasure Island this weekend. You'll like her, I swear."

"Treasure Island?" I repeat.

"Oh, that's right. You weren't there when Eli was telling us about it. Lots of local bands will be playing." She eyes a woven pillbox hat on a mannequin's head, but her arms are too full to reach for it. I laugh at her pouty look and pull the hat down for her.

"Is Eli's band playing?" I ask, adjusting the hat on top of Leyla's pigtails.

She catches sight of herself in a mirror and frowns. "Not sure. Madison would know. I don't really care about the lineup, anyway. I'm just going for the post-apocalyptic atmosphere."

Of course she is. Treasure Island lies halfway between Oakland and San Francisco, in the middle of the bay, and has an ironically jolly name for an abandoned military base. It sounds like the kind of place that would have roller coasters and funnel cakes, but it's actually full of graffiti-ridden barracks and broken glass.

"I'm in," I say. "And I'm sure I'll like Rebecca, if you think she's so cool."

"If you can't trust your best friend, who can you trust?" She smiles. "I'm going to go try these on."

Leyla disappears into the dressing room, and I wander aimlessly around the store, her last question echoing in my mind. Can I trust Leyla? She seems so . . . *Leyla*, but she hasn't said anything that proves she isn't Cyrus.

The salesgirl is parked behind the counter, playing with her phone. She must feel me staring, because she looks up. "Can I help you find anything?" she asks.

"Just looking around," I reply. She shrugs and hits a button on the CD player behind her. The store fills with the sounds of the Clash, trying to figure out if they should stay or if they should go.

Cyrus's note weighs heavily in my mind as I drift over to a pile of screen-printed T-shirts by the window. *Love never dies.* How wrong he is. My love for Cyrus died ages ago.

When, exactly, I can't say. I remember the first time I left him, perhaps thirty years after he made me immortal. I had kept in touch with one of the younger servants at my parents' estate, posing as an old family friend and benefactor who sent money and gifts and who wished to remain anonymous in exchange for regular updates of Lord and Lady Ames. I no longer cared what happened to my father after he threw me out of his house, but my mother was blameless.

Then one day a letter arrived at our home in France telling me that Lady Ames was very ill. I wanted to go to her immediately, but of course Cyrus forbade it. It was too dangerous, he said. Need he remind me that the last time I was in London I was nearly killed? I didn't care; I couldn't lose this chance to say good-bye to my mortal life.

So I left. I slipped out when Cyrus was away. But by the time I made it to London, my mother was already dead.

I kept waiting for tears, for sorrow, for some sort of release, but it never came. I felt nothing. Far more painful was returning to Cyrus and finding him utterly broken, gaunt and devastated and hurt. He was certain that he would never see me again, that I had left him alone. He wrapped his arms around me like a drowning man when I walked in, choking with sobs. *I was so alone, Sera. Please don't ever leave me again.* I held him in my arms, whispered how sorry I was, how much I loved him. And at the time, I meant it.

Being alone is Cyrus's greatest fear, and he's always done his best to instill it in the rest of us. I remember him giving the same speech to the other coven members when he made them immortal: *You can never leave. If you do, there's no guarantee you'll find us again. What if we took new bodies, new names, a new city? We'll have disappeared into the world, and you'll be all alone. There are no others like us.*

Only Cyrus had the elixir, the alchemical formula that severs the connection between body and soul, leaving our spirits free to move into new bodies. He wore it around his neck on a silver chain. I knew his father was the one to give him the vial, and he was also the source of the knowledge for making more. Though in truth, Cyrus stole the formula from his father, Johann von Hohenheim, renowned alchemist and scholar. *And killer,* I remember. Johann wanted me dead almost as soon as Cyrus made me an Incarnate. Cyrus took the blue book from his father's house the night he ran away with me.

Since that night, I have never seen Cyrus without the vial of elixir around his neck. He would never let any of the others touch it. Keeping the elixir from them was his insurance policy. *Even if you had the formula, none of you could ever make the elixir,* he used to remind us. *It requires a skilled alchemist. You could never make new companions.*

How could we leave, knowing we would be doomed to walk the earth alone?

No one ever left the coven. Until me.

My phone buzzes in my pocket, pulling me back to the present, to the world I wish would absorb me and keep me secret. A smile plays across my lips when I see who's calling.

"Is this the unicorn hotline? I'd like to report a sighting." Noah's voice breathes in my ear.

"You've got the right number. Give me the details."

"I'd prefer to report them in person, over dinner tonight."

"The unicorn hotline will send a representative to your house at eight," I answer.

A pause. "You don't have to do that, Kailey—"

"I know, but I want to. See you soon!" I tap the END CALL button before he can protest. It's true—I *do* want to see his house. I'm in love with Noah, and I want to know everything there is to know about him.

"The gods of fashion are smiling upon me today," Leyla declares, emerging from the dressing room with a pigtail askew. "Operation Retro Chic is a success."

I make the appropriate admiring sounds as she heaps her finds on the counter and chats with the salesgirl. When

Leyla finishes paying, she tosses her purchases into the huge canvas tote that hangs off her shoulder. "I'm so glad we got the chance to hang out, just the two of us," she says, linking her arm through mine.

"Me too," I answer.

"Just because we both have boyfriends doesn't mean we can ignore girl time," Leyla says, pulling me out to the sidewalk.

"Wait—does that mean Bryan's your official *boyfriend*?"

"Um," she stalls, a blush stealing across her cheeks. "Yes? That's okay, right?"

"Of course it is! You two were clearly meant for each other." I laugh. "But if you start coming over only to see Bryan and ignoring me, then you're in trouble."

"Never!" She gasps theatrically. "You're right, though. I think the last time we hung out alone was, what? Three weeks ago, when we got coffee? Way too long." My heart lifts as she speaks. There's no way Cyrus could know that.

"Yeah, what was the name of that café again?" I ask. I need to be sure.

Leyla stares at me. "Seriously? You don't remember?"

My heart starts to pound. "It's on the tip of my tongue." My voice sounds strangely high-pitched.

"Jeez, Kailey," she admonishes. "We've only been going to Caffe Strada for three years."

"Right! Duh. Of course." I clap my hand to my forehead. Leyla's shaking her head and laughing at what an airhead I am, but I can't stop smiling.

"You know what? I think we should hit up Caffe Strada right now," I say. "Gelato on me."

It's a small victory, but I need to celebrate it. Noah isn't Cyrus, and neither is Leyla. This knowledge makes me feel much less alone in the world: the opposite of how Cyrus promised I would find myself.

It makes me wonder what else he was wrong about.

ELEVEN

When Noah's father answers the door later that night, I'm blasted with the smell of whiskey on his breath. "Kailey!" he shouts. "Come in, come in." He closes the door behind me with a slam, the hinges creaking in protest. "Guess I should oil that," he says.

I just nod. I've never actually spoken to Mr. Vander before or seen him up close. He's got Noah's deep blue eyes, but his skin is sallow, his nose a garden of broken capillaries. He's tall, though, like Noah, and strong. His beard covers up what I suspect to be a twin to Noah's sculpted jawline. It's grizzled and shot through with gray. He's wearing shorts and a stained T-shirt, despite the late fall chill that hangs in the air. The house is freezing.

Noah's dog Harker bounds into the room, eyeing me suspiciously. He backs up slowly, tail bristling, a deep growl emanating from his throat. "Stop it, you jerk," commands Mr. Vander. "It's just Kailey." Harker yelps and sits down but doesn't move his eyes from my own. I subtly bow my head, trying to show canine submission in my body language. I don't blame the dog for not liking me. Most animals don't.

"I swear, that dog's insane. He doesn't like anyone but Noah," Mr. Vander says, folding his arms across his chest.

"He doesn't bother me," I say, looking around. I've never been in Noah's house before. The foyer is covered in dark wooden wainscoting, its oiled finish dull in spots. To my right is a staircase leading to the second floor and Noah's room. To my left, an open door reveals a small living room, where a TV fills the room with cold blue light. The oak floors are scratched and warped.

"Well," says Mr. Vander, focusing on me with bleary eyes, "I should go get Noah. It's not polite to keep a pretty girl like you waiting." He looks me up and down, and I momentarily regret the dress I chose to wear. Fitted around the bodice before flaring out at my waist, it's a robin's-egg shade of blue that reminds me of Noah's eyes in the sunlight. I wouldn't call the neckline indecent by any means—it's just low enough to frame the birdcage necklace that Noah gave me, on its long silver chain. But the way Mr. Vander looks at me makes me wish for a jacket that buttoned up to my neck.

He puts his hand on the banister of the staircase for balance, running his hands up and down the smooth surface. I shiver. He never breaks eye contact with me. I wonder how he's even upright. Judging from the whiskey fumes that emanate from him, he's been drinking all day. But he doesn't slur his words, not a bit. And somehow that's more unnerving than if he had.

"Kailey, sorry, I didn't realize you'd be here so quickly." Noah appears, clomping down the stairs. "Do you . . . want to come up for a few?" He locks eyes with me, and I nod.

"Yeah." I have the strange sensation that he just rescued me from something. I could tell when we spoke earlier that he didn't want me to come over, and now I'm beginning to see why. I follow him up the stairs, turning for one last look at Mr. Vander, but he's already returned to his ripped leather chair in front of the TV.

Noah's house has an air of faded grandeur. The stained-glass window overlooking the landing is streaked with dust; the faded Persian runner in the hallway rubbed almost down to the cotton backing in parts. There's no smell of food cooking, like there is at the Morgans' house. No clatter of conversation.

No Mrs. Vander. I recall Noah saying she threatened to leave when his father lost his job and started drinking again. It looks like she did, though I'm ashamed to realize I never asked Noah what happened. He doesn't talk about his family much.

Harker lopes up after us, but Noah stops him when he goes to follow us into Noah's room. "Stay," he commands. The dog lies down on the rug in the hallway, watching me warily.

Noah's room fits him perfectly. It's cozy, with low, angled ceilings. A huge oak desk holds an old desktop computer, a pile of books, and an open sketchpad. My eyes are immediately drawn to the walls, covered in framed photographs, beautifully arranged.

Some are reprints from famous photographers—Man Ray, Robert Mapplethorpe, Diane Arbus, and a few others I can't immediately place. Others I instinctively recognize as his own work. There's a portrait of Harker, his dark eyes liquid and full of love, rendered in black-and-white. There are shots of various locations I recognize from around Berkeley and Oakland: the clock tower at the UC Berkeley campus; a group of kids riding bicycles; birds clustered on a liquor store sign while a man with sad eyes stands underneath.

On the wall above his dresser is a painting, the only

nonphotographic piece in the room. It's unmistakably one of Kailey's. I move closer to study it.

The painting shows Kailey from behind, in her room, looking out her window toward the Vanders' house. The only source of light is the soft glow from Noah's window, outlining his silhouette—but then I see the small dots of light surrounding the window, illuminating the gutters and the eaves. I smile. They are tiny fairies, their translucent wings delicately rendered. Kailey's signature touch: magical creatures thrown casually into the real world.

"I like your dress," he says to my back, and I turn around.

"Thank you," I answer. "You too." His brown shirt and dark pants follow the line of his lean, muscled frame. The scuffed combat boots peeking out from beneath his cuffs are the only indication of his usual rumpled style. It looks perfect.

"Oh?" He arches an eyebrow. "You like my dress?"

"Shut up," I say. "I meant that you look nice."

He grins. "I was going to wear a tie, but I realized I don't really know how to tie it."

"A tie? How fancy is this place?"

He looks down, suddenly embarrassed. "It's not, but I was having fun with the whole date thing."

"I'll tie it for you," I offer, picking up the tie draped over the back of his desk chair. "You're going to have to sit down, though. I don't think I can reach that high."

He obliges, and I wrap the tie under his collar, brushing his hair back with my fingers. A shivery feeling takes root in my belly. I can feel his breath in the air between us.

"Where did you learn how to do this?" he asks. His voice is low, soft.

"Um, I've seen Bryan do it?" I offer. My voice catches as I see the books on his desk and realize what he's been reading about.

Every one of them is about alchemy. Thomas Vaughan's *Coelum Terrae*, George Ripley's *The Mistery of Alychymists*, a title called *The Alchemical Practice of Mary the Prophetess*. I recognize some from Cyrus's own collection, though these copies have Berkeley library stickers on them. I look past them to the sketchbook and almost gasp at what Noah was drawing—two people standing at the top points of a downward-pointing triangle, silver cords curving out from their navels toward strange symbols in the air. The cord connecting body and soul, the bond that the elixir is designed to destroy.

My god. I hadn't realized how much Cyrus taught Noah before he vanished. He was clearly grooming Noah for the coven. I'm not surprised—Cyrus loves intelligence and beauty. He especially loves those who are lost and confused, those he can rescue and brainwash and turn into his loyal followers. Noah is all of those things—although Cyrus would have never accepted Noah if he'd known I'd loved him.

I want to reach out and grab Noah, keep him safe from Cyrus forever. But all I say is "How's that?"

Noah rises and studies himself in the mirror on the inside of his closet door. "Bravo. Should we go?"

He leads me back downstairs, where Mr. Vander is passed out on the leather chair. I'm surprised, considering how alert he seemed only a few minutes before, but Noah barely gives him a second glance. Harker whimpers when Noah opens the front door. "It's okay, buddy. I'll be back later," Noah says quietly. Harker settles down to wait, and I have the feeling he'll still be right there when Noah gets home.

We drive to downtown Oakland, toward Lake Merritt. It's hard to be in this area without thinking of Cyrus—he staged his death so close to here—but I try to brush those thoughts away. I'm with the boy I love tonight. Noah sees me looking out the window and must sense my trepidation. "I swear I'm not taking you here because of Mr. Shaw."

"I didn't say anything," I counter softly. "Besides, it's okay if you want to talk about him. I . . . I know he was important to you." I realize that more now than ever.

The restaurant is at the end of a long pier that extends over the lake. From the outside, it looks like a cottage out of *Grimm's Fairy Tales*, with its river-stone walls and alpine beams. The interior glows with hundreds of strands of Christmas lights, criss-crossing the ceiling in a hopelessly tangled web. Metal sconces light the way to our table, which sits next to a large window. Outside, the water ripples underneath the nearly full moon.

"I love it," I tell him. It feels like we're on a boat.

The waitress brings us mint tea in delicate porcelain cups. "I had a feeling this was your kind of place," says Noah.

The air is redolent with cardamom and nutmeg. I sink back into my chair, holding my teacup in a decidedly unladylike fashion, fingers of both hands wrapped around its smooth surface to soak up the warmth.

"What should we order?" asks Noah, holding up his menu.

"You pick." I'm so happy to be in this magical place. I can almost believe in safety again.

"What if I pick lamb brains?" he asks.

I've eaten those before, simmered in butter and garlic. I've lived all over the world and eaten meals that would probably terrify Noah. "Yum" is all I say, then, "Wait. Do they have that?"

"No," he replies. "Lucky for you."

"Don't hold back on my account." I scan the menu, and a thought occurs to me. "Wait, Noah, this place is expensive.

How are you paying for this?" Cyrus had extravagant tastes and bottomless wealth, but Noah's family certainly isn't rich.

"You're not supposed to ask that, Kailey!" he protests. "It's a date. I'm a man of means." I raise an eyebrow. "Okay, okay, I shot some photos for the restaurant last summer. They're using it in a brochure or something. My dad knows the owner and hooked me up with the gig. Anyway, it's taken care of."

I've been observing humans for a very long time, and I don't miss the fleeting shadow that moves across his eyes when he mentions his father. It's like a wayward cloud on an otherwise sunny day.

"He's not doing well, is he." I say it like a statement, not a question. Noah meets my eye and shakes his head. "You don't have to talk about it if you don't want to," I add, but I hope he will.

"No . . . I *want* to talk to you. I'm just not sure it's that interesting. He's a drunk, my mom's gone, and I'm stuck there." His jaw tightens. I don't say anything, hoping he'll continue. "I think he wishes she'd taken me with her. So there'd be no one around to make him feel guilty. I know he blames me. He always tells me never to have kids because they ruin your life. Nice thing to say to your son, right?" His eyes are full of pain, shimmering in the candlelight that moves over them like moonlight on a lake.

"Where did she go? Your mom?" No matter how much she hated her husband, I find it hard to understand why she'd leave her son behind.

"She's in Arizona with my grandparents. When she left, she said she was just going to stay with them for a while. She said she didn't want to take me out of school. She said she'd call me every day." He takes a sip of his tea. "I haven't heard from her once. She's not coming back. I'm not stupid."

"You never know," I offer weakly.

"No, I do know. And I don't care. Things weren't much better when she was here. But it doesn't matter to me what they do. Next month I'll be seventeen. And that means I only have one more year before I can do whatever I want. I can leave, I can travel—" He stops talking abruptly as the waitress interrupts to take our order. Noah lists several dishes, but I'm not listening.

Noah and I have another year of high school—but what then? He wants to leave. We could go together. But how long could that last? *How long before he finds out I'm not human?*

I don't want to think about the future anymore. All I want is for this moment, right now, to last forever. I want it always to be the November that I fell in love with Noah.

The waitress leaves. "Where would you go?" I ask. "If you could travel."

He smiles and looks out the window. He has a faraway

look in his eyes, like he can see coastlines in other countries, like he's memorized every map. "I don't know," he admits. "It's a big world. I've always wanted to see the northern lights."

I desperately want to tell him about their colors, their shifting electromagnetic dance. I watched them with Charlotte from the middle of a volcanic hot spring, its steam billowing in a similar shape to the aurora borealis, our long hair trailing in the water like Nordic mermaids.

"I'd like to see them with you," I say instead.

"Mr. Shaw used to talk about all the places he'd been. That guy was really well-traveled for being so young."

"He was certainly . . . interesting," I say diplomatically.

He reaches across the table and takes my hand. I feel my skin come alive under his touch, a feathery sensation that climbs up my arm to my chest. "*You're* interesting."

"Oh, yeah?" I reply.

"Yeah." He lets go of my hand and reaches for my face, tucks a loose lock of hair behind my ear. "You know, honestly—this is going to sound really weird—but I always kind of assumed you liked girls."

"Why? Because I wasn't obsessed with you? So typical," I say smoothly, though his comment makes me wonder. I know so little about who Kailey was.

He laughs. "No, I'm not that egotistical. It's just that,

well, you always had tons of guys asking you out. And you turned every single one down. I figured you must have some reason. And, you know, you're kind of a private person."

I take a sip of tea, considering. It was certainly possible. I'd had the impression that she was hiding something from her family. Could this explain where she was going the night that she died?

"Well, the last time I checked, I like *you*." I feel bold. "So hopefully that answers that."

"Good. So . . . there's that dance coming up at school. Would you go with me?" He lowers his chin slightly and regards me, and I'm surprised to see that he actually looks nervous.

Seraphina Ames at a high school dance? The idea is comical.

But dancing with Noah? Being in his arms? Being *normal*? The idea is intoxicating.

"I know you're Little Miss Rebel and stuff, but—"

"I'd love to," I answer quietly, and he grins at me with obvious relief.

After we eat, we walk hand-in-hand along the footpath surrounding Lake Merritt. Noah makes sure to avoid the shore where Cyrus was supposedly killed.

The temperature fell while we were inside, but with Noah next to me I can't even feel it. Thoughts about our future keep arising in my mind, unbidden and undeterred by the moonlight. But when he pulls me into the shadow of a cypress tree I forget everything but now, this perfect moment. Because Noah's hand is at the small of my back, and his lips are searching, and the lights of the downtown buildings are flickering across the lake. Our bodies are pressed together like a flower between book pages.

I only wish I could tell him who I really am, *what* I really am. Because how can he love me without knowing my true name?

Since I can't tell it to him, I kiss him instead.

TWELVE

The next day after school, Noah raises his head from a nineteenth-century microscope in the antique store where I work. "This is the best toy ever," he informs me. I laugh.

"I dare you to find a kid outside who agrees with you," I tease. I'm grateful for his company. There's been only one customer all day, a thirty-something woman who was in the shop just for the five minutes it took her to pick out an Edwardian ivory hand mirror. I'm always amused at the things people buy in here.

Noah pulls a piece of paper from his pocket and slides

it under the microscope's lens. "Did you know that paper is hairy?" he asks.

"I think they're called 'fibers,' not hair," I say.

"Okay, smarty-face. Come here," he demands, waving me over.

"You want me to look at hairy paper?"

"Why not?" But when I approach him, he takes my hand and places it under the lens. The cold brass surface chills my skin. "Hmm, interesting."

"What do you see?" I move my body closer to his. I can smell the tea tree oil soap he uses. I want to run my fingers through the dark, tangled waves of his hair.

He fiddles with the knob. "There," he says finally. "I see it. It's all silvery."

"What do you see?"

"Your soul," he answers.

I rip my hand away.

"Wh-what are you talking about?" I stare at him.

"Jeez, Kailey. What's wrong?" He looks hurt.

"That's just a really weird thing for you to say," I answer, rubbing my hand. There's a scratch on it from the sharp brass edge of the microscope.

"It was something Mr. Shaw told me about," he explains. "He said that the human soul isn't a religious myth—it's something physical. There was even a doctor who measured it. Did you know that the average soul weighs 21 grams?" He looks at me nervously.

I force myself to be patient. I understand that he needs to talk about Cyrus. He's grieving a friend. It's not Noah's fault that he has no idea that Cyrus is actually alive—or what a monster he is.

"I didn't know that," I lie. I remember Cyrus's brilliant smile in March of 1907, when Dr. MacDougall's research was published. *You see, Sera? Modern science is finally catching on to what the alchemists have known for hundreds of years.*

Noah leans back on a Victorian fainting couch, abandoning the microscope. I curl up next to him, and he puts an arm around my shoulder.

"Yeah, Mr. Shaw told me that there's no difference between the spiritual world and the physical one. He said that most people think of alchemy as a cheap trick. Turning lead into gold—that sounds so selfish, right? Like . . . the medieval equivalent of a get-rich-quick scam." He strokes my hair as I bite my tongue. "But it was so much more. When the alchemists talked about transforming one thing into another, they were also talking about spiritual transformation. It was noble."

I have a bitter taste in my mouth. "They were looking for immortality. I can't think of anything more selfish."

"I don't think it's selfish, not in itself. It would depend on how you spent it, whether you used all that time for good or evil." He pauses. "A lot of things are like that, I guess."

"Immortality is tragic, if you think about it." My throat grows thick with unshed tears, and I swallow hard. "Can you imagine being forced to stay young forever, watching everyone you know die? How pointless would life seem if you saw that?"

Noah's arm tightens around me. "Hey," he says. "What's wrong?"

"Nothing," I whisper. Now that I've tasted it, I want nothing more than to keep talking with Noah about alchemy, no matter the risk. My heart yearns to tell him everything, to let him see what I carry inside me. All my years, all my lifetimes.

He's so close to the truth and doesn't even know it.

"Of course, immortality would only be bearable if you had the right person to share it with," he says, and my heart catches. I stare straight ahead, but I close my eyes when he turns and kisses me on the cheek.

"Would you choose it, if you could?" My voice is barely audible.

"I would," he answers. "Maybe I'm just being romantic about it, but to me, immortality means *freedom*. You don't have to get old. You don't have to get a job you never wanted. You don't have to regret the places you've never been, the things you missed out on. You could really, truly follow your dreams. Most people's lives are a lot more tragic than that."

There's a truth in what he says that resonates on the silver strands of my soul. "It sounds like Mr. Shaw gave you a lot to think about," I say. "I'm starting to understand how much he meant to you." And I do. Cyrus knew just how to play Noah, I think bitterly. He knew how attractive all of this would be to a boy whose home life was falling apart, a smart and sensitive and passionate boy whose world was just a bit too small.

"I had a dream about him last night," he says, and I stiffen. "I dreamed he was in my room, sitting at my desk. It was really weird—he looked completely different. Somehow I knew it was him, though."

Goose bumps rise on my bare arms. "Strange," I say, resisting the urge to ask what the dream Cyrus looked like.

"You know what's really strange, though? The police haven't found his body. It makes me wonder." He rakes his hands through his hair.

"Makes you wonder what? Oakland homicide is pretty busy, you know. I'm sure they'll find it eventually." I'm sure they won't.

He shakes his head. "It's not that. They dredged the lake.

I mean, his death was a huge deal. Public-school teacher shot in cold blood—the news people have been all over it."

"What are you getting at?" I ask, almost afraid to hear his answer.

"You're going to tell me I'm crazy," he says, jumping up from the couch and pacing back and forth.

"I won't," I tell him. "Swear."

"It can only be two things. Either someone doesn't want the police to find his body. Or he's still alive."

My heart starts to pound. "There were witnesses," I say, my voice quavering.

"But maybe the witnesses kidnapped him and made up the whole story of the shooting to cover it up? Or maybe they were his accomplices and helped him fake his death." He stops pacing and wraps his arms across his body.

"Why would he do that?" I hate where this conversation is going, but I'm gripped by the destructive urge to continue it, the same way people can't help but stare at car crashes.

"Who knows? The guy was obviously brilliant. What was he doing teaching high school biology anyway? Maybe, once he couldn't find the girl he was looking for, he wanted to disappear and start over. Maybe he thought Seraphina had left Berkeley. Or *maybe*"—he looks me in the eye—"he finally found the secret to immortality." He grins, as though he's said something amusing, but I'm shaken.

"You're giving me the creeps," I say. "Come sit next to me."

He obliges, and I'm immediately warmed to the core. "Thanks for listening," he says, cupping my face.

The bells hanging over the front door jangle, startling me. I whip my head around to see Kailey's brother entering the store.

"Sorry to interrupt you lovebirds," he says with a smile that reads as anything but.

"Hey, Bryan," Noah says awkwardly.

"We were just having a conversation, I'll have you know," I tell Bryan primly.

"Mmm-hmm," he answers. "I'm not staying. I'm on a mission."

"Which is . . . ?" I ask.

"Mom wants to know what time you're coming home. We're going to see that play tonight—*The Nutcracker.*"

"I think it's technically a ballet," I tell him. "Anyway, why didn't she just call me?"

"First off, stop trying to make me feel dumb. And second, she *did* call you. No answer. I see now why you didn't pick up." He winks.

"Oh," I say, defeated. "Well, my phone is on *silent.*"

"Sure it is." Bryan wanders over to one of the store's many bookshelves and studies the volumes.

Noah clears his throat. "I should probably get going, Kailey. Let you finish up here. Have fun tonight."

"Hey, why don't you come with us to the show?" Bryan offers.

"No, that's okay. I don't want to intrude on your family tradition."

"You're not intruding. I'm sure our parents wouldn't mind, now that you're Kailey's boyfriend and all."

Noah just shakes his head. "I'm supposed to have dinner with my dad tonight—he'd be really disappointed if I ditched him." I wish he would change his mind, but I understand that Noah needs some time to himself right now.

"Right, say hi to your dad for me," I say, playing along.

"Sure. I'll call you later." He kisses me and heads out the door.

I turn to Bryan with a sigh. "Brother dear, you have terrible timing."

But Bryan is too busy flipping through the pages of a leather-bound book to pay any attention to me. "You should reduce the price of this book," he says instead. "It has a typo."

"A lot of old books have typos," I say in exasperation. "They spelled things differently back then."

"No, I mean this is a chemistry book with a mistake in it. It says here that copper sulfate turns fire blue. But copper sulfate turns fire *green*." And with that, he snaps the book shut and makes for the front door, throwing it open with a bang.

Just before he walks out, he winks knowingly at me.

Long after he's gone, I remain frozen, staring at the door in a state of shock. I think of Cyrus, pulling a pinch of powder from his leather satchel to toss on the fire. *I burn for you, Seraphina. I burn in different colors. Flowers don't do you justice, so I bring you a garden of flame.*

THIRTEEN

Please not Bryan, please not Bryan. The phrase slams through my head as I make my rounds, quickly closing up the shop: dragging the sale pieces in from the sidewalk, counting the day's meager profits, and turning off the lights.

Out on the street, I can see my exhalations in rapid white puffs as I lock the front door. It's dark and deserted in the late November gloom. *Please not Bryan,* I think again as I hurry back to the Morgan house.

Kailey's family has already lost so much, even though they don't know their daughter is dead. I can't bear the thought of them losing their son too—and to Cyrus.

I plod up the wooden stairs to the front door. Just as I reach for the handle, it opens, and I come face-to-face with Bryan.

"How did you know I was here?" I ask.

"You underestimate me."

I stare at him. I watch. I wait.

He steps outside. "We're out of horseradish. And apparently our father sees this as a great emergency. I'm going to the store."

"It's his favorite," I say. Even I know that, and I've only been around for a few weeks.

"Is that right?" Bryan smirks. "You want to come with me?"

"No," I say, more sharply than I meant to. I move past him and inside, where I'm greeted by the scent of beets roasting with garlic, but all I can think about is Bryan. How badly I want him to be safe. How worried I am that I'm too late to do anything about it.

"Kailey? That you? Come set the table." Mrs. Morgan's voice wafts out from the kitchen.

"In a minute," I promise. In the hallway, I pause in front of Bryan's room, seized with a sudden urge to go in. To investigate. It's what Cyrus would do. Before I can argue with myself, I slip inside, shutting the door quietly behind me.

Bryan's room is a mess, the unmade bed covered in dirty

clothes and mismatched sheets. The walls are lined with posters for the Oakland A's. An empty aquarium sits on the desk next to a lifeless laptop. I peek into the closet, where potato chip bags vie for space next to piles of sweatshirts. I try to imagine Cyrus here, and fail.

But then again, what was I expecting to find? Alchemy texts? A well-tailored suit, a briefcase made of fine leather?

My head starts to hurt from thinking about all of it, and I sink down onto Bryan's bed with a sigh, only to jump back up again. Something is digging painfully into the under-side of my right thigh. I drop to the floor and run my hand between Bryan's mattress and box spring—and immediately come into contact with something hard.

I shove my arm under the mattress and lift it up. The entire space is lined with books.

And right at the top, underneath the spot where Bryan's pillow would be, is a beat-up leather-bound journal. It opens easily to the page that was last written in, thanks to a Taco Bell receipt for two Doritos Locos Tacos. The receipt is printed with yesterday's date.

And the contents of the journal? Not a list of suspects, their names crossed out one by one like the pictures in the yearbook that Cyrus marked off when he was Mr. Shaw. Not a formula for an elixir that grants immortal life.

It's a poem. Dedicated to Leyla.

I know it's wrong. But I read it anyway. And my grin grows wider with every line.

Lady Leyla Ladybug

Super awesome insect girl
splashing in my muddy heart
candy-apple carapace
softer than spider's lace
you've got a crazy pretty face
land on me anytime, little bug
keep on flashing, flashlight girl
and keep me in your magenta world

"Not cool, not cool at all."

I snap my head up. Bryan's face looms coldly in the open door.

"I'm sorry, I—" My voice falls off. I really have no excuse.

Bryan steps inside and closes the door behind him. "You *so* owe me. That's number three, if I'm counting right," he declares, sitting heavily above me on the bed.

I open my mouth but nothing comes out. And then finally, weakly, I repeat after him: "Number three?"

"Mmm-hmm. *First*, I covered for your car accident. And *second*, I sneaked you out of the house when you were grounded."

Oh. *Oh.* Relief breezes through me. I look down, smile, remembering the night he took me to the party in Montclair. This is Bryan.

"I *do* owe you," I admit. "What do you want me to do?"

He considers this. "Nothing. I'm earning chips."

"Chips?" I briefly think of the snacks he has hidden in the closet.

"Like in poker. Just letting them pile up. No need to cash in yet." He ruffles my hair. "But for a start, how about you don't tell me how bad that poem is."

I follow his gaze to his journal on my lap. "I thought it was pretty good, actually."

"Shut up," he says, not unkindly, and snatches the journal away. "You've told me plenty of times how awful my writing is. You're the artsy one in the family—I get it."

I feel a pang of sympathy for Bryan and his über-jock shtick, his room plastered with athletic paraphernalia while his books are hidden under the mattress.

"Every writer gets rejected," I say. "I was just trying to toughen you up."

"Pretty twisted, Kailes."

"What can I say—I can be mean sometimes." I stand up, smoothing my skirt. "But seriously, I think you should give the poem to Leyla."

"And *I* think this conversation is over," he counters,

standing next to me and throwing an arm around my shoulders. Before I can react, he digs his knuckle into the top of my head.

"Hey!"

"Oh, you *totally* deserved that noogie."

"Okay, okay," I say, rubbing my head. "I mean it about the poem, though." I quickly dart out of reach toward the door. "Leyla would love it."

"Out!" he yells even though I'm already in the hallway. I steal a glance back, but Bryan's no longer looking at me. His eyes are trained on the page.

I can't contain my smile. Bryan isn't Cyrus—he's just regular old goofy, messy, adorable Bryan, who happens to write secret poems comparing his girlfriend to insects. And I love him for it.

FOURTEEN

"*The Nutcracker* is my favorite part of the holidays," says Mrs. Morgan as we walk toward the theater after Bryan and Mr. Morgan. Her cheeks are rosy from the clear cold air, and her eyes are shining. The combination makes her look girlish.

I love this ballet too. Charlotte and I attend a performance every year at the War Memorial Opera House in San Francisco. *Used to attend, that is*, I think sadly. It was our tradition, just the two of us. Amelia came with us one year, but then she spent the entire evening critiquing the dancers' athleticism under her breath. "Circus performers get no respect," she sniffed, referring to her previous career as an aerialist. "They can do everything these ballerinas can do, all while swinging in the air from a trapeze." We left her at home after that.

Mrs. Morgan loops her arm through mine. "I've told you how my father used to put this record on when I was a little girl, haven't I? And my sisters and I would dance around the living room pretending to be Clara and the waltzing snowflakes?"

Mr. Morgan chuckles. "You tell us every year, Lisa." And with that, I've crossed Kailey's parents off my list of suspects.

The theater is in a converted church, a solid-looking Craftsman building with thick eaves, dark wood siding, and leaded-glass windows. It's beautiful, but nothing like the grand theaters I'm used to. I think of when I attended the premiere of *George Balanchine's The Nutcracker* performance in New York City with Cyrus. He stroked my dark hair and whispered to me that I looked just like Maria Tallchief, the prima ballerina who danced the role of the Sugar Plum Fairy. "Except more beautiful, of course," he added. "Perhaps your next body should be that of a dancer?"

Bryan and I follow Mr. and Mrs. Morgan to our seats. I settle in and study the crowd, spotting Leyla with her

parents several rows up, close to the stage. They're carrying an enormous bouquet of poinsettias and brilliant orange
dahlias.

The curtain rises, and the familiar playful strains of the
overture fill the theater. I steal a glance at Mrs. Morgan,
whose rapt gaze follows every movement on stage. I imagine her as a young girl in Milwaukee, pirouetting with her
sisters around a 1970s living room with avocado green shag
carpet, their parents trailing them with cameras. In my
mind, she looks just like Kailey.

On stage, Leyla's sister is beautiful, maybe thirteen, and
a perfect Clara. Before long I'm lost in the story, delight-
ing in the family's Christmas party, dismayed when Clara's
brother breaks her toy, goose bumps rising on my arms as
the Nutcracker comes to life and battles the Mouse King.
By the time the Nutcracker prince whisks Clara away to the
magical Land of Sweets, I've almost forgotten about Cyrus.
Almost.

I catch myself thinking about escape. So many of my
favorite stories are about escaping to a fantastical world:
Dorothy rides a tornado to Oz, the Pevensie children find
the portal to Narnia inside a wardrobe.

My life here with Kailey's family *is* my magical world.
Noah wants to escape, to travel to other countries and leave
his family behind, and I understand why. But as far as I'm

concerned, Kailey's life is wonderful. Kailey's life is my Oz, my Narnia, my Land of Sweets.

The orchestra swells, and I feel tears in my eyes. I blink them away as the curtain drops and the lights come up for intermission.

"I thought that would *never* end," says Bryan. "I'm starving. Meet you outside." He dashes off to the concession stand before it's fully bright in the theater.

"Anna was fantastic, don't you think?" Mrs. Morgan says of Leyla's sister as we squeeze out of the theater. She yawns. "Eric, would you get us some hot cocoa?" she asks Kailey's dad. "I'm so sleepy. Maybe the sugar will wake me up." He nods and strides away.

Groups of Berkeleyites mill about outside the theater, their outfits running the gamut from floor-length evening gowns to frayed Levi's, everyone's breath forming white clouds in the chilly air.

"*There* you are!" I hear Leyla's voice and turn around to see her waving at us. "Come here," she says. "These heels are impossible to walk in."

I burst out laughing as Mrs. Morgan and I push through the crowd to Leyla. She's wearing the dress she bought yesterday and teetering in a pair of three-inch beige leather pumps.

Mrs. Morgan frowns at me. "Why are you laughing? Leyla looks lovely."

"Thank you, Mrs. Morgan," says Leyla sweetly, putting her hand on my shoulder for balance. "No thanks to your mean daughter." She winks.

"No," I protest. "You look great. Just a little . . . unsteady."

Leyla sighs, shifting uncomfortably and tugging at the hem of her dress. "I know, I know. You're right. I have my cowboy boots in the car, but I'm determined to make it through the night in these torture devices. Where's Bryan?" she asks.

"Attending to his appetite," I reply.

"I heard that, Kailey." I whirl around to see Bryan and Mr. Morgan, each carrying two cups of steaming hot cocoa. Bryan has a soft pretzel tucked into each pocket of his jacket and a brownie cradled in the crook of his arm. "I can't help it if this play—sorry, *ballet*—makes me hungry," he says. "Sugar plums, candy canes. It's like they designed it to sell food at the concession stand."

"I hear Tchaikovsky made a fortune in the soft pretzel business," Mr. Morgan adds.

"Chai who?" Bryan's voice is muffled as he stuffs half a pretzel in his mouth.

"The composer," Leyla says with a laugh. "Now give me a bite of that brownie."

"I was just kidding," Bryan protests as he splits the brownie in half, handing Leyla the larger piece. "I knew this was by Chailovsky."

I have to giggle. Now that I've seen the hidden side of Bryan, I wonder if he's only pretending to forget the name, clowning for our amusement.

"Hey, artist girl," a voice breathes in my ear, and I stiffen.

It's Reed, wearing a charcoal wool suit with a forest green handkerchief poking out of the breast pocket. "Hi," I say cautiously, taking a step back and resisting the urge to wipe my ear where he breathed on it.

His sister, Rebecca, trails behind him. She's wearing a vintage plum-colored satin dress that's gathered at the waist with a jeweled brooch, complete with a fur stole. Dainty gold hoops flash in her ears.

"How's everyone doing this fine evening?" asks Reed.

I stiffen, annoyed at their intrusion. *They just moved here,* I remind myself. *They're trying to make friends.*

"Great." Leyla immediately stands up straighter, eying Rebecca's retro-chic fashion.

"And you, Kailey?"

"I always love the ballet," I say calmly, meeting his gaze.

"Have you been to *The Nutcracker* before?" He leans closer to me.

"Yes," I reply but don't offer anything further.

But he presses on. "Do you come every year?" Behind him, Rebecca watches me with her huge, long-lashed eyes, waiting for my answer.

I pause and look around at the group. I'm almost certain that someone said this was a Morgan family tradition—but I can't remember.

Mrs. Morgan comes to my rescue. "We do," she answers, "though some of us enjoy it more than others." She shoots Bryan a pointed look, and he grins, shrugging his shoulders.

Reed barely glances at her before returning his attention to me. "So what else do you do for fun? Besides painting murals and making people think they know you from a past life."

"That's pretty much it," I say flatly.

But Reed's undeterred by my lack of enthusiasm. "How long have you and Leyla been friends?" This is getting ridiculous.

"Oh, forever," I lie. I turn to Rebecca, hoping to deflect some of the attention Reed seems determined to direct my way. "How are you liking the ballet so far?"

"Well, the second half is always the best part," she says.

"When Clara and the prince dance the *pas de deux*. It's so romantic." She has a trace of an accent, and I wonder if she's one of those people who try to sound European to make themselves appear more cultured.

"That's not Clara and the prince," says Mrs. Morgan gently. "It's the Sugar Plum Fairy and her cavalier."

Rebecca purses her heart-shaped lips. "That can't be right. The prince falls in love with Clara when she kills his enemy, the Mouse King. He loves her because she's so loyal to him."

"You might be mixing up the ballet with the original short story," Reed says. "By E. T. A. Hoffmann. I think it came out in 1816? There are several differences in the plot."

"You're pretty smart," Bryan tells Reed. "Maybe you should go on *Jeopardy!*" I smile at the distinct note of sarcasm in his voice.

Mrs. Morgan yawns, triggering a sympathy yawn from her husband. "Okay, we're leaving as soon as this is over. The old folks over here are clearly out too late for a Wednesday. Kailey, I think you're going to have to drive us home. It's dangerous to get behind the wheel when you're sleepy."

"Sure," I answer.

"Kailey's driving?" Mr. Morgan raises an eyebrow at me. "Better buckle up."

"Oh, stop," Mrs. Morgan says to him. "She needs to

regain her confidence. Don't make her nervous." My heart starts to thud in my chest. I don't like the way this conversation is going.

The car accident that Kailey was in the night I found her is the one thing that completely, irretrievably connects me to her. If Cyrus found out who was in that accident, he knows who Seraphina Ames is pretending to be. And while I trust Leyla and the Morgans, Reed and Rebecca are question marks at best.

"Are you a bad driver?" asks Reed.

Behind him, Rebecca cocks her head. "Were you ever in an accident?" she asks.

"She's usually a great driver," begins Mr. Morgan, with an exasperated smile. "Except—"

Before he can say anything else, I do the first thing I can think of. I fake a sneeze. A big one. And in the process, spill hot chocolate all over the front of my shirt.

"Ow!" I yell.

"Are you okay?" gasps Leyla.

"Here." Reed presses his silk handkerchief into my palm. I dab at the spreading chocolate stain, but the minuscule swatch of silk doesn't do much good.

"Thanks, but I think I need to go clean this up in the bathroom." I try to give Reed his handkerchief, but he shakes his head.

"No, keep it," he says in a low voice.

My skin crawls. I stuff the silk square in my pocket and hurry off. Even in the middle of the crowd, I feel the hairs on my neck stand up. I don't turn around to confirm what I already know: Reed is watching me walk away.

I turn the corner toward the bathroom and hear the girl's voice before I see her. "No—not her. *Definitely* not her." It's the accordionist from Eli's band. She's pacing in the empty corridor, a cell phone glued to her ear. Without thinking, I take a step backward so she won't be able to see me and peer carefully around the wall. "I'm narrowing it down," she hisses, blond dreadlocks shaking impetuously. A chill runs across my body.

"Yes, there are a lot of girls. Which is why there can be no mistakes." My eyes widen. I think of the yearbook in Cyrus's hotel room, with the girls' faces marked out one by one in black Sharpie as Cyrus continued his deadly search for me. "No, I can't come to San Francisco tonight. You need to handle this on your own."

I gasp, and her head shoots up. "Hang on," she says. "I need to check on something."

I don't wait to hear more. I turn and run down the stairs, breathless, my chocolate-covered shirt sticking to my skin as I stumble back into the theater.

FIFTEEN

The next day, Madison sits at the head of her family's dining room table and clears her throat. "The inaugural meeting of the winter dance committee shall now come to order," she says grandly, tucking her shaggy hair behind one ear.

It's been raining all day, and the Victorian wood-paneled dining room is dark, just the gloomiest bit of gray light falling on our faces from the large bay windows.

It seems like Rebecca's style is rubbing off on everyone. Madison has traded her usual lipstick and chunky necklaces for simple pearl earrings and a silk scarf. Leyla is still making an effort, but she's abandoned the heels for maroon combat boots that are somehow charming underneath her black vintage gingham dress. And Chantal has always had the ladylike thing down pat, so today's periwinkle sweater set and pressed trousers aren't out of character.

I feel a grudging appreciation for Nicole, the only one who's refused to become a Rebecca clone. She's sporting her usual haute-yoga look, flowing cotton pants and a fitted Lululemon top that leaves little to the imagination. "Maddy, I think you need a gavel or something," she says wryly. I can tell the whole group is amused at how seriously Madison's taking her position.

Madison flashes a brilliant smile. "That is an excellent idea. Why don't you be in charge of that? I'll write it down." She pulls her clipboard out of her backpack and sets it in front of her with a flourish. "On second thought—why don't *you* write it down? You can be secretary of the committee."

Nicole accepts the clipboard, clearly annoyed.

"The first thing we need to decide is our theme," Madison says.

Reed immediately leans forward. "I have a few ideas," he says eagerly.

We're interrupted by Madison's mother, who sweeps into the dining room with a tray in her hands. "I thought you guys could use some snacks," she says.

Madison nods. "You can put it down right over there,"

she tells her mother coolly, in a way that suggests she's used to being waited on. Leyla and Bryan perk up, grabbing handfuls of chips and nuts as soon as Mrs. Cortez leaves.

Reed adjusts the tie he's wearing, a paisley number that's screen-printed with the image of a rose. "How about a Twenties theme?" he proposes. "Flappers, fedoras, ragtime?" Of course he'd want that. He and Rebecca could probably costume all of us with the contents of their closets.

Bryan looks confused. "I thought this was supposed to be wintery? Like . . . snowmen?"

Leyla cracks open a root beer. "Wait, wait, I've got it: 'Silent Night, Deadly Night.' It'll be like a Santa Claus horror movie theme. Bloody bowls of punch, evil elves." Chantal curls her lip in disgust. Nicole just shakes her head. "I'm totally serious, you guys," Leyla adds.

"I'm sure you are," Madison replies, looking completely unamused. "But it can't be a Christmas celebration. This is nondenominational."

"Roaring twenties isn't religious," Reed presses.

Madison shakes her head. "I'd rather not listen to old-timey music all night."

An idea occurs to me. "What about 'Winter Solstice'?" I offer, remembering how Echo mentioned it in art.

Chantal scoffs. "That's so . . . *hippie-dippie.*"

But Madison is nodding slowly. "Not bad, Kailey. We can

celebrate the return of the sun. That's really what Christmas is about, anyway—just recycled pagan mythology. But we'll concentrate on astronomy instead of myth. I like it." I wonder if she and Echo have been talking.

Reed looks disappointed but doesn't protest.

"Kailey, you could do an antique astronomical chart for the mural," Madison suggests. I was hoping she'd forget about that. I smile and nod, though I have no idea how I'll pull it off.

"Excellent. Nicole, write that down. Kailey's in charge of the astronomy mural."

As Madison begins assigning tasks to everyone else, I let my mind drift on the warm buzz of conversation. I can't stop thinking about what I heard Eli's bandmate saying last night at the theater. I don't even know her name. But her words are engraved in my mind: *Yes, there are a lot of girls. Which is why there can be no mistakes.*

Her words are a wake-up call. I've been limiting my search to Kailey's friends—clearly, I need to cast a wider net. But I'm not sure how I could approach the blond girl, or where to even begin.

On the other side of Noah, Nicole is scribbling frantically, copying Madison's assignments for the group. Leyla and Bryan will be in charge of food, of course. Leyla's already suggested several different food trucks that could cater the event. Noah's hiring a photographer to take pictures of couples standing in front of my mural. He offered to take the photos himself, but Leyla squashed that idea, declaring that Noah must be free to dance with me all night long. I had to smile, both at the way Leyla looked out for me and at Noah's furious blush.

Madison declares that she'll be in charge of booking the band—no big surprise for the indie rock queen. But it gives me an idea.

"What about Eli's band?" I say quickly. Madison's head swivels in my direction, and she fixes me with her brown eyes. I wonder if she's annoyed that I'm treading on her area of expertise.

"Interesting idea," she says coolly.

"Why don't I talk to them? You're so busy, and I don't mind." My words come out in a rush.

She stares at me for a long moment, her expression unreadable, then nods. "Thank you, Kailey. Yes, please talk to Eli. Or better yet, Julie. She's the one who books their gigs."

Julie. There's only one girl in the band—that must be the accordionist's name. "I'll talk to her tomorrow," I promise, a thrill running up my limbs.

"All right, then if there's nothing else, I think we're done here," Madison says. Noah jumps up.

"We should go." He nods at me. "Before the rain starts again."

"Wait," Madison interrupts. "Before you all leave—is everyone coming to the Treasure Island party tomorrow night? There are some *excellent* bands playing." Her brown eyes sparkle in anticipation. "Including the Travelers. You know," she says to my blank expression, "Eli's band. Kailey's *favorite*." Her voice is laced with sarcasm, and I wonder again if I've pissed her off.

"I'll definitely be there," I answer in a neutral tone. There's a rumble of *yes*es as everyone else follows suit.

"Well, Rebecca and I must be going," Reed says stiffly. "Our parents are taking us to dinner at Range & Saddle. It's the latest Michelin-starred restaurant." He smiles, pleased with himself, but no one reacts. I don't suppose average high-schoolers even know what Michelin stars are. "It's my birthday," he adds.

"Happy birthday," I say finally, when no one else speaks.

"Thank you, Kailey," Reed says warmly. "Do you want to join us?"

I freeze. "Sorry," I manage. "Homework."

"Another time, then," Reed demurs.

Not if I can help it.

* * *

Back in Kailey's room, my phone buzzes with a text from Leyla: *new boy luvs kailey, kailey perfects her ice queen bitchface.* I would normally laugh, but I don't share Leyla's belief that Reed has a crush on me. I'm worried it's something far more sinister, more . . . predatory.

I plant myself in the desk chair and flip open Kailey's laptop, typing Reed's name into the Facebook search bar and pulling up his profile. Apparently we have dozens of friends in common already: Leyla, Madison, Chantal, even Echo, the ethereal boho girl from my art class.

Should I be relieved that he hasn't asked to be my friend? Somehow being ignored feels more ominous. Why is he treating me differently than the rest of the girls in the group?

Reed's profile page has his Berkeley address listed. I've never seen a home address on Facebook before, and it makes me wonder. I thought most people were afraid of identity theft and Internet stalkers.

Suddenly, I'm determined to go see Reed's house. I realize this makes me the kind of bona fide Internet stalker that people worry about. Well, serves him right.

Before I can change my mind, I'm outside, wheeling Kailey's bike out to the street and consulting Google maps on her phone in the deep twilight. I refuse to think about the possibility that it could all be a trap; that if Reed is Cyrus, he might have listed an address *knowing* that I would go there.

When I finally reach the Sawyers' street, I'm so warmed by the exercise that I stop to take off my jacket. Mediterranean bungalows loom on both sides of the street, perched above beautifully terraced front yards. The Sawyer house—all soaring glass and slate walls—could not look more out of place. Its sleek front yard is full of smooth gray pebbles instead of grass and dotted with cacti in square orange planters, their color barely discernible in the dark.

It appears to be completely deserted. There are no cars in the driveway, no lights on, inside or out. If I'm going to see anything, I'll have to try the backyard. I tuck the bike behind a neighbor's tree and approach the house, walking softly.

I'm filled with a strange sense of excitement. For once, I'm the one in pursuit, the stalker outside the house, the monster in the shadows. I'm so used to it being the other way around.

The side gate is locked, but I easily climb over it, landing with a soft thud in the backyard. I move carefully toward a floor-to-ceiling glass wall and peer inside, using Kailey's iPhone as a flashlight.

I don't know what I expected to find—Cyrus's bulletin board, covered with girls' faces marked through with *X*'s? A makeshift laboratory? But all I see is a kitchen with gleaming copper pots above the stove and a pile of papers on the granite counter. Framed family photos decorate the wall leading into the family room, where a pair of slippers sits next to a white leather couch in front of an enormous television. In the corner, a neat pile of moving boxes waits to be broken down and recycled.

I let out the breath I'd been holding, and the window immediately fogs up. I back away, sliding my phone into my pocket and retreating toward the street.

I'm almost at the gate when I feel a tickling sensation in my hair, like a cat whose tail puffs up to twice its normal size. I whip my head around so quickly that my ponytail slaps my mouth.

A curtain moves in an upstairs window. Someone was watching me.

I hurry over to where I hid the bike, yanking it roughly toward me and banging my shin on the pedal. Tears sting my eyes, and I mash my lips together to keep from yelling.

Just then, I feel a vibration coming from the phone that's wedged against my butt. I tug it out from my pocket and squint in the screen's sudden brightness. It's a new e-mail.

The subject line reads, *Reed Sawyer wants to be friends on Facebook.*

SIXTEEN

Julie's barely five feet tall, but she moves through the after-school throng with remarkable speed. I nearly lose track of her sunny blond dreads more than once. Finally she glides through the oak doors that lead to the music classroom, and I swiftly follow, pausing at the entrance.

From within, I hear the muffled notes of a piano. I cock my head, surprised to find that I don't recognize the song.

Cyrus can play the piano. All of us Incarnates can, to one degree or another. When you're alive for as long as we are, you find ways to keep occupied. Cyrus could perform a Chopin nocturne as well as a Satie *Gnossienne*—with impeccable technical skill but not an ounce of passion.

I pause, my fingers tracing the handle of the oak doors. Cyrus could never play the piano with such deep sorrow. It resonates with emotion, with humanity—and what's more, I think it might be an original composition. I take a deep breath and go in.

Inside, I find Julie hunched over the piano, her small frame swallowed up by an oversized blue poncho and baggy, patched jeans. Her hands roam over the keyboard with practiced grace, the melody veering from major to minor keys, from classical impulses to a vaguely jazz-influenced storminess.

I approach, making no effort to conceal my presence, but she doesn't seem to realize I'm there till I'm right in front of her. Her hands jerk away from the keys as she gasps.

"Kailey! You scared me."

"Sorry." I smile. "I didn't mean to. I just wanted to ask you something. The winter dance is coming up, and we need a band to play. At the dance. We were all hoping you guys— you and Eli and—" I break off when I realize I don't know the name of their third member, the boy who plays banjo.

"It's not a good idea," she says quickly, her lips set in a thin line.

"It's a great idea," I counter, surprised. Cyrus would have leapt at the chance, knowing it was a perfect way to observe students. "Everyone loves you."

"We can't." Her voice quavers, sounding suddenly fragile.

"But—" My voice halts when, to my utter confusion, she begins to cry.

"I'm sorry," I say and hurry to her side, patting her shoulder awkwardly while she shakes. "What's wrong?" I ask, after a moment.

"It's Eli," she manages to say finally. "I'm just . . . so *worried* about him." She turns her teary face to the window. My heart ricochets inside my chest.

"What do you mean, you're worried about Eli?" I ask. I'm suddenly on high alert. She draws her knees up to her chest. "He's just . . . not himself lately. He's being distant. And mean. And he keeps forgetting the words to our songs." She wipes her eye with her wrist. "Sorry to unload on you like this."

"No, it's fine." My heart takes off like a horse, like a jet engine. I throw out a hand to brace myself. "When did this start?" I hear myself ask.

"Ever since that teacher got killed," she whispers. "And at first I could understand—we were all shaken up, you know?"

"I know." The sun shifts. The beam of light disappears from the window.

"Anyway, we've been looking for another female singer. We were supposed to meet on Wednesday for auditions. He never showed, which is *so* unlike him."

Yes, there are a lot of girls, Julie had said in the hallway the night of the *Nutcracker*. *Which is why there can be no mistakes.* They were auditioning singers.

"The worst part is, we're playing tonight on Treasure Island. It's our biggest show ever. I just hope he can get it together. If he can't . . . well, we may have to replace him. He can't even perform anymore. It's almost like he's become another person. I just hope he's not, you know, *on* something." She wraps her arms around her knees, looking even smaller as she pulls herself into a tight ball.

Fear and certainty explode across me like a dying sun. An easygoing violinist is suddenly mean to his friends? Forgets his songs? I think of how he couldn't remember loaning me his instrument at the party in Montclair. *Destiny*, he said, when I collided with him in the hallway. *As if there was such a thing.*

Eli is Cyrus. I know it like I know that thunder follows lightning.

"I'm sure he'll be fine," I say quietly, fingers losing purchase on the slick surface of the piano. "I can't wait to hear you guys play."

"Thanks for letting me talk," she answers, but I'm already halfway out the door.

Tonight, on Treasure Island, I'm going to kill Cyrus at last. I've found him before he found me.

I'm closing in. I just pray he isn't doing the same.

SEVENTEEN

Outside, the sun lingers even while the sky roils with purple clouds. It's my favorite kind of weather, my favorite kind of light. It's just past four, and the late November sun will be going down soon, but for now it washes everything with gold.

As Noah drives me home, I watch his profile. After tonight, there will be nothing to keep us apart. He pulls up to the curb outside my house.

"Wait," I say. "I don't want to go home yet." Something unspoken passes between us, some agreement, and we head silently down the street, our feet padding lightly over the leaves that stick to the pavement in an organic, earthy collage.

Noah pauses and pulls me with him toward a stone staircase, a pedestrian shortcut up the hill to the next street over. I must have passed it a hundred times, but somehow I never noticed it before.

I follow him, trees dripping leftover rain onto my forehead. At the top of the hill is an abandoned fountain surrounded by trees. He pulls me toward him, blue eyes sparkling in the gold light.

When his eyes are like this, I want to tell him who I am, so badly. How can he look at me this way when he only knows a hundredth of my being, when he doesn't even know my name?

Noah pulls away from me. "What's wrong?" he asks, searching my expression.

"Nothing," I answer. "Absolutely nothing."

"You're happy, right? With me?" His eyes darken to a bluer shade.

"You make me happier than anyone else I've ever known," I answer, my voice low.

"That's all you have to say," he answers, stroking my hair. I lean against his chest, hearing his heart beat under his sweater. "I want this moment forever. This light, you. This place."

I laugh when he pulls his camera out from the messenger bag he carries. He tells me to sit on the edge of the fountain while he fiddles with the lens and various aperture settings.

He comes closer, closer, till he's standing right in front of me, looking down. "Just look at me," he instructs. "Forget the camera's here."

I do as he says, looking past the lens to his forehead, to his hair. *I love you,* I think.

Click. "Perfect," he says.

Back at the house, I slip unnoticed into the garage. I'm hit with the smell of dirt from Mrs. Morgan's gardening equipment and an acrid mixture of paint and cleaning chemicals. I run my hand over the nearest wall, recoiling when I touch a thick, sticky spiderweb, but then I find the light switch and flip it up.

In the corner, on a shelf that sags beneath the weight of camping equipment and power tools, I see Mr. Morgan's fishing tackle box. I hurry toward it, brushing against a rusty pink cruiser bicycle, staining my jeans with grease and rust. It must have been Kailey's when she was younger.

I pick up the knife carefully and slip it out from its leather sheath. It's sharp, serrated, and shines brightly in the overhead light. Perfect. From outside, I hear the familiar rattle of Mr. Morgan's Volvo pulling into the driveway, so I slip the sheathed knife into my knee-high boots, slip through the garage, and turn off the light.

I dart through the hallway and back into Kailey's room, exhaling as I flop onto the bed. The weight of the knife feels comfortingly solid against my calf.

Having it there reminds me of my early days with Cyrus. I used to carry a knife at all times. That was before Cyrus brought Jared and Sébastien into our coven, before I was told that keeping me safe was the men's job. Before Cyrus stopped trusting me with my own weapons.

I think through my plan for tonight. It won't be too hard to find Eli backstage after their set. But what will I say? *Oh, Eli, your music is so incredible. I've never felt more alive.* Truthfully, it doesn't matter what I say. Cyrus has never been able to resist flattery, especially from a pretty girl.

I wonder if, in the last few moments, as I lean in for a kiss and pull the knife from my boot, he'll realize his mistake. I want him to know that I'm the one who finally succeeded in killing him. I want him to realize how much he's always underestimated me.

EIGHTEEN

The cold ocean breeze sweeps across Treasure Island as though we were on a boat tossed by salty waves. I'm glad I listened to Leyla and dressed warmly—even with my wool hat, coat, and scarf, I'm chilled to the bone when the wind gusts, but Noah doesn't seem to mind when I lean into him.

"C'mon," Leyla urges us. "I see fire over there."

In the distance I spot the abandoned naval barracks, orange flames flickering up their graffiti-covered stucco walls and silhouetting the profiles of hundreds of kids who are here for the music.

I take Noah's hand and follow Leyla, Bryan a few steps

ahead of us. The wet grass has been trampled to mud by hundreds of feet, and it tries to suck my boots off as I walk. According to the texts everyone has been sending, Reed and Rebecca have already joined Madison in the crowd, and Nicole is on her way with Chantal.

We reach the barracks and slip through the crowd in a human chain. There's a makeshift stage on the steps of one of the abandoned dormitories, and the first band is already playing. It consists of three bearded, skinny guitarists and a drummer. They don't appear to have a singer but don't need to, the guitars weaving a chiming wall of sound that's as complicated as a Bach fugue.

Madison's standing on a crate so she can get a better view of the band, Reed and Rebecca stationed in front of her like guards.

"This place is amazing," Bryan admits, and Leyla grins triumphantly.

"I *told* you. Broken windows, graffiti, spookiness galore. And all right next to San Francisco! You guys, we should pretend this whole crowd is a horde of zombies." She cocks an imaginary shotgun.

"You gotta aim for the head," adds Bryan, doing the same. "Otherwise they won't die."

Madison shakes her head. "You guys both know that zombies are scientifically impossible, right?"

"Science has nothing to do with monsters," Leyla retorts. Oh, how wrong she is.

"You clearly haven't read *Frankenstein*, if that's what you think." Reed shoots Leyla a smile that verges on a smirk.

"Good point. Let's toast to experiments gone wrong, then," says Leyla, pulling a bottle of wine out of the voluminous folds of her coat—though it might be more apt to call it a cloak, the red wool falling around her like she's Little Red Riding Hood. She passes it around, and we each take a long swallow. I feel its warmth reaching down into my chest as the song finally comes to an end.

"We're Firestorm, and we're from Texas," announces the lead guitarist to a roar of applause, before beginning the next song, his fingers coaxing an achingly sweet motif from the instrument that's soon joined by a throb of drums.

I lean over to Madison. "When is Eli's band coming on?"

"They're next," she informs me, with a wide smile. "I'm really excited to hear them play."

"Me too," I respond. And I am, though not for the reason she thinks.

Although *excited* is not quite the right word for how I feel, this wrenching combination of dread and anticipation. I'm not looking forward to killing Cyrus, to watching his stolen body disintegrate into dust.

I never wanted to be a killer, even though I've killed countless times, just to stay alive. But this is different. Cyrus has already killed Eli. How many more will have to die before he's satisfied?

I throw my head back as the next song begins, the tops of the buildings looming over me like trees. Noah's hand finds mine. He squeezes my fingers, then hands me the bottle of wine. I take another drink, watching his profile in the flickering light, before passing it along to Reed.

It's amazing to think how much has changed since I first heard Eli's band play at Dawson's party. It was only a month ago, and Kailey's friends were strangers to me. I wanted to escape, I wanted to die. Her life was a prison that I'd unwittingly locked myself into.

Now I can't imagine leaving this life. I would fight for it. I *will* fight for it.

The song ends, and my heart floats back to earth. The band waves good-bye, and the crowd sends them off on an eruption of cheers and applause.

Silence descends as people bustle around on stage, changing out instruments and adjusting wires.

"Their set went by so quickly," I say.

"Don't worry," Madison replies. "The next act is going to be even better." She wraps her arms around herself. A chill of danger bubbles through me. As soon as Eli's band goes offstage, I'll make my move. Lure Cyrus into a shadowy corner, and end it.

Rebecca nods. "The Travelers are *really* good." I stifle a laugh. Looks like Madison's found the perfectly obedient assistant. I don't think I've heard Maddy say one thing that Rebecca hasn't agreed with.

Reed takes another swig of wine, his teeth slightly purple when he smiles. "You know, I don't usually go in for this indie rock scene, but that last group was pretty good."

Just then the crowd cheers as Eli's band walks out on stage. I see Julie, a fedora perched on top of her hair, and the boy with the stretched-out earlobes who plays banjo. There's another boy I haven't seen before who sits behind the drum kit with an inexplicably sad expression on his face.

I don't see Eli—*Cyrus*—anywhere.

My heart starts to thud.

"Where the hell are Nicole and Chantal?" Madison muses. She pulls out her phone and begins texting furiously.

Julie straps her accordion to her chest slowly, her back to the crowd. She looks at each of her bandmates, who nod to her in turn. She turns around, walking up to the microphone. She adjusts it down for her size and offers a wan smile to the audience as she does so, earning her a cacophony of claps and cheers.

"Hi," she says into the mic. The crowd welcomes her with more applause.

"I'm afraid I have some bad news," she continues. Everyone falls silent. "Our lead singer, Eli, is missing."

No. Not again.

A low murmur of concern rumbles through the crowd. The wind is nothing to the cold that runs through my veins.

"We talked about canceling our set, but we know that's not what he'd want." She takes a deep breath, and I can tell she's holding back tears. "So we're going to play anyway." The crowd cheers. The sound is poisonous. "And we're going to start with a song that he just finished. Eli, if you're out there, this one's for you. Please come home."

The banjo player walks across the stage to stand next to her, putting his arm around her and taking the microphone out of its stand. She backs away, tears shining in her eyes.

The banjo player holds the mic to his mouth. "Julie forgot to tell you the name of Eli's song." She nods gratefully, and he continues. "It's called 'Seraphina.'"

My heart nearly stops.

"I wonder if Mr. Shaw told Eli about Seraphina, too," Noah murmurs in my ear. I am too stunned to answer. The band starts playing. Julie's accordion emits a low, mournful hum as the boy plucks out a melody on his banjo in a minor key. After a few bars, he leans into the microphone and sings:

She gave me poison wine
She climbed the stair at night
She set my blood on fire
Before she took flight

Seraphina, I know you're still there
I know the light that falls upon your hair

At the chorus, Julie leans in and harmonizes with him, her thin soprano wavering above his warm voice. I force myself to stay calm and listen, though every muscle in my body is telling me to run.

She burns in different colors
She sees with different eyes
Her body is a vessel
for different colored skies

Seraphina, I'll love you till I'm gone
I'll search the world till you're where you belong

She's an old soul by starlight
with my blue book beside her
She's made a mistake
and it fills me with fire

Seraphina, don't you dare kiss another
I'll kill him myself if you take a lover

At this, I suck in my breath, looking at Noah out of the corner of my eye. The wind shifts, sending a column of smoke into my face.

She's my past, she's my future
She's my Renaissance bird
I won't rest till she's back
Take me at my word

Seraphina, be faithful. Be true, little girl
I won't stop with him. I'll destroy your whole world

She loved me in the garden
She kissed my silver soul
Without her, I am nothing
So I'll never let her go

The crowd explodes with approval as they finish. Every muscle in my body is rigid, my blood running thick and slow. I briefly wonder if I might faint, might sink into unconsciousness the way a stone drops into deep water.

"Are you okay?" Noah asks me, his turquoise eyes flickering with worry, his eyebrows pulled low over them.

"I'm fine," I whisper, but I can tell he doesn't believe me.

The wind blows, lifting his crow-colored hair behind him, individual tendrils backlit by fire.

"Your eyes are wet," he says.

"I . . . I think it's the smoke from the bonfire," I lie.

"Do you want to go get some air?" he asks.

I shake my head. I want to run. But I can't. It would reveal me to Cyrus, whoever he is now. I have no doubt that he's close by, scanning the crowd to see which girl trembles, which girl is obviously shaken.

I feel Reed's hand on my arm. "That song was beautiful, wasn't it? It reminds me of traditional murder ballads." A bomb goes off inside me. Shrapnel pumps in my heart.

"I don't think threats are beautiful," I say.

He smiles. "Whoever this Seraphina is, she'd better watch out."

This conversation just became very, very dangerous. "Maybe she doesn't love him anymore," I whisper weakly.

"I don't think that's an option," Reed replies, never breaking eye contact. "He said he'll never let her go."

The flames from the bonfire dance in his eyes. And for just a moment, they look ice blue.

NINETEEN

The rest of the set passes in a nonsensical wave of static. I wait as long as I can stand it before tugging on Noah's hand. "I need to get some air," I murmur, choking on my own voice. When we turn to leave, Reed grabs my shoulder once more.

"Where are you going?" he demands.

"She needs a minute away from the fire," Noah says roughly.

"I'll see you later." I force myself to sound casual.

"You better come back," he says, tightening his grip on my upper arm, then smiles warmly to show he's only kidding, to disarm me.

Noah pulls me away, shoving his way through the crowd with ease, his broad shoulders clearing our path, till we reach the edge where San Francisco is visible.

"I need you to take me home," I tell Noah. "Now."

"What's going on, Kailey?" His forehead is furrowed, his lips tight.

"We can talk in the car," I answer, my heart breaking. Cyrus's message is clear. I know what I have to do.

I watch Noah's profile as he drives us back to Berkeley in silence, remembering the night we hiked to the top of the cliff, the night he saved my life, the night I almost killed him. If I hadn't stopped when I did, he'd be dead now.

But he's alive. And I need him to stay that way.

I look out the passenger side window, the world passing in a blur of lights. I open the window, and the wind stings my eyes. I wish I were high above the Arctic Circle, where the winter air would freeze my tears, where I'd suffer some frostbitten consequence on my face to match the way I feel inside. I want to be in a place where the winter solstice means darkness twenty-four hours a day, the sun only circling the sky, keeping far away from me like the curse I am.

I remember the cramped jazz club in Paris that I used to drag us to, back when the coven lived there in the nineteenth century. I'd insist that we stay out till dawn, till everyone else's eyes were drooping with exhaustion. It was tucked away behind an old stone façade on Rue des Âmes. *Look at the street's name!* I said to Charlotte. *Yes,* she agreed. *Street of the souls, the perfect place for Seraphina Ames to drink pastis.*

And I remember, too, the night one trumpet player kept making eyes at me. I was grateful for the dim, smoky room that hid my blush; but Cyrus noticed, of course, and accused me of being unfaithful later that night when we returned to our flat. *I've never spoken to him!* I cried, earning me a slap across the face. *You're lying,* Cyrus told me. His apology didn't come until two weeks later, in the form of a grand piano in our parlor.

It's my fault, I thought at the time. *Cyrus is sensitive. I should be more careful not to hurt him.* I forgave him and gave myself over to the sickness that was our centuries-long relationship.

Cyrus must have guessed that he'd find me among Eli's friends, knowing how much I always loved music. When he didn't, he left Eli's body and found another, killing yet again in the process. But who?

Murder ballads, Reed whispers in my mind.

"Pull over," I say to Noah when we're a few blocks from our houses. He does. Up the street I can see the staircase leading to our fountain. Only yesterday we were there in the fading sunset.

"Please," he says, when he turns off the car, taking my left hand in his. I put my right to my brow, and I cover my face. "Tell me what's wrong. Don't shut me out."

If only I could stop time, if only I could keep us here, in the car, by the staircase where we loved each other.

But I can't.

Because I love him, I can't. I shiver and roll up the window.

"Noah," I begin, his name like honey in my mouth. "We need to break up."

"What are you talking about?" His eyes are so hurt, so confused. Outside, the wind gusts, shaking the car. Leaves fall on the windshield like pages of a book ripped from their spine.

"This thing—you and me—it's not working out." I tremble but force myself to say my next words. "I don't love you."

He turns away, leaning back in his seat like he needs something solid to prop him up. "I don't believe you," he whispers.

"You should," I answer.

He slams his hand against the steering wheel, the sound making me jump. "Stop it, Kailey. Just stop." His voice cracks, and he finally looks at me, his eyes so sad in the streetlight's beams that turn them the color of beach glass from another time.

He reaches for me, pulls me toward him, finds my mouth. I am caught, caught in his warm hands, his hungry lips, his photographer's eyes, their blue pummeling me like warm Diablo winds at the end of November, ruining groves of eucalyptus and ruining my resolve, as fragile as an old window.

I tear myself away.

"You can't kiss me like that and not love me." His voice cracks. "You can't."

He's right. I can't. I can't let him touch me again.

Seraphina, don't you dare kiss another.

I'll kill him myself if you take a lover.

"You're wrong," I breathe. "You don't mean anything to me." Cyrus won't hesitate to kill Noah. I know that. I've seen him kill before for much less.

Noah's face is pale. "Does this . . . does this have anything to do with Reed? I'm not blind. I see the way he looks at you." He closes his eyes, waiting for my answer.

I think of Reed's face by the fire tonight. *Whoever this Seraphina is, she'd better watch out.* I briefly consider letting Noah believe I have feelings for Reed. He'd hate me, and he'd stay far away. But then I picture Noah saying something nasty to Reed, with no idea that an evil, ruthless spirit now possesses his body. He'd be in too much danger.

"No. It has nothing to do with Reed," I answer, and his jaw clenches.

"Is there someone else?" He wraps his arms around himself. He's shaking. I want to touch him, to kiss him back from this abyss, but I can't.

I breathe in, breathe out, breathe in, summoning the strength I need. "Not yet," I say.

"But you told me earlier that I make you happy. Were you lying when you said that?" His voice is red with pain.

"Yes," I say.

He stares, his mouth trembles. I've hurt him. But it's for his own good. "But I love you," he says, his voice breaking.

"I'm sorry," I say. "It's over." My words slam into the side of his face. The death blow to our relationship.

"Get out," he says, reaching across me to open the door. The wind takes it, ripping it backward so it bounces on the vintage hinges. I see a tear run down his cheek, and I resist the urge to smudge it away with my thumb, to take him in my arms.

I slam the car door. I run down the street, boots slapping on the pavement, finally alone in the dark. Eli is dead, Noah's heart is broken, and it's all my fault. I don't stop running. At last I start to cry the tears I couldn't shed in front of him, their salty heat immediately feeling like ice in the cruel November wind.

TWENTY

In Kailey's room, I hunch by the window, feeling minute currents of cold air sighing through the tiny gaps between the sill and the old wooden sash. I think of Kailey's painting, the one that hangs in Noah's room, the way she painted herself from behind, watching his window. Right now it is nearly recreated as I stare across the street, past stupidly happy gusts of wind throwing handfuls of leaves around in circles. I can't tear my gaze away from Noah's window. But in the painting, his shades glowed a creamy yellow from the light behind them, surrounded by a swarm of Kailey's magical creatures, fairies coalescing around the eaves. And now it's just dark.

I don't see his car—he must not have come home. I wonder where he went, fully realizing I've lost the right to know. I lost it the moment I told him I didn't love him anymore.

Ragged tears slide down my face, a sob crumpling my face like something that should be thrown away. Regret blooms inside of me, watered by pain. I want to take it back, to take back the whole damned night, to erase the chain of events that led to this hurt that I've caused. For once, knowing I did the right thing doesn't dull the pain.

I make my way across the room to Kailey's dresser. There's a candle on top of it, sealed with its wax drippings to the large abalone shell it rests in. The surface is coated with dust that I wipe off with my fingers. I find some matches tucked behind a jewelry box and light the candle. The air fills with the scent of roses, the firelight playing across the iridescent surface of the shell.

I carry it across the room and place it on the windowsill, driven by an urge to warm up the glass, to send some kind of light out into the world.

It flickers briefly before an unseen tongue of wind snuffs it out.

And somehow, *this* is what makes me start to cry again.

I throw myself on Kailey's bed and turn over on my back, looking up at the glow-in-the-dark stars that dot her ceiling, her artificial constellations rearranging themselves through the veil of my tears.

I hurt. I say it aloud, though there's no one to hear.

And I'm scared. Scared of what will happen to me if Cyrus finds me. I don't think he'll kill me. He'll do something much, much worse.

When we lived in Berlin in 1917, he caught our human servant Greta snooping in the library. She had figured out that something was different about us and confronted him. She wanted to become an Incarnate too.

"Oh, I'll make you an Incarnate," Cyrus said. He gave her the elixir—then forced her into the body of a sick, elderly man before locking her up. She was imprisoned for years. Whenever her body began to fail, Cyrus made her take another one, equally as decrepit and ill. And the torture would begin anew.

I shudder at the memory. It's too dark in here. I feel my way to the window and retrieve the failed candle, bringing it back to Kailey's bedside table and relighting it. I sit up in the bed, leaning against the wall with my knees drawn up under my chin, inhaling breath after breath of the candle's sweet air as I try to calm down.

It's Reed. You know it is. Just go to his house, tonight, and kill him, says a voice in my head, the voice that craves certainty, proof, evidence.

Except I have none. Nothing except a hunch, a creepy feeling. I was wrong about Noah—I could be wrong again. I don't know Reed very well at all. No one does.

That's exactly why Cyrus picked the new boy. No way for you to figure it out.

And even if I *could* figure it out—so what? I deduced that he took Eli's body, and what did that get me? Too little, too late. I'm always one step behind.

I smash my fist onto the silk green coverlet, suddenly so overcome with frustration I want to scream.

I settle on pacing back and forth on the rug in my stocking feet. Kailey's bedroom has never felt smaller. My eyes play over the paintings that adorn the walls, lingering over the one next to the window. I've stared at it several times before: the girl with shaggy black hair, balanced on the roof of a cathedral, a guitar strapped to her back. And the other girl flying in the air above her, wings outstretched, arms reaching.

Something about it stops me in my tracks.

I cross the room swiftly for a better look, blinking slowly, trying to understand why this painting feels so important.

Suddenly, it hits me.

The night I ran away from the coven, my body on the verge of death. The dive bar in Jack London Square. The girl inside, her feathered earrings. A bright red T-shirt, slipping in and out of view through the fog. Green eyes, shining with pain. Wind whipping her black hair around her face as she faced me on top of the shipping container cranes.

The girl who watched me take Kailey's body after the car crash.

The girl who stole Cyrus's book after I stupidly left it on top of the crane.

Taryn.

My mind reels. The implication is staggering. I clamp my eyes shut, remembering the night Kailey died. Remembering Taryn's sadness. The way she insisted she was alone in the world, with nothing to live for. The way Kailey's broken body drove me out of my mind with pain, a whirlwind of blood and gasoline and jasmine perfume clouding my vision. The way Taryn's tiny frame stood across the road, watching me.

The only witness to that night's events wasn't a random stranger, a lost junkie girl who just happened to be in Jack London Square.

Taryn *knew* Kailey and saw me take her body. She's yet another link to me, another bread crumb in the trail I've left behind, leading straight to the Morgans' door.

I tried so hard to save Taryn, only to let her friend die in my arms. Suddenly I'm back on the crane, the rain lashing at me, whipping my hair. I'm standing over the river, ready to throw the book in the water, ready to leave it all behind forever—

Wait. The *book*. Cyrus's blue book of alchemy, his most treasured possession aside from me. He even mentioned it in his song tonight. The book he took from his father, Johann, the night we escaped London more than six hundred years ago, that contains the formula for making the Incarnate elixir and who knows what other alchemical knowledge.

If I can find Taryn, maybe I can get the book back. It's the one thing that would tempt Cyrus, that might make him do something stupid. The perfect bait.

After all, there is more than one way to hunt.

In our first century as Incarnates, Cyrus returned home one day, ashen and shaking, certain that he had seen his father selling scrolls at the market. *I know he's in a new body by now, just like we are, but I recognized the cadence in his voice, the words he used. It was him, I swear it.* Seeing as how Johann threatened to kill me the last time I saw him, I put up no argument when Cyrus made us leave.

Our new home in the Black Forest was isolated, a rough abandoned cottage in a forest that was rumored to be full of werewolves and vampires, witches and ghosts. Of course, Cyrus found this hilarious. But it was the perfect place for us to hide.

That's when Cyrus taught me to hunt.

"There is more than one way to bring down prey, Sera. Strength, stamina, even weapons—these things are not always needed," he told me, kneeling by my side in the frosty, overcast forest. I watched, rapt, as his fingers expertly twisted the leather cords that would make our snare. "You can kill without a bow, without a knife, and without hounds, as long as you know how to set a trap."

When we returned to the snares a few days later, we would find them full of small animals, mostly rabbits.

I scramble to my feet, fumbling through Kailey's purse till I find her phone. I don't really expect to find anything useful—I searched through Kailey's contacts the first day I was in her body, and I would have remembered if I'd seen a Taryn. But one thing I've learned about Kailey is that she was a girl with secrets.

And there it is, in her contacts. Just one letter. An unassuming *T*. With a phone number, and an address. It was right there, the whole time. If it had said "Taryn," I would never have missed it. But I never thought to worry about who T was until now.

I tap on the number and hit SEND MESSAGE, then pause. I have no idea what to say. No idea what went through Taryn's mind after she witnessed me, kneeling over Kailey's broken body, transferring my soul in a dizzying whirl of sparks. From everything I know, Taryn is a drug addict. She was certainly high that night. She can't know the truth of what she saw.

Best to keep it simple. *hey, how're things?* I type.

Almost immediately, the phone buzzes with a reply: *hey stranger. been a while.*

can we meet? I type back, holding my breath as I hit SEND.

Wasteland tomorrow?

I frown. I'm not sure how to parse this response, but I have the sense to flip open Kailey's laptop and google "Wasteland Oakland."

My eyes widen at the first search result: "Jack London Square's original gothic, steampunk, and industrial dance club."

Jack London Square is where Kailey had her car accident. Could she have been going to this venue to meet Taryn? I sit up straighter, clicking on the club's name. *The Wasteland.* The poet T. S. Eliot must be spinning in his grave.

Dark jangling beats erupt from the laptop as the screen fills with a deep shade of purple, and I quickly turn down the volume. THE WASTELAND is displayed at the top of the page in a black typeface, thorns entwined around each letter.

An intricate motif of rotating gears, skulls, and black roses surround a scroll, which slowly opens to reveal a list of upcoming events. Apparently someone named DJ Mittens will be spinning synthpop darkwave—whatever that is—this evening, and tomorrow night Lady Elektra will be providing industrial cabaret.

At the bottom of the page is a button bearing a pale blue gothic *F*, with mysterious instructions underneath: "For photographic evidence of our events, consult the Book of Faces."

Clicking on the *F* brings me to the club's Facebook page. I chuckle—"Book of Faces," how impossibly pretentious.

I click to the photo albums, filled with thumbnails of heavily made-up boys and girls, their thick smears of black eyeliner and wildly colored hair completely incongruous with Facebook's cheerful blue-and-white background.

I scan face after face. The screen passes in a blur of fishnet stockings, corsets, top hats, and pierced everything— eyebrows, lips, noses, even cheeks.

My eyes catch on a group photo with perhaps fifteen people in it, some standing and others kneeling in front. I recognize the two girls in the front center immediately. Taryn's pale, scarred arm is slung around a blond whose face is turned away from the camera, her loose curls covering the side of her face. But I know her. I know her throat, her chest, her belly, the tanned arms hiding inside her long-sleeved shirt with its plunging neckline, far more revealing than anything I'd expect her to wear.

Because they are mine, now. My arms, my throat.

Kailey.

Puzzle pieces slide into place.

Kailey and Taryn were most definitely friends. And judging from their body language in the photo—the subtle arch to Kailey's back, the way she leans into Taryn's side—they may have been *more* than friends.

Heart racing, I compose a reply to Taryn: *awesome. see you then.*

I'm going to get hold of that book, and then I'll use it to bait the snare and lure Cyrus out of hiding.

TWENTY-ONE

By the time I leave for The Wasteland the next evening, the mist has given way to a downpour, wind ripping the leaves off the neighborhood trees and water flooding the gutters. I don't mind, though. The noise makes it easier to sneak out.

I fake-yawned through dinner until Mrs. Morgan practically ordered me to bed. Bryan raised an eyebrow at me and accused me of trying to get out of doing dishes but let me go without complaint when he saw the dark circles under my eyes, courtesy of the lightest touch of Kailey's matte black eyeshadow. Once in Kailey's bedroom, I turned off the lights and waited for the house to go quiet, watching the rain stream against the window and bounce off the asphalt on the street.

I considered telling Mr. and Mrs. Morgan that I was going out with Leyla, but I'm worried they might stay up waiting for me to come home, and Lady Elektra doesn't even come on until eleven. I have a feeling that most of the people who go to The Wasteland aren't exactly worried about breaking curfew. Kailey's parents would never let me stay out that late even on a Saturday.

Rain pelts the windshield of the cab I called, and I wonder how the driver is able to see anything through the blur of constant water. Windshield wipers are a joke in this kind of weather.

I catch sight of myself in the rearview mirror and cringe. I haven't dressed this way since the coven went through our goth phase in the early eighties. I did my best to approximate the style of the girls I saw in The Wasteland's photo albums, pairing a low-cut, midriff-baring velvet tank top that I found stuffed in the back of Kailey's dresser with a short lace skirt. The loosely crocheted tights I've got on do little to keep me from feeling naked. I lined my eyes with liquid black and coated my lips with nearly the same shade.

As the car approaches Jack London Square, I smell the familiar reek of the saltwater estuary and overripe produce from the wholesale markets. We turn a corner and I see a line of dressed-up people huddling against a wall, trying in vain to keep dry. There's no sign, but I can tell by the corsets and platform boots that we're in the right place. The club is only a few blocks from where Kailey had her car accident. I'm surer than ever that she was heading here the night she died.

But why was she by herself? Why hadn't she brought Leyla or any of the other girls? What was she hiding?

"You're sure this is where you want to go?" The driver meets my gaze in the mirror, concern flickering in his eyes. *I'm more than six hundred years old*, I want to tell him. *Don't worry about me.* But I just nod and pay the fare.

21 PLUS, reads a small sign by the door. WE CARD EVERY-ONE. *Shit.* I forgot to bring the fake ID I bought from Lucia. I'm not used to worrying about being underage.

I slip inside and am immediately stopped by a boy wearing a pair of cut-up fishnet stockings as a shirt. It barely covers his otherwise bare torso, smooth and muscled. I assume the fingerless gloves he's wearing are just for visual effect, since they won't do much against the damp cold.

"ID?" he asks. Or at least I think that's what he said—the music is loud, sped-up jazz horns and honky-tonk piano accompanied by a pounding electronic bass line that makes my legs feel weak.

"I left it at home," I yell back, making a pouty face.

"I'm just messing with you, Kailey," he replies, pulling me toward him in a tight hug and ruffling my hair. My cheek slides against his chest, slick with a fine sheen of sweat. Gross.

I pull back, forcing myself to smile. *Play along*, I remind myself. "Where have you been, anyway?" the boy asks me. "Haven't seen you down here in forever."

"Oh, y'know, busy . . ." I let my voice trail off.

"Well, get in there." He laughs and waves me inside.

The interior is dim, lit by several flickering chandeliers, their light bouncing off the tin ceiling and casting a diffuse glow on the crowd. The air is heady: Patchouli and sandalwood and lavender mingle with clove cigarettes and sweat. Another scent floats over these—the unmistakable waft of kerosene.

On a stage there are two girls dancing with scarves on their heads and contraptions on their hands, long wires extending from each fingertip and covered with burning wicks. They dance, their fingers transforming their hands into fans of fire. Orange light plays across their bare stomachs, each punctuated with a jeweled belly ring.

Above the stage is an empty balcony that rings the room. If I can figure out how to get to the second level, I'll have the perfect vantage point to observe the crowd and hopefully to spot Taryn.

I slide through the bodies, dodging waitresses carrying precariously balanced trays of drinks and countless elbows and swinging hips. I see every gender configuration possible as I make my way across the floor: boys with girls, girls with girls, boys with boys, and mixed groups next to solo dancers doing their own thing. Several people make eye contact with me and nod in a way that suggests they may know Kailey, but I just smile and press past them.

Finally, I reach a staircase in the corner of the room, quickly stepping over the velvet rope that marks it as off-limits and darting up to the balcony. It's swathed in shadows, and I hide behind undrawn silk curtains.

I scan the crowd for several minutes, but I don't see Taryn anywhere.

She's not here, I finally admit to myself, disappointment curling inside my chest.

"I can't believe you actually came."

I whip my head around. There she is, in skintight leather pants and a ribbed white tank top, eyes just as vividly green as I remembered, like emeralds beaming from her gaunt face. The last time I spoke with her I was in a different body. And the last time she saw Kailey's body, there was a different soul inside.

"How have you been?" I ask. She was close to killing herself that night.

Taryn curls her lip and laughs bitterly. "As if you actually care."

"That's not true," I protest.

She shakes her head and wedges her hand in her back pocket to pull out a pack of cigarettes. "I'm over it, Kailey. You don't need to bullshit me."

I'm not positive what she's talking about, but the barest glance at her body language tells me that whatever it is, she is most certainly *not* over it. She lights her cigarette and takes a deep drag, crossing her arms across her chest.

"Why are you so angry?" I ask, knowing it will probably piss her off. I need her to reveal what she knows.

"Are you serious?" She laughs, a short, harsh sound. "You're so hot and cold. One night you love me. And the next? You stand me up and make me look like a complete fool." She takes a deep breath and blows a stream of smoke at my face.

"When did I stand you up?" I ask, processing the fact that Kailey loved Taryn, or said she did.

She fixes me with those incredulous, feline eyes. "A month ago. I waited around the bar for hours. We were supposed to go dancing." She pauses, waiting for a reaction from me. But I have none. I'm replaying the events of that night in my mind. Remembering Taryn at the bar, how upset she was. How doomed she would have been without me to pull her back from the ledge. How doomed Kailey was, regardless.

"Don't pretend you don't know what I'm talking about," Taryn continues. "You are so manipulative, I never believe you." She pauses, and her voice drops a few octaves. "I can't even believe myself."

I take a step toward her. "What do you mean?"

She shudders. "It was nothing. I was messed up. It was a dream."

"Was I in it?"

She throws her cigarette on the ground, grinding it out with a steel-toed boot. Nods. "I imagined I saw you die in a car accident. It seemed so real. You were bleeding. There was fire. And there was this girl, with long brown hair."

Now I shiver. "And then what?"

"I thought she was an angel at first. It wasn't the first time I saw her. She—" Taryn breaks off. "She talked to me earlier that night. When I went outside. For . . . fresh air."

She's lying, but I understand why.

"I dreamed that she kissed you—and then she . . . turned into dust." Her lip trembles.

I put a hand on her shoulder, feel the bone so very close to the skin. "I'm sorry I didn't meet you. I wish I could explain why."

She jerks away. "In some ways, I'm glad it happened like this. You know the phrase *rock bottom*? I was there, but now

I'm getting better. I'm writing, stories like that one about the angel girl and the car accident. I may even start blogging them." She pauses again. "My stories are kind of like your art, actually."

My heart catches in my throat. Taryn, blogging about car accidents in Jack London Square? About mysterious girls and electromagnetic kisses and bodies that crumble away and vanish on the breeze? Cyrus would see through that immediately. Taryn would be dead minutes after she'd clicked the button to publish.

"That dream sounds scary and dark," I say carefully. "Maybe you should write about something else."

"I'm not crazy!" Taryn snaps, and I worry that I've pushed her too far. "I found her stuff!"

"What?"

"That night! Up on the crane!" My heart beats faster as I remember that my book wasn't the only thing I left behind—it was inside my getaway bag, alongside clothing, my car keys, and, worst of all, an ID bearing the name Jennifer Combs. The last in a series of false names I went by. A name, I recall bitterly, that Cyrus gave me.

"What did you find?" I press.

"Lots of things. The angel girl left a bag. She was *real*. I mean—she was, like, a real person. I have her ID, her money, her journal." My breath explodes out of my chest. "At least I thought it was a journal, at first. But the book dealer said—"

"Did you sell it?" I ask, grabbing her arm more roughly than I meant to.

She throws my hand off. "No," she says, rubbing her arm.

"Can I see it? The book? Is it at your place?" My words come out in a rush, sounding as out-of-control as I feel.

Taryn stares at me. "I don't think that's a good idea," she says levelly.

A voice interrupts us from the staircase. "You should ask her about the money she owes you." The man who steps out from the shadows is familiar, but it takes me a moment to place him. He's wearing the same leather jacket as the last time we met. The same nose ring, the same frayed knit hat.

He'd approached me at the coffee shop in Berkeley when I went with Leyla. I remember what he said: *Hopefully you make it back down to the club one of these days. I miss dancing with you.* I wondered then how he knew Kailey—he seemed so much older than her.

"What money?" I ask. Taryn doesn't reply as she rushes to his side. My eyebrows rise as she gives him a long, lingering kiss.

The man locks eyes with me. "That's right, Kailey. Sorry I stole your girlfriend. I guess that's just how irresistible I am." He laughs, and the sound rises above the din of music below. "But then again, I hear you're into boys now, too.

Which is fine with me." A chill runs up my spine. Has he been watching me? Seen me with Noah?

He takes a step toward me. I back up but run into the railing of the balcony, its sharp edge jammed into my lower back.

"What money?" I ask again.

He shakes his head, amused. "And that's why *you're* just the user, and I'm the drug dealer. I never forget a debt."

What? "I owe you money? For drugs?" This is certainly a new side to Kailey.

"You owe *me* money," Taryn clarifies. "You were just supposed to hold on to it for me. You don't remember?" *Damn,* I think, remembering the wad of bills I found in Kailey's closet, the money I paid Lucia for erasing my records and procuring my fake ID.

"S-s-sorry," I say reflexively, though I'm not. "I don't have any money."

The man inspects his fingernails. "You gonna take that for an answer?" he asks Taryn.

"I guess so," she ventures.

He licks his lips and runs his eyes over my body. "Because we could *make* her pay you back." I narrow my eyes. The way he says it sounds like a threat.

He pulls a flask from his pocket and takes a long swallow. "Amateur hour. No offense, babe. But you're letting her walk all over you."

I have an idea. "Maybe I could get the money together, if you could show me that book?" I direct the question to Taryn, who locks eyes with me, her expression full of . . . what? Sadness? Longing? "I can come by," I continue, sensing she's about to cave. "And we can talk."

But the man steps between us, advances toward me. "No more talking. When you get the money, you give it to *me*." His breath reeks, hot on my face.

I look past him. "Taryn?" But she just shakes her head. Her face closes like a door.

"Taryn's done with you," he answers for her.

"But—"

"Don't try my patience," he sneers. "I don't care if you're just a little girl."

I am *not* a little girl. But his face is cold. And I suddenly realize how much bigger he is than me. The threat is written in his eyes, his body, the way we're so close to the safety of downstairs and yet so far away.

"We're leaving, Fisher," Taryn says suddenly, her voice sharp as a whip. "Now."

He reluctantly follows her toward the staircase. I don't try to stop them.

"Hey, Kailey?" Taryn calls, turning back to look me in the eye.

"Yeah?"

"Stay the hell away from me."

And then she's gone, taking my one chance with her. Stomping out my plans to beat Cyrus, leaving me once again with nothing.

I slump to the floor and rub my throbbing temples. My loneliness hangs around me like a cloud of smoke. And then I start to cry—for Taryn, for myself, but mostly for Kailey.

Kailey clearly liked girls. And no one else in her life knew. Even in Berkeley, the most liberal place in America, she felt she had to hide who she really was. She sought refuge at The Wasteland, the one place she could be herself.

But even though I never met Kailey, I've lived as her long enough to feel certain that she never did drugs. The painting on her wall shows her as an angel, arms outstretched, trying to save Taryn from falling. That could be why she held on to Taryn's money: She didn't want her girlfriend to buy any more of the drugs that would ruin her life.

You don't know that, Sera. She could have been doomed, even without the car accident. But the world will never know how Kailey would have turned out. The world doesn't even know she's gone.

Eventually I pull myself up. I plod down the stairs and begin to drift through the crowd, jostled and slammed by dancers, by people in love with each other and with life. Complete strangers who smile at me and say "Hey, Kailey."

And somehow that makes it so much worse. The loneliness gains strength, fills my eyes, and begins to spill down my cheeks. I shove through the people and make my way outside into the freezing rain.

"I know how you feel." Surprised, I look up to see Echo. Her deep red dress is covered with tiny silver stars that sparkle in the muted glow of the streetlight. Her hair clings to her high cheekbones, drenched by the rain. And yet she seems somehow more brilliant than I've ever seen her, like a dried-out shell from the beach that shows its true color only when dipped in the sea. Echo is a watercolor, and I . . . I look like a drowned cardboard box: covered in mud and close to falling apart.

I'm suddenly embarrassed. I wrap my arms across my chest. "I'm fine," I lie. I've been doing that a lot lately.

She studies my face, then smiles. It's almost enough to penetrate my iced-over solitude. "That's a good attitude, to remember that everything happens for a reason."

If Cyrus were here, he'd laugh in her face. But somehow, I don't think she'd care. "I wish I could believe that," I reply.

She shrugs. "It doesn't really matter if you believe it or not. That's the cool thing about life. None of us has any real clue what the meaning of it all is."

"Good point," I say with a laugh. And it is. I've been alive for more than six centuries, and I'm no closer to the answer.

"Except—if everything happens for a reason, why try to do anything?"

"Because fate isn't something that just *happens* to you. You're part of it. For example, I felt incredibly lonely today. I couldn't stop thinking about Eli—wondering where he is, if he's okay." Her face briefly darkens, and I remember that she was good friends with him. "So I came here to be less alone."

"I can relate to feeling lonely," I say.

She looks me in the eye. "The crowd makes it worse." I nod. "But then again, if I hadn't come here, we wouldn't be having this conversation."

I allow a small smile. Circular logic, to say the least. "So this conversation is my fate?" I ask.

"How else would you get home?" she tosses back, then plunges her slim hand into the leather purse that's strapped across her body. She pulls out a set of keys that dwarfs her palm, exploding with more key chains and charms than I've ever seen in one place. No wonder she needs such a large bag. "You need a ride, right?"

I nod, and she loops her arm through mine. "Let's go, then."

"So, wait," I muse, as we traipse through the rain, "if you hadn't shown up here tonight, I would have been stuck without a way of getting home. Would that have been my fate?"

She throws her head back and laughs. "Of course not. It would have simply been fate telling you to get creative."

She's right. There's more than one way to solve a problem. Taryn has the book. That's all that matters. *Get creative, Sera*, I tell myself. There's more than one way to get it back—especially if you're willing to add breaking, entering, and robbery to an already extensive list of crimes.

TWENTY-TWO

On Monday, the school is deluged with a storm of rumors. That Eli killed himself, that he ran away to join a band in L.A., that he was spotted busking in the New York City subway. Several classmates try to involve me in conversation, but I stay out of it. I'm too busy thinking of how to convince Taryn to let me see Cyrus's book.

A voice over the school's intercom informs us that third period's been canceled for an assembly. I turn around on my way to Art and change directions, glad that I won't have to spend a class with Reed.

The auditorium is eerily quiet even though it's jam-packed

with students. I spy Leyla and Bryan sitting near the front and go to join them but stop short in the aisle when I realize that Noah's sitting directly in front of them. Even worse, Nicole is right next to him, their shoulders touching as she leans to whisper something in his ear. I grit my teeth and crane my neck behind me, looking for anywhere else to sit.

"Kailey! Over here!" Leyla waves at me and pats the seat next to her. Noah's posture stiffens as she calls Kailey's name, and my chest tightens. He clearly doesn't want anything to do with me. Nor should he. But it still hurts.

I slide into the open seat, trying not to watch Noah, the way his messy black hair falls in waves around his neck. The way Nicole's fingers dance on his arm as she speaks, her nails painted the same deep red as the curtain on the stage.

News of my breakup with Noah has saturated our group of friends, and the resulting whispers and concerned glances have cemented it into utter, heartbreaking finality. I texted him yesterday to tell him I'd find another ride to school, which thankfully Leyla was willing to give me. I'd had no option but to tell her and Bryan the news while squeezing my hands into fists in the pocket of my coat.

"But . . . why?" Leyla had asked me, her dark eyes searching. "I thought you guys were perfect for each other. Did something happen?"

"No . . ." My voice trailed off. "I just . . . decided that I was leading him on. I didn't care about him as much as I originally thought."

"Uh-huh," she'd responded, sounding unconvinced. "Well, I suppose that's fair."

"Right, I didn't want him to waste his time with me. We should both see other people."

Bryan never spoke—I'm sure he didn't want to get in the middle of his sister and his friend. He'd just ruffled my hair. Somehow, the gesture had choked me up more than talking about Noah did.

"Is this seat taken?" Reed doesn't wait for my answer before settling into the seat next to me. I have never considered myself claustrophobic—when I was a little girl, I used to wedge myself into the tightest places I could find to hide from my mother and my nurses. But now, with Reed's solid presence effectively penning me in, I start to panic.

Rebecca follows Madison into the open seats in front of us, right next to Noah and Nicole.

"What happened to you the other night?" Reed asks. I can feel his eyes on the side of my face. I don't want to look at him, but the only alternative is to stare forward at the back of Noah's head.

"What do you mean?" I ask. I haven't forgotten the things he said on Treasure Island.

He shrugs. "You never came back to hear the rest of the

music. I was worried about you, but Bryan said you'd be fine. You seemed so upset, though." His deep-set brown eyes radiate concern, but I know better.

"Well, yes, the news about Eli—"

"Oh, of course. Who wouldn't be upset? I hope they find him." He leans in conspiratorially. "My parents don't know yet. My mom's going to lose it when she hears a kid went missing. I just hope she doesn't yank us out of school."

Before he can continue, the speakers crackle as the principal steps onto the stage, and the room falls silent. "Most of you have already heard the news, but I wanted a chance to talk to you myself." He takes a deep breath, and the microphone picks up the sound. I can see the deep shadows under his eyes, the coffee stain on his pale olive dress shirt, the slight tremor in his hands.

"So soon—too soon—after the death of Mr. Shaw, another tragedy mars our community. A student, Eli Macgregor, has gone missing." He takes another shaky breath as a murmur goes through the crowd of students.

"I can't believe there's anyone who doesn't know yet," whispers Leyla, to my left.

I just nod wordlessly.

"The police have launched a comprehensive investigation," the principal continues. "And they are doing their absolute best. Let's have a moment of silence for Eli. I know we are all praying that he is found right away."

There's a low rustle as the group lowers their heads. I do the same, though I know he's long since turned to dust. I steal a glance at Reed. His head is bowed, eyes closed.

I am incredibly conscious of Noah's presence. Only a few feet from me, but the gulf feels much wider. Especially when Nicole leans into him again and murmurs something in his ear, making ice crystallize in my heart. But what can I do? I can only hope that common decency will prevent her from making a move on him anytime soon. I doubt it, though.

The principal leans into the microphone once more, earning him a high-pitched squeal of feedback that makes us jump. He laughs nervously before continuing. "Officer Spaulding is here from the Oakland Police to fill us in on the search for Eli. Officer?" He nods to a man who stands in the shadows offstage. The familiar policeman strides into the light.

He steps to the podium, a bounce in his step, his sun-glasses pushed up on his bald head, its shiny surface reflecting the theater's lights the way sun bounces off a windshield late in the afternoon.

"Thank you, sir," he says to the principal, snapping a piece of gum as he talks. "I'm sorry to be speaking with you under such terrible circumstances. But know that the Oakland PD won't rest until Eli is found. And we need your help to accomplish that. If any of you has any information that might help us out, we'd appreciate hearing from you." Next to him, Principal Gutierrez mops his forehead with his beleaguered tie.

"And we're continuing our investigation into the death of your teacher, Mr. Shaw. There have been some developments in the case—I can't give you the details, since the investigation is ongoing. But we're lucky to have some very helpful witnesses, a young man and woman from San Francisco, who are working with us to find the person who did this." His gaze sweeps across the auditorium, and although I know that the theatrical lights must be shining in his eyes, preventing him from actually seeing our faces, I swear he makes eye contact with me.

I shudder, imagining Amelia and Jared lying to this officer. The more he deals with them, the more danger he's in. And I'm certain he's completely unaware.

Reed rubs my arm in a consoling gesture. I want to yank my hand away, but I don't.

"Rest assured that we will do *whatever* it takes to find Eli," Officer Spaulding is saying. "That's—that's it for now. Remember: Any information might help. Thank you." He turns his whole body to face me, and a beam of light catches his badge, momentarily blinding me, making me think of bright lamps punishingly aimed in interrogation chambers.

I bring my hand up to my face to shield it, and when I lower my arm, he's gone.

Whatever it takes, I repeat in my mind, knowing what I need to do. Get that book back from Taryn. By whatever means necessary. All this wondering, this second-guessing and reverse psychology—it won't mean anything once I have that book in my hands. Taryn's address is listed in Kailey's phone contacts, and I'm going to go to there this afternoon, with or without Taryn's permission.

The principal is standing again at the mic. "Thank you, Officer Spaulding, for keeping us up to date." A glistening layer of perspiration covers his face, bringing the crow's feet at his eyes into sharp relief. "I'd like to invite anyone who would like to say a few words about Eli to come up to the stage. Of course, if you'd rather speak with me privately, my door is always open."

The low sound of movement surrounds me, a scuffling of sneakers on the floor and knees turned to the side to allow students to pass by. A line is quickly forming down the aisle as boys and girls approach to speak about Eli. I'm touched that he's inspiring so many people to speak. Touched—and horrified. He has so many friends who don't know that he's gone and never coming back.

"Excuse me, I need to get out," I mumble. Reed stands up, and I shove past him, fighting my way through the stream of students who are lining up to speak about the boy that no one knows is dead.

I'm halfway to the door when I hear Noah's voice behind me. "Kailey, wait." My treacherous legs turn of their own accord, move forward slowly toward him.

"Can we talk?" he asks softly.

Talk? I want to do more than talk. I want to pull him to me, to feel our puzzle-piece lips locking together. I start to lean toward him—and then I see Reed, watching us, and I snap together.

He'll kill Noah if he realizes you are in love with him. He's made his intentions painfully clear. It will end up just like the jazz musician in Paris. When we went back to the club after that night the trumpet player and I made eye contact, he was nowhere to be seen. *Must have left town,* Cyrus said with a smug grin. As if I didn't know. Cyrus had him removed— just as he would do to Noah if given the chance.

"No." My throat is so parched that my voice is barely audible. "I already told you everything I had to say."

Noah flinches. The lights shiver on his crow-black hair. He stares down at his grubby red sneakers, then pushes past me toward the door.

Nicole follows a beat later. When she catches up with him, she takes his hand and leads him away. I want to scream. I hate what I've created, but there's no turning back, not now.

The book, I tell myself. *Get the book, draw Cyrus out, and hopefully Noah will take you back.*

But the way Nicole touched Noah, the way he let her touch him, pokes a million holes in my certainty. What if, by the time I beat Cyrus, it's too late?

TWENTY-THREE

Taryn's apartment is on Hannah Street in West Oakland, a mixture of hundred-year-old houses wedged in next to warehouses and the occasional brand-new condominium building. The neighborhood is far grittier than where Kailey lives—trash collecting in the gutters, potholes scarring the asphalt, and wrought-iron bars covering most of the houses' windows.

The concrete steps leading to Taryn's building are stained and cracked, with weeds growing in the corners. It's a three-story building that was probably beautiful at one point, before someone painted the ornate Victorian woodwork a garish combination of bright yellow and grape. A window downstairs is missing its glass, a piece of plywood nailed in its place.

I set out for Taryn's place as soon as I got home from school, telling Mrs. Morgan the almost-truth that a friend of mine had a book I needed. She let me borrow the car, assuming the book in question was for school. I didn't correct her.

I approach the front door, scanning the hand-written names that appear above each unit's buzzer. And there it is: Apartment 3A is occupied by a T. Miller. I raise my finger to the buzzer, letting it hover for a long moment. Then I take a deep breath and push.

I wait, rocking back on my heels, wondering what I will actually say to Taryn if she answers. She doesn't.

I ring again, but still nothing.

I release the breath I didn't even realize I was holding. Damn it. I can easily pick the lock, but the entryway is completely visible from the street. I don't want the neighbors seeing me break in.

I catch a movement out of the corner of my eye from behind the glass door. I press my face between the metal bars, cupping my hand around my eyes and straining to see into the dim interior.

Inside, an older woman is locking the door to one of

the ground-floor apartments, an enormous sack of laundry slumped at her feet. She heaves the bag into her arms and heads straight for me. The front door opens.

"Let me get that for you," I say sweetly, moving to her side and holding open the door.

"Why, thank you," she says, breathing hard as she wrestles with the lumpy bag of laundry. She doesn't even look up at me. I slip past her up the staircase and climb to the third floor. The carpet is worn and stained, black splotches blending in with the floral pattern. Despite my soft steps, the stairs erupt in violent creaks with every footfall.

The door to Taryn's apartment is locked, so I fish the paperclip out of the pocket of my jeans and pick the lock in less than a minute.

It's dark inside. The only light leaks through the thread-bare spots in the drawn curtains. I feel for the wall next to the door and flip the light switch, and the room comes into sharp, well-lit focus. It's a disaster.

The first thing that hits me is the smell: a combination of stale air, rotting food, and something else. Something that makes me retch.

I bury my nose in my shirt, lurching forward to the window, and frantically rip open the curtains to crank the old casement handle. Clean, fresh air wafts over me, and I inhale gratefully.

When my stomach settles, I turn around and survey the filthy room. A brown corduroy couch sags against one wall, covered with junk: candy wrappers and greasy paper plates, dirty socks, unopened mail. The coffee table in front of it is a forest of beer cans, wine bottles, and candles serving as makeshift ashtrays. A puddle of some former, unidentifiable liquid has dried in its center, criss-crossed with trails of ants.

I move to the kitchenette. The tiny stove is painted in drippings and littered with rusty pans holding uneaten food in various stages of decomposition. The trash can is over-full, an avalanche of garbage spilling to the floor.

I regard the only other doorway in the small apartment. It must be Taryn's bedroom. There's a short hallway with a sharp turn at its end, effectively blocking any light from the living room, or any fresh air. The awful smell gets stronger as I step into the darkness, running my hand over the wall next to the door for a light switch. But I can't find one. I take another step, once again pulling my shirt up over my nose and nearly tripping over debris as I feel my way deeper in. I climb over soft piles that I assume—that I *hope*—are clothes. The smell is so strong, I fight not to gag.

My knee bumps into something solid—I throw out my hand and realize it's a bed. I run my hand along the side and follow it to what must be a nightstand. Wildly, I grope its surface, hoping I don't cut myself on the broken glass that my fingers brush against. I make contact with something thin, flexible, plastic, and close my hand around it, triumphant.

The electrical cord is attached to a lamp that's fallen to the floor, and I quickly locate its switch, blinking as the room is filled with light.

A beat-up suitcase yawns out from the open closet door. And next to that is the source of the smell. The carpet is covered with feces and, judging from the ammonia fumes that sting my eyes, urine. *Not human*, my rational brain tells me through my growing dread. I hurry to the room's one window and throw it open as well.

I lean against the bare wall next to the window, closing my eyes. I knew Taryn was a junkie, but somehow the squalor she lives in makes it much more real—and more hopeless. I picture Kailey's cozy, colorful bedroom. What was she doing with someone like this?

I feel something wet trail down my cheek, a rogue tear that welled in my closed eyes and escaped. *Poor Taryn*, I think. *Poor Kailey.* Two lost girls who found each other. One of them is gone forever. And the other can't be far behind.

I'm about to give up the search when I hear a rustling noise from the closet. I freeze.

"Who's there?" I demand, as I slip the knife out from my boot.

There's no answer, but I see movement—the pile of clothes on the floor undulates. An errant hanger on the top of the heap loses purchase and slides to the floor.

"I have a knife," I add, my voice braver than I feel. "And I'll use it."

No response. A shoe in the clothes heap shifts, falls away, and I find myself staring into two bright green eyes. A small, furry thing pokes its way out, holding its tail erect with all the grace of a princess.

It's a cat. A damn cat.

I exhale in a huge gust, collapsing against the side of the bed. The tiny kitty approaches my outstretched feet, sniffing my sneakers. I brace myself for the inevitable hisses, the predictable claws and fangs that animals always show me.

But they never come.

Instead, the cat arches its back and lets forth a volley of outraged meows. She comes closer, right up to me, and sniffs my arm, my hip. I slide my knife back into my boot and put out a tentative hand. The cat walks right into it, pushing her head into my palm. A small pink tongue laps my wrist, and I laugh. It tickles. I don't think a cat has ever touched me before, not in six hundred years.

"What's the matter, huh?" I coo, running my hand experimentally down the cat's furry side. Her coat is light gray, with just the hint of lighter gray stripes. Her body is so thin. I rub down her spine to her hips, tears blurring my vision as I feel each vertebra, the jutting bones to either side of the tail. The cat meows again—not in fear. More like she wants to yell about how hungry and neglected she feels. I pick her up gently. The poor thing can't weigh more than five pounds.

"Come here, little baby," I say, cradling the ball of fur in my arms and stepping carefully out from the bedroom. I set her down on the kitchen counter and scour the empty shelves, the pile of trash on the floor. She watches my every move, her huge, pale green eyes looking like two full moons. I swear they look hopeful, like she knows what I'm searching for.

Next to the dented microwave that sits on the counter I finally get lucky, unearthing an unopened can of cat food.

"You're about to have 'ocean whitefish and tuna with gravy,'" I tell the cat, reading from the label. "Now if only I could find a can opener," I murmur, regarding the trashed kitchen in despair. The cat meows again. Loudly.

"Okay, okay, you're hungry, I get it. I can be inventive." I pull my knife from my boot, piercing the lid in several places, then peel it back with my fingernails. I dump the unappealing contents onto a plastic Tupperware lid and push it in front of the cat.

She buries her face in the mush and takes huge bites,

her tiny body racked with purrs. The food is gone in minutes, and she regards me again with those huge moon-round eyes, meowing. She makes it sound like a question. "More?"

"Poor thing," I say, petting her again and looking around Taryn's apartment. I can't leave the cat here—that much is obvious. Judging from how emaciated she is, plus the mess on the bedroom floor, Taryn's been ignoring her for quite some time.

I remember the suitcase in the bedroom and quickly retrieve it. The cat follows me, staying inches from my heels. "You're going to come with me, okay?" I ask her.

She meows agreeably.

With my knife, I poke air holes in the side of the suitcase, then open its flap. "Hop in," I tell the kitty.

And then I see it. A glimpse of blue out of the corner of my eye, a blue I know as well as I know its owner's original eyes. On the bookshelf, wedged next to a stack of scratched CDs, lies Cyrus's book.

"Yes!" I whisper, triumphant, as I slide it off the shelf. I chuckle softly in disbelief—the bookshelf, of all places. The one object in the entire apartment that's in a logical place. I had assumed it would be hidden.

I tentatively sit down on the couch and run my fingers over the cover, the blue leather worn and supple, the broken lock that was added far after the original manuscript was bound, once its owner had descended well into paranoia and secrecy. The lock that I myself broke when I smashed it against the sea-damp metal surface of a shipping container crane, moments before I intended to leap into the Oakland Estuary and end my life.

If Taryn had been able to offload the book, it would have changed her life. A complete alchemy text from the fourteenth century? An auction house or museum would have paid hundreds of thousands for something like this. Taryn could have gone to rehab, moved away, gotten the fresh start she deserved.

The cat, I realize, is scratching and whining at a door I hadn't noticed earlier, half-hidden behind a purple velvet armchair. "Come back here," I tell her. "We need to go."

But she just meows louder, sticking her paws under the door. My arms erupt in goose bumps for no reason. "What's in there?" I whisper, stepping toward her, foreboding raising the hairs on my neck.

More scratches.

I wipe my clammy forehead, take a deep breath, and open the bathroom door. The opaque orange shower curtain mocks me. I don't want to see what's behind it. I don't.

I don't have a choice. The cat bolts toward the bathtub and leaps up to its chipped porcelain lip, batting at the shower curtain with her paw.

When it briefly moves aside, I glimpse lank, dark hair surrounding a complexion as pale as the tile behind it. I run toward the tub, yanking the shower curtain from the wall. The entire rod crashes to the floor with an echoing metallic clang.

"Taryn!" I yell. She's fully clothed, a rubber strap tied around one pale, scarred arm sprawled on the soap dish next to a blackened spoon and a needle.

I drop to her level, banging my knees on the tub and jamming my fingers into her neck. Her flesh is ice cold.

But dimly, faintly, I feel it. The small, slow, thrum of her pulse. She's alive.

"Taryn!" I yell again, pulling my hand back and smacking her across the face, hard. Her head lolls heavily to the side.

I twist the faucet knob and cover her in a spray of hot water, trying to raise her body temperature as quickly as I can. I shout her name. "Wake up!" I tell her.

And then, to my surprise, she does.

Her mouth moves for several long moments before any words come out. Then: "Kailey?"

"Yes, it's me." I turn off the shower and stroke her clammy forehead.

"No, it's not." She opens her eyes, stares at me. "I know who you are. You're the angel girl."

"Stay awake," I command her.

"Angels don't get to boss me around," she sighs. "I'm tired." Her eyelids flutter, then close.

"Taryn, no! Don't fall asleep. Stay with me."

"But you're not Kailey. I just saw her. . . . You took me away from her. She's dead." My stomach drops. My skin breaks out in a sweat. Freight trains screech through my head.

"We've got to get you to the hospital," I say. "I'll help you get up."

But she doesn't respond. I put my hand on her shoulder, shake it roughly. Nothing.

I scramble from the bathroom and dig my phone from my bag. I'm about to dial when I realize I can't use it—I can't be traced here, to Taryn's apartment. I hurry back to the kitchen, where I saw a landline phone next to an old pizza box on the counter.

With quavering fingers, I dial 911. "Help," I say, when the man answers, my words tumbling out. "There's a girl. She's unconscious. Drug overdose. I think she's about to die. In the bathroom."

"Can you describe—"

But I've already hung up. I scoop up the cat and drop her in the empty suitcase. To my surprise, she doesn't fight. I zip it closed and run out the door, leaving it unlocked, and stumble down the stairs with the suitcase in hand and the

193

book under my arm. I can already hear sirens wailing in the distance.

I explode out the building's front door and down the stairs to the street, breath tearing holes in my chest as I scramble down the block to Mrs. Morgan's car. Ignoring the cat's frightened mews, I strap the suitcase into the passenger seat and start the ignition.

And then, without really knowing why, I pause, sliding down in the seat so I won't be seen as the first ambulance tears around the corner. EMTs burst out the doors and into the apartment building in a crackle of walkie-talkie feedback and red lights.

Several police cars pull up as I throw the car into gear. I need to leave. I can't be questioned. But some instinct tells me to wait. The officers jump out of their cruisers and I recognize one of them: a lean, powerful figure with mirrored sunglasses over his eyes, despite the deepening dusk. I hold my breath as Officer Spaulding takes the stairs two at a time, then disappears inside.

I drive the whole way home with the book in my lap. Its weight feels solid, like an anchor. Or a weapon.

Mid-Continent Public Library

Checked Out Items 3/30/2019 13:24
XXXXXXXXX2372

Item Title	Due Date
30007133431535 The adoration of Jenna Fox	4/27/2019
30004001623004 The impossibility of tomorrow	4/27/2019
30004003505845 Before I fall	4/27/2019

Amount Outstanding: $4.95

A New Library Experience is Coming!
Get updates on what's happening with
branch construction projects and
other enhancements at MCPL. Visit
mymcpl.org/community or like us on
Facebook to learn more!

TWENTY-FOUR

"No way. You're *allergic* to cats, Kailey." Mrs. Morgan's hands are on her hips as she eyes the little ball of gray fur that I'm cuddling in my arms.

Oh. Kailey's body may have been allergic when she was alive, but the alchemical process of transferring my soul would have healed any such maladies. "Not this one, apparently," I say with a smile. "Which means I'm *meant* to keep her."

She doesn't say anything but tentatively reaches out her hand to scratch the cat's ears, earning a loud, rumbling purr.

"Please?" I whisper.

"Where did you find her, again?" Mrs. Morgan asks, continuing to stroke the cat's chin.

"On the street, by my friend's house. Feel how skinny she is, Mom. She would have died if I hadn't found her." I feel tears burning my eyes. I'm not sure why, but I *need* this cat. I don't know if it's because she belonged to Taryn, the girl whose life I've tried to save twice, who might already be dead. Or is it because no other animal has ever shown me affection?

"Aw," Mrs. Morgan murmurs, as the cat arches her back and closes her eyes. "Poor little baby. She's definitely a stray."

"Please?" I repeat. "Can we keep her?"

She looks at me for a long moment, but I know I've already won this battle. I don't see how anyone could fail to love this cat. "Okay," she says. "But *you* have to take care of her. Feeding, litter box, everything. And if you start getting asthma attacks, we're taking her to the shelter, straightaway. Deal?"

I nod vigorously. "Deal." I hug the cat to my chest, cradling her thin body, then set her down on the checkered linoleum floor. "Go ahead, little kitty," I say. "Explore your new house." The cat begins to sniff everything in sight, rubbing her head against the table legs, the cupboards.

"You're going to have to give her a name, you know," says

Mrs. Morgan. "'Kitty' is a bit common, don't you think?"

"Right," I answer, kneeling down next to the cat to stroke her head. "What's your name, huh? What should we call you?"

She stares at me, her huge green eyes reminding me, not for the first time, of twin full moons. Suddenly I know exactly what to call her. "Luna," I say solemnly. "Her name is Luna."

"Perfect," says Mrs. Morgan. "And very Berkeley." This comment makes me unaccountably happy. Luna, my little Berkeley cat, meows, as though to say she's pleased with her new name.

"I think the drugstore might still be open." Mrs. Morgan pulls on her coat, her purse already dangling from her arm. "We should go get Luna something to eat."

Luna meows in agreement, casting me an accusatory glance. I can't help but chuckle softly at her outraged feline expression.

"I don't think I've seen you this happy since—well, since last week," Mrs. Morgan says carefully as she fishes her car keys from her purse.

"You can say it," I tell her. "Since Noah and I broke up."

Her cheeks relax. "I didn't want to say anything," she admits. "I figured you wouldn't want to discuss boy problems with your mom."

"It's okay," I say, though I'm not very convincing. "We're still friends. We just weren't meant to be together."

She regards me for a minute, then reaches out to tuck a lock of hair behind my ear. "Kailey, I've known you your whole life. I know when you're sad. I hope you know that you don't have to keep up the tough-girl act around your own mother."

I can feel my shell cracking, can feel the tears I can't shed for Noah threatening to break through my fragile composure. *Be a hawk*, I command myself. Luna rubs against my leg, and I sink back down to her level, grateful to have an excuse to hide my face. Her fur is so soft, like a rabbit's.

"We should take her to the vet," I say, swallowing the lump in my throat and feeling Luna's jutting ribs. "What if she's sick?"

Mrs. Morgan kneels next to me and pets Luna. "I don't think she's sick, honey. She's just hungry. But you're right, we should take her to the vet to be sure. I'll call first thing tomorrow." I nod gratefully.

"You know what else we should do this weekend?" she continues. "Take you shopping for a dress. The dance is next week, right? The stores will be crowded, with all the after-Thanksgiving sales, but we can go early . . ."

I stare at her. Does she really think I'm still going to the dance?

Her face falls. "What? Oh, you probably want to go shopping with Leyla. I get it."

I stand up. "Mom, I'm not going to the dance. I don't have anyone to go with." I try to keep my tone light.

"So?" She smiles. "Bryan's taking Leyla, why don't you just go with them?"

"It doesn't work that way. I don't think they'd appreciate me tagging along on their date."

"They're your best friend and your brother. They love you. Why wouldn't they want you to come?" She frowns, like she's honestly puzzled.

"Look, I know you're worried about me. But you don't have to be. Really." From the floor, Luna meows, as if echoing Mrs. Morgan's concern.

"But you're on the committee," she protests. "It doesn't seem right for you to miss the actual event."

"I'll help with the decorations, but that's it. I'm not going." My voice sounds sharper than I intended.

"It's up to you," Mrs. Morgan says, putting her hand on my shoulder and pulling me toward her. "But just . . . think about it. All your friends will be there." She hugs me. "I'm going to play the I'm-your-mother card here, Kailey. You don't want to miss out on memories like this. When you're my age, you'll realize how fast time goes by. How years pass by in an instant, and how happy you are to have these memories of being together with your friends. You're only sixteen once."

I inhale, smelling her rosemary-mint shampoo, and am surprised to feel my eyes pricking with tears.

You're only sixteen once, unless you're me.

TWENTY-FIVE

"Interesting technique, Kailey," Madison says drily the next day, nodding toward the drawing I'm working on. When Mrs. Swan assigned us a still-life sketch of flowers today, my stomach immediately tied up in knots. This was the only solution I could think of on short notice.

Kailey would have faithfully reproduced the lilies, irises, and silver-hued roses in the angular glass vase, deftly shading their petals and stems. She had a real talent for making a drawing that looked almost like a photograph—except, knowing her, she would have added fairies or angels or other winged creatures, little bits of magic darting through reality.

I can't begin to approximate her style, so I refuse to even try. Instead, I've covered my sketchpad in an abstract design, just the barest suggestion of leaves rendered geometrically off the harsh, slashing lines that pass for stems. "Yeah, I'm trying something different," I inform Madison in what I hope is a confident tone. "Realism isn't everything, you know."

"Mm-hmm," she responds, sounding unconvinced, and returns to the clipboard in front of her, covered with notes and checkboxes. Apparently she's not interested in this assignment, either. She's been covertly working on dance committee business for the whole class period, quickly sliding her sketchbook on top of her clipboard whenever Mrs. Swan walks by.

"I like it," Reed says, standing to get a better view of my drawing. "Very Russian avant-garde." I just smile sweetly and wait for him to sit back down. I let my hand drift to my boot and run my finger over the reassuring hardness of the knife tucked inside.

Mrs. Swan saunters by, and Madison quickly switches her attention to her sketch, sighing dramatically once our teacher moves on. "This class is such a waste of time," she complains. "I mean, really: flowers? I have more important things to be thinking about."

I stifle a smile at how seriously she's taking her job, but

I know how she feels. I can't wait for this day to be over, either, so I can finally put my plan for Cyrus's book into motion. I just need to make sure I keep the entire thing anonymous. Luckily, I know just the person who can help with that. Lucia, who helped erase the police records from the night I became Kailey Morgan.

I think of Taryn again and wonder how she's doing. This morning, I finally caved and called the hospital from a pay phone. I can't let myself be connected with her, but I needed to know what happened. The receptionist told me she's in a coma. She hasn't woken since they brought her in.

"That reminds me," says Madison, sticking her pencil behind one ear, where it pokes through her shaggy hair like an oddly limbless tree. "Can you make a dance committee meeting on Friday? There are so many details we need to work out."

I pause. I looked forward to having the long weekend to myself, to concentrate on trapping Cyrus. "I'll have to check with my parents," I say. "Since it's a holiday weekend and all. I'm not sure what they have planned."

"Oh, Thanksgiving. Right. Well, Bryan already said he'll come. So I assume that means you're off the hook." She smiles sweetly.

"In that case, I wouldn't miss it," I reply.

"Kailey, you're not fooling me. I can tell you don't want

to go. And I know why." I turn to meet her gaze, noticing for the first time that her eyes aren't completely brown. The tiniest flecks of blue hover around her iris, catching the light that streams in through the classroom's tall windows.

"What do you mean?" I stammer, feeling like she caught me doing something wrong.

She cocks her head, the tiny piercing below her lip glinting in the sun. "I heard about you and Noah. The breakup. He tried to get out of the meeting too."

Through the barrier of flowers, I can feel Reed's eyes on me. He doesn't speak. The sound of Noah's name sends a bolt of pain through me, but I will my face to remain impassive. The more emotion Cyrus sees from me about Noah, the greater danger he's in.

"Oh, *that*." I wave my hand dismissively. "Don't worry about me and Noah. We're friends." I plaster a big fake smile on my face. "We just weren't meant to be more than that."

"You don't have to lie to me, Kailey." Madison's voice is warm, caring.

Across the table, I can *feel* Reed and Echo eavesdropping.

"I mean it," I answer. "Noah's great as a friend. But that's it. For me, at least."

"So you wouldn't care if he went out with another girl?" she presses. "Hypothetically speaking, of course."

"Nope," I say, perversely proud of how casually I'm able to get the words out. "I want him to be happy."

"That's very mature of you," Madison says. "I wouldn't be able to stand it."

I open my mouth, about to spill forth another batch of lies, but Echo speaks instead. "If you love somebody, set them free," she opines in her high-pitched, breathy voice.

"That's a famous poem, right?" asks Reed, scrunching up his forehead.

"It's a Sting song," Madison, the resident rock music expert, informs him. "From *Dream of the Blue Turtles*. Nineteen eighty-five."

Echo clasps her hands together, obviously pleased that Madison caught her reference. She's wearing grubby overalls with a fitted blouse underneath that reveals two smooth reaches of skin at each hip. Her hair appears to have gained a few more colors of yarn since I last studied it, violet and golden threads added to the rest. It's pulled up in a dramatic bun at her crown, the better to show off her enormous silver earrings. They're easily three inches in diameter and bearing what I assume to be her astrological sign: Aquarius.

"I never understood that concept," Reed replies, dropping his eyes to his drawing. "If you always set the ones you love free, you're doomed to be alone."

"Agreed," says Madison. "It doesn't make any sense."

Echo scoffs. "It makes complete sense. If you set the person free, but they come back to you, well, *that's* love." Reed swivels his head to stare at her, but she doesn't look at him.

"Excuse me, class." Mrs. Swan claps her hands at the front of the room, and I'm grateful for the interruption. "I have some inspiration for you. Our next project is a personal favorite of mine. We're going to partner up for this one."

I feel Reed's eyes on me and know without a doubt that he'll ask me to be his partner. I refuse to look at him, keeping my eyes trained on Mrs. Swan, who's reaching into a cardboard box that lies on her desk.

The class collectively *oohs* at the object she thrusts into the air. But not me. My breath is caught in my throat.

It's an antique Venetian mask; an exquisite one, bone-colored leather molded into the shape of a bird's beak and intricately painted. When I look at the two dark circles meant for the eyes, I shiver. They remind me of a skull's eye sockets.

I'm sure I'm as pale as the mask. To the rest of the class, this is nothing more than a costume, a work of art, a remnant of an elegant past.

But to me, that mask brings back a torrent of memories. The masquerade ball where Cyrus made me immortal. The plague-ravaged London where I came to terms with my fate.

The young girl in the garden whose body I took, my first true victim as an Incarnate.

Madison's posture is stiff, her cheeks flushed. "Those things give me the creeps," she admits. "They're almost as bad as clowns."

"Masks are a very powerful archetype," Echo agrees.

"I think they're fantastic," says Reed. "Perfect for a masquerade ball."

"Have you ever been to one?" Madison asks.

"Maybe in another life," he says, and smiles. Inside my boots, my toes curl up. "I suppose we should pick our partners? Kailey, do you—"

"Kailey's with me," Echo interrupts, catching my eye. I nod, sending her a silent *thank you*.

"Oh, well then, Madison, I guess that leaves us?"

She shrugs nonchalantly. I doubt she's even paying attention to us anymore.

The bell's shrill tone precludes anything further he may have said. Finally. I affect great absorption in the packing up of my belongings, grateful that our conversation is apparently over. When I look up, I realize that Echo's already left.

I hurry out into the hallway and quickly spot her wildly colored hair up ahead, rising above most of the other girls. Her platform clogs add at least four inches to her already impressive height.

I slip through the crowd and catch up to her. She whirls around when I tap her on the shoulder. "Well, hello," she smiles. "It's you."

"It's me," I agree, tilting my head upward to meet her eyes. "I wanted to thank you. How did you know I wanted to be your partner?"

"Body language," she says, shifting her army green canvas backpack. "You turned gray when Reed started to ask you. I don't know why, though—I think he's kind of sweet." I just stare at her in shock.

"There you go again," she laughs.

"Am I that easy to read?"

"Only to me. So, do you want to start today? On our project?" I hesitate. I meant to spend the afternoon putting Cyrus's book for sale online.

Echo seems to read my silence as agreement. "Let's go to my house," she offers. "Did you know my dad's a medieval literature professor, and my mom's an artist? She actually works with leather a lot. We'd have reference material and supplies all ready to go."

"And I just so happen to be an expert on the history of masks," I say archly.

"Now we're talking," she says, rubbing her hands together.

Have I said too much? I try to backpedal. "I'm just kidding."

"No, you're not," she deadpans. "So, are we on?"

I haven't technically crossed Echo off my suspect list, but I feel like I can trust her implicitly. And I like spending time with her, I realize. For the first time, I have a friend who wasn't friends with Kailey—someone I can talk to without the burden of a shared history. It's a relief not to be constantly worrying about saying or doing the wrong thing, giving myself away in some way I can't even anticipate. "Okay," I relent. "I'll meet you at your car?"

"Sounds like fate," she replies in her musical voice, as she walks away.

TWENTY-SIX

I run into Leyla in the parking lot on my way to meet Echo. "Open it," she says, thrusting a folded-up piece of paper in my hands. "This is a historic occasion. Excuse me, *an* historic occasion, which is what literary people say."

"So you're literary now?" I ask, unfolding the paper, already knowing what it's going to be.

"I think someone who gets a *poem* named after them counts as literary," she replies with a grin.

"'Lady Leyla Ladybug,'" I read. "Wow."

"I know, right? I'm going to have to wear more red to live up to my reputation." She's obviously delighted. I'm happy for her, even if I'm not in the best state of mind to tolerate loving couples.

"Come on," she says, grabbing my hand. "Let's go find Bryan and get out of here. And don't you dare breathe a word about this to him."

"I wouldn't," I swear. "But actually, I'm meeting Echo. We're working on an art project together."

"Oh," she replies. "Okay. Have fun with Echo. But let's hang out soon. I miss you, Kailes."

I nod and depart, averting my eyes as she catches up with Bryan and throws her arms around him. I quickly spot Echo's car, a vintage teal Karmann Ghia covered with bumper stickers. GOT MAGIC? reads one of them. MY OTHER CAR IS A PUMPKIN, reads another. Its charm didn't quite register with me the other night, when she drove me home from The Wasteland.

"Nice car, by the way," I say.

"Thanks. My parents hate it," she tells me, when I'm seated in the front seat next to her. "It's not very fuel-efficient, I'm afraid." The dashboard is strewn with dried flowers, crystals, and lollipops. "Want one?" she asks, handing me a cherry-flavored sucker.

I start to unwrap the lollipop and look out the windshield when I see Noah standing next to his car. He's talking to Officer Spaulding.

"Why is he talking to Noah?" I muse, only realizing seconds later that I spoke out loud.

Echo shrugs. "I think he's questioning everybody. Your friend Chantal said a police officer showed up at her house this morning, too. I hope it helps them find Eli."

I shiver, suddenly anxious to leave. After everything that happened at Taryn's apartment last night, being questioned by Officer Spaulding is the last thing I want. "Shall we?" I prod Echo, hoping my voice doesn't give away the pounding of my heart.

"We shall," she agrees, pressing the key into the ignition.

I feel better as soon as Echo directs the car out into traffic. She drives us to West Berkeley, expertly parallel-parking on a street that's an incongruous combination of industrial warehouses and gingerbread Victorians. The architecture is similar to Taryn's neighborhood but minus the security bars covering most windows. I follow her to the unmarked doorway of one of the warehouses, where she pulls out her keys and lets us into a hallway. She turns right, then left, down another hallway, and finally unlocks the door to her loft.

A pile of shoes lies just inside. Echo kicks off her clogs, adding them to the heap. I hesitate—it won't be easy to explain why I have a knife tucked into my boots. But Echo's already disappeared into the loft, so I quickly tug off my boots, leaving the knife inside.

"Some tea?" Echo's voice resonates from the kitchen. "I would offer you something more exciting, but my parents won't allow us to buy anything that comes in a package." I nod yes to the offer of tea, looking around the kitchen as she fusses with a kettle. It's true; I don't see a single commercial food product. Instead there are bowls of fruit, glass jars of grains and nuts, and papery cloves of garlic huddled next to a bottle of oil. None of the cupboards have doors. Echo pulls two ceramic mugs down from a high shelf and adds loose-leaf tea to them. Earl Grey, I think, judging from the bergamot scent in the air.

Beyond the kitchen, I can see the main living space. One soaring wall is covered with books, a ladder leaned against the top shelf, nearly brushing the twenty-foot-high ceilings. "Go ahead and make yourself at home," Echo says. "I'll bring this over when it's ready."

"Okay," I say, too curious to protest. The other wall of the main room is covered with art, traditionally framed paintings as well as stretched hides with primitive-looking designs drawn in charcoal. I approach them for a better look. The figures on the hides look like women surrounding a wounded mammoth, a spear protruding from its side. Family portraits are sprinkled amongst the art. Echo must get her height from her father, I decide, sizing up the professorial-looking man who appears in several of the photos. I assume that the woman in the shots is Echo's mother, half a foot shorter than her daughter and crowned with frizzy light brown hair.

At the far end of the room is a large table, its surface covered with books, candles, unsteady stacks of paper, and even a reptile skull. A cutting mat lies at the center of a cluster of linen thread and bookbinding needles. An X-Acto blade completes the scene.

I take a seat on one of the leather couches, tucking my sock-clad feet underneath me. I don't see a TV anywhere. Instead, the couches face a wall of glass doors that lead to the family's small balcony space. Above one of the doors is the taxidermized head of a deer, its antlers stretching two feet across. Flanking the couch where I sit are several female-looking sculptures, goddess figures rendered in marble and granite.

"It's very Paleolithic girl power around here," says Echo, carrying a tray with two steaming mugs over to where I sit and setting it upon the gnarled and shellacked redwood tree stump that functions as their coffee table.

"I like it," I say truthfully. And I do. Girl power is exactly what I need right now. I picture the circle of ancient women attacking Cyrus with their blunt spears.

Cyrus has always insisted that I am weak, whether out of genuine concern or an urge to control me, I don't know.

Probably both. His belief was cemented the night I was attacked in New Orleans. It was 1726, and Cyrus left our plantation with Jared, attending to "business matters." I knew that was polite code for gambling and general thuggery. An opera was playing in the French Quarter, a debut from a young Italian composer that I desperately wanted to see, and I went alone, ignoring Cyrus's orders to stay at home.

When the men grabbed me from behind, under the flickering light of the gas lamps, I fought back hard. But it was Sébastien, unknown to me at the time, who stepped from the shadows and saved me. That's how I met him, covered in my attackers' blood. And that's what led to Cyrus's decision to bring him into our fold. *You need constant protection, Sera. Constant surveillance.* Cyrus never thought I could take care of myself.

"Okay, so. Masks." Echo lifts the mug to her mouth and takes a tentative sip.

"Works of art designed to hide who you really are," I comment.

"I completely disagree," she smiles. "The best masks allow you to be who you really are, without all the hang-ups."

I cock my head. Cyrus had said something very similar at the masquerade ball.

"So who would you be?" I ask Echo.

215

She thinks for a moment, sipping her tea. "I know you expect me to say something really weird, like I want to be a wise woman or a priestess."

I laugh. She's right.

"And I *do* want those things, but honestly, I'd rather have a mask that made me normal. Like . . . one of those girls who can be a sexy witch for Halloween."

"That's silly," I declare. "I *like* that you're not normal, whatever that even is. And anyway, you're already kind of a sexy witch."

"Hand me my broom," she cracks. "Who would you be?"

"A warrior," I answer without hesitation.

"Who do you need to fight?" she asks. "Noah?"

I look down at my lap, shaking my head. "No, I'm not mad at him."

"I didn't think so," she replies. "What's Noah's birthday, anyway?"

What an odd question. I think back to our date at the restaurant on the pier. "Next month," I answer. "December."

"December what?" When I just shrug, she forges on. "I'm going to guess early December. Sagittarius. Noah's no Capricorn. He's into philosophy, yes? And travel?"

My neck prickles. "Yes to both," I say.

She nods with satisfaction. "Definitely Sag. What's your birthday?"

I pull my mug of tea to my face, taking a long, burning swallow, stalling. I picture Kailey's driver's license. "June . . . nineteenth," I answer slowly.

"Interesting," she responds. "I wouldn't have thought of you as a Gemini. But it totally makes sense now, about you and Noah. Air and fire are a combustible combination, you know. Doesn't work for the long haul."

I think of my real birthday, my mortal birthday. Early August, the last gasp of summer, which makes me a Leo. Fire on fire. I know more about astrology than I'm letting on to Echo. Cyrus believed in it with an intense fervor. "These so-called empiricists think astrology is a joke," he'd scoff. "The stars and planets are much larger than any of us. To ignore their influence is quite literally to tempt fate."

"Okay, so a sexy witch and a warrior mask it is," says Echo, deftly changing the subject. "I know! You can be Athena."

"The goddess of wisdom and warfare. I like." I remember one myth where Athena turned a particularly awful man into an olive tree. I could use her influence right about now.

Echo claps her hands in excitement. "Okay then. How about I work up some drawings?"

"We'll need a few days, I'm sure. I know Thanksgiving is tomorrow—"

"Oh, don't worry about that," she cuts me off. "My family doesn't celebrate Thanksgiving. My father says it's disrespectful to Native Americans. We do a harvest feast when the moon is in Cancer. Abundance, nurturing, you know."

"Makes sense," I reply, stifling a smile. She might be the most Berkeley-esque person I've met here.

"Besides," Echo continues, "it's good for me to keep busy. Otherwise I'd just think about Eli and be sad."

Eli. It hurts to hear his name. But it's also a good reminder for me to be strong. "Are you guys close?" I ask gently, using the present tense on purpose.

"We were," she corrects me. "I know he's gone. I can feel it." She looks out the window at the quickly darkening sky, and I think I see her eyes fill with tears, though it may be a trick of the light.

A thought occurs to me. "I know another way you can keep busy, if that's what you want. Why don't you join the winter dance committee?"

She tilts her head. "Madison's in charge of that, right? She seems kind of bossy lately. What would I do, anyway?"

I laugh. She's right about Madison—being the chair of the committee has certainly gone to her head. "Well, there is a mural that needs to be painted. It's supposed to be a solstice theme. Astronomy, astrology."

"In other words," she smiles, "right up my alley. Okay, I'm in."

218

I resist the urge to hug her. I can't believe my good luck—Echo's willingness to sketch the masks already made my day, but getting out of painting the mural is an unexpected bonus. I decide to take it as a good omen.

I wish Charlotte and Sébastien were here, to fight Cyrus by my side. But they're not, and Echo is. And as far as allies go, I could have done a lot worse. She has a quiet strength to her, a confidence that's rare to find in someone so young.

"Hey, Echo," I say on a whim, "do you like tacos?"

"Hell to the yes," she answers.

"Good," I respond. "I'm starving. And there's someone I want you to meet."

TWENTY-SEVEN

The smell of cilantro and poblano chilis greets us the moment we enter the Fruitvale market. "I thought I'd been to every taqueria in Oakland," Echo remarks. "I've never heard of this place."

"It's amazing," I tell her. The man at the front register doesn't appear to recognize me, giving a disinterested nod as we breeze by, but Lucia definitely does.

"Well, well. If it isn't Señorita Jane Smith," she says, stepping out from behind the taqueria counter at the rear of the store. I smile at the reference to the name on the fake ID she sold me nearly three weeks ago. As before, her espresso-colored hair is piled on top of her hair in a tight bun, though it's now held in place with a pair of red chopsticks. She's wearing a black, bateau-necked top and jeans that hug her hips like a second skin, emphasizing her slender frame. Bright pink high heels lift her several inches, though she's still not as tall as Echo.

Echo cocks her head. "Jane Smith, eh? Just how many names do you have?"

I hold a finger to my lips, and Echo nods, playing along.

"What can I get you two secret agents?" Lucia asks.

"Two chile verde for me," I say, taking Echo's elbow and scooting her closer to the menu, posted on the wall behind Lucia. "We're hungry."

"I'll take two lengua tacos," Echo says, and Lucia raises her eyebrows. "I love tongue," Echo adds. "My parents are really into weird meat." Lucia writes our order down on a notepad and disappears into the back.

Echo's eye is drawn to a display of saints' candles. "Go ahead, take a look around," I tell her, and she wanders down one of the crammed aisles.

The rich smell of meat intensifies, and my stomach grumbles. Lucia pokes her head out from behind the wall, and, seeing that I'm alone, gestures for me to move closer. "I know you didn't come all this way just for the tacos," she hisses. "What are you really here for? You need me to erase more police records?"

I shake my head. "No. I . . . I need to sell something. On the Internet. And I don't want anyone to be able to trace it back to me. Can you call your hacker friend?"

Lucia crosses her arms across her chest. "First of all, he's not a 'hacker,' he's just really smart with computers."

"Okay, your computer-genius friend, then—"

"Secondly," she cuts me off, "what are you selling?"

"I'd rather not say," I reply, looking down at the counter.

She shakes her head. "No way, sweetie. I don't get involved with drugs or guns." She counts them off on her fingers.

"No," I protest, "it's nothing like that."

"You're going to have to give me some more details, then." She purses her lips and cocks her head, keeping her arms firmly crossed.

I pause, considering. I *need* Lucia's help, and no good lie springs to my mind. I am the worst secret agent ever. I sigh, deciding to go with the truth. Or a version of it.

"It's a book. I need to sell a book," I say weakly.

"Nobody comes to see Lucia just to sell a book," she says, fixing me with an intense stare. "There's more to this story. I can smell it."

"It belonged to my ex-boyfriend," I continue. "And he's dangerous."

Her face softens, and she hurries around the counter that

separates us, pulling me into a hug. She smells like meat and roses. "Oh, sweetie," she breathes. "I'm sorry." She's gripping me tightly, and I wonder if I hit a nerve.

"No one can know," I whisper. "Not even my friend."

I feel her nodding. "Don't worry," she says. "I'll call my guy."

She heads again to the taqueria's kitchen, emerging minutes later with two heaping plates of food, plus a sheet of folded notebook paper that she drops into my pocket. I wave Echo over, and she joins me at the counter, a selection of saints' candles in her hands.

"Mmm," Echo breathes, setting her candles on the counter and scooping up one of her tacos. She takes a huge bite. Incredibly, she doesn't spill a single onion or drop of salsa verde.

"San Miguel y Nuestra Señora de Guadalupe, eh?" Lucia murmurs, reading the labels on the candles Echo's chosen. "Someone needs powerful protection."

Echo laughs. "My dad's obsessed with the Virgin of Guadalupe. He says she's the symbiosis of indigenous goddess worship and Catholicism."

Lucia and I both stare at Echo, who finishes her taco in one more huge bite. "What?" she asks, her voice muffled.

"He sounds like a smart dude," Lucia says wryly.

I pay for the tacos and Echo's candles, thanking Lucia

again. She grabs my hand as we leave, pulling me close. "Listen," she whispers in my ear, "you need any more help, you come see Lucia, okay?"

"I will," I promise.

Back in Echo's car, I'm dying to open the note Lucia gave me, but I resist. I guess it contains instructions to elude detection online, but I expected the matter to be a bit more complicated than a single scrawled note.

"You shouldn't worry so much," says Echo, pulling up to the Morgan house, and I jerk my head to look at her, surprised. It's like she can read my thoughts.

"How did you know I was worried about something?" I ask.

She pokes my shoulder, its tight ball of muscle. "Look at you. The way you hunch over, the way your hands keep fidgeting."

She's pretty damned observant, I think. For a human.

"Thanks again, Echo," I tell her. "This was fun. I'll see you tomorrow? And don't forget about the dance committee meeting on Friday."

"Definitely," she answers, tucking a lock of yarn-wound hair behind her ear. I hug her and climb out of the car, watching till it disappears around the block.

In Kailey's room, I study Lucia's instructions. They're not too difficult, even for me—a proxy server, an IP address scrambler, and a couple of fake e-mail addresses later, I'm in business. I spread a white sheet on the floor and arrange the blue book in the center, snapping a few photos with Kailey's phone.

Even though part of me doesn't want to look at the book any closer, I can't help it. I pull the book into my lap and start to turn the pages, noting, as before, the illustration of two people with the braided silver cord between them. It's the same image as the one I saw in Noah's room. *Cyrus was going to recruit Noah*, I think again with a shudder, imagining Noah's fate as one of Cyrus's henchmen.

Although I'm well-versed in Latin and Greek, I haven't read either language in years, let alone spoken them. And the old-fashioned black-letter characters—I recognize Cyrus's father Johann's handwriting—are frustrating to my modern eyes. Still, I am able to make out some of the text. There are sections on the mercurial nature of the human soul, the metaphysical properties of lightning, and the assertion that no change can be enacted upon the human body without also similarly transforming the spirit.

On another page I find the formula for making the Incarnate elixir. It's written in a confusing tangle of languages, and I can only translate bits and pieces: "the Essence of Silver," "the furnace of Balneum Vapori," "the Salt of Quicksilver." I shake my head. It would take a true medieval scholar, someone like Echo's father, to figure this out. Possibly several scholars, plus a team of chemists.

I flip a page that feels thicker than the rest. The second half of the book is entirely in Cyrus's handwriting. I find myself returning to the thick page, running my finger round its rough vellum edge for several minutes before I realize why it's so much heavier than the rest: It's actually *two* pages, fused together.

I slip my knife from my boot, but the heavy blade was meant for gutting fish, not delicate cuts. I rifle through the plastic box that contains Kailey's art supplies until I find what I need: a razor-sharp X-Acto blade with a very fine point.

Carefully, I run its edge between the pages. Despite my caution, some of the fibers rip and minute flakes of centuries-old ink sift to the floor. The process is painstaking, but finally, I'm able to separate them with a minimum of damage.

I stare at the writing within for several long minutes, trying to comprehend what it says. The strokes are thick and crowded together, and a deep sense of vertigo makes me glad I'm already sitting down.

It's backward, I realize. No wonder I can't read it. I rise to my feet and hold the manuscript up to the mirror over

Kailey's vanity, blinking my eyes as the words become clear. It's written in what modern scholars would call Middle High German. Or, as I knew it, simply German.

"The Alchemical Order of the Incarnates," it reads, "and its Brothers and Sisters in their respective Covens, those whose Souls may Travel between corporeal Beings, never Departing." Below that is a list of names, perhaps fifty, and locations all over the world. And, at the very bottom, in different-colored ink: Cyrus von Hohenheim, of Caffa. Seraphina Ames, of London.

My jaw drops. I immediately understand what it is, though the implications take much longer for my mind to grasp.

There are other Incarnates out there. Others like me. This list was compiled close to seven hundred years ago— who knows how many there are now?

And Cyrus kept this a secret from me—from all of us, Sébastien and Charlotte, Amelia and Jared. *There are no others like us*, he would say. *And only I have the elixir, so you can't make new companions.* He was so certain, so convincing. We believed him. We believed that the only alternative to staying with Cyrus for eternity was being completely alone in the world.

The enormity of the betrayal is incalculable. Charlotte

and Sébastien could have left together. Even Jared and Amelia, as much as I despise them, might have turned out quite differently without Cyrus's influence.

It's clear why he did it. Being alone is Cyrus's greatest fear. This way, he could ensure we would never leave him.

Still shaking, I log on to the antiquarian book auction site, typing in the book's details: blue leather-covered alchemy codex with illuminated vellum leaves, circa fourteenth century, binding repaired in the eighteenth-century style and historically inaccurate with the original text, complete manuscript. I decide not to list a minimum bid, knowing that any serious offers will be at least $40,000. This way I can weed out any bids that aren't worth my time. I set the auction timer for four days. I'd rather do even fewer, but I need to make sure Cyrus sees the listing. Though I don't doubt for a minute that he'll find it. He probably has Google alerts on every single antique book site on the Internet right now.

Here goes nothing, I think as I flop onto Kailey's bed. Luna immediately hops on my stomach, kneading her paws into my sweater with a satisfied purr. I remember that this is, in some ways, the hardest part for a hunter. The trap has been set; now all that's left to do is wait.

So I'm startled when Kailey's iPhone buzzes against my hip, not five minutes after I posted the book for sale. I unearth it from my sweater and bring it to my face. "New e-mail," the notification reads. I immediately tap through with trembling fingers, their tips leaving smudges on the glass.

There's a bid on the book. For $50,000.

TWENTY-EIGHT

"Kailey, what is *wrong* with you?" Mrs. Morgan asks. "Did you *completely* forget how to peel an apple? And put on an apron, you're going to ruin your shirt."

I sigh, looking at the gummy, ruined fruit in my hands. "I'm out of practice," I offer, though it's a lie. Cooking is a skill I've never had to learn. Other people have prepared food for me my whole life.

I eye the apple warily. *Cooperate!* I order it, silently, then attack once more with the peeler, wishing I could remove the skin in long, continuous spirals like Mrs. Morgan does. "Ouch!" I yell as my hand slips and the peeler slices into my finger. Bright red drops of blood immediately stain the white ceramic sink.

"That's it—you're done," says Mrs. Morgan, removing the peeler from my hand and covering the cut with a paper towel.

"As bad-ass as it would be to have bloody apple pie, I agree with your mom," chirps Leyla, pulling an apron from a wall hook. "Let me help, Mrs. Morgan."

Bryan claps. "I gotta give you credit, Kailes. You're committed to getting out of pie duty. I mean, cutting your own finger? That's dedication."

I shake my head. "I'm not *trying* to do anything," I protest. "Let me give it another shot."

Mrs. Morgan shoos me over to the kitchen table. "Just sit," she orders me. "As much as I appreciate the offer, I refuse to serve biohazard pies for Thanksgiving dessert."

"Biohazard pie?" Mr. Morgan repeats, stepping into the kitchen. "Sounds like something Leyla would like. Oh, *hi*, Leyla." He feigns surprise.

"Very funny," she retorts. "It was your lovely daughter who started the idea."

"What can I say? I'm a monster." I bare my teeth at Leyla. "*Rar.*"

"Rar indeed," Leyla agrees, turning back to her peeling.

I lean back in the chair, inhaling the sweet scents of

cinnamon, clove, and caramelized brown sugar that mingle with the roasting turkey. Mr. Morgan sits next to me and starts snacking on a bowl of pistachios, arranging their shells in two neat piles. I smile, watching him. I love this family, this kitchen. I love the mixing bowls stacked on the messy counter, the clatter of cooking and conversation, the smudge of flour on Mrs. Morgan's cheek that I don't have the heart to wipe away.

Luna seems to feel the same way, purring and rubbing against our legs, constantly underfoot.

Bryan joins Leyla at the sink and begins cutting the apples into thin slices. They're standing very close together, and I feel a wave of bittersweet happiness. They're obviously crazy about each other, but Kailey never would have allowed them to date. That's one good deed I can give myself credit for, I suppose.

But I can't deny that watching them hurts me too.

I can't stop thinking about Noah—what he's doing, how he's feeling. I'm sure this holiday must be tough on him. I don't exactly picture his father whipping up a Thanksgiving meal. I wish, not for the first time, that he was here with me, in the Morgan's kitchen. *As soon as Cyrus is gone, you can get him back*, I promise myself.

Maybe. Maybe he will. If he's not in love with someone else first.

Leyla told me earlier that Nicole was planning on asking Noah to the winter dance. I nearly died when I heard the news and instantly hoped he would turn her down. Then I felt even worse for being so selfish. He deserves happiness—and a girlfriend who doesn't come with six hundred years' worth of deadly baggage.

But I can't help it. I still love him.

I should know better by now. Happily ever after is a silly dream. What kind of happy ending can Noah and I have—a mortal boy and a girl doomed to live forever?

Yet I can't stop believing in it. Otherwise I would have nothing left to live for.

My reverie is interrupted by the low chime of the doorbell. "Kailey, can you get that?" Mrs. Morgan asks me as she heaves the turkey out of the oven for basting. Luna sniffs the roasting pan and announces her interest in the turkey with a plaintive meow.

"Of course." I jump up, happy to have something to do.

I open the door to a grinning Officer Spaulding. His eyes are inscrutable behind dark sunglasses, and he's holding a mustard yellow envelope. "Hello there," he says. "Kailey, right?" I nod. "This was on your doorstep."

"Thanks," I say, taking it from him. KAILEY & BRYAN MORGAN is written on the front in scrolling maroon ink. "Did you need something else?"

Despite the cold, overcast day, he's wearing the short-sleeved police uniform, revealing thick, muscled arms and a tan that has no reasonable explanation at this time of year. "I actually came here to talk to you, Kailey. And your brother." He consults a notepad that he pulls from his breast pocket. "Ryan, is it?"

"It's Bryan," I say flatly. "With a *B*." Some detective.

"Right, Bryan. I guess I'm just better with girls' names." He pushes his sunglasses up on his bald head.

"May I come in?" he asks, his smile revealing a row of sharp, white teeth. I'm reminded of the old legends about vampires—that they're not able to enter a human's home unless they're invited. I'm well-versed in their mythology, thanks to Cyrus's obsession with the writer Anne Rice.

"She's surprisingly sympathetic to her vampires," he used to say wistfully. "Even though they're murderers, just like us." He would smile, as though he'd said something funny. "We should go find her, don't you think? I hear she lives in New Orleans. Damn fine city for immortals. We could turn her into one of us. Blow her mind. Too bad there's no such thing as vampires; I wouldn't mind being one."

Cyrus had a way of missing the point.

"Come on in," I say hesitantly. Officer Spaulding is already through the door before I finish speaking, headed straight for the kitchen, as if he's already familiar with the layout of the house.

I follow his powerful-looking back, massive shoulders tapering to a slim waist, feeling like I just let the coyote into the henhouse. I'm nervous about what he might ask me in front of Kailey's family.

"Hello, Morgan family," he says, entering the kitchen. Bryan and Leyla turn to see who it is, their eyes wide. Worry flickers across Mr. Morgan's face, and he makes to stand up from the kitchen table. "No, no, don't get up," Officer Spaulding continues. "No need to panic. I'm just here to ask a few questions."

The kitchen, which was already crowded, now feels positively claustrophobic. I squeeze past Officer Spaulding and join Mr. Morgan at the table, scooting my chair back toward the wall.

"Can I get you some coffee, Officer . . . ?" Mrs. Morgan offers.

"Officer Spaulding. Thank you, but no, ma'am. I'm sorry to barge in on Thanksgiving, but I'm afraid that my business is far more important than good manners." He pulls a chair out from the kitchen table and sits across from me. We all jump when Luna, who was hunkered under the table, explodes with an angry yowl.

"Oh!" Officer Spaulding exclaims. "I'm so sorry." He peeks

under the table and appraises Luna, who rewards him with a furious hiss before darting out of the room. "I think I set my chair on your cat's tail," he explains, his face pale. "Should I go see if she's okay? I can't believe I did that—I love cats."

I want to run after Luna and make sure she's not injured, but Mr. Morgan shakes his head. "She'll be fine," he replies. "And I think she just learned not to hide under tables with a room full of people."

Officer Spaulding nods. "Is she still a kitten? She's so small."

"We're not sure," Mr. Morgan answers. "We've only had her a couple of days. She was a stray."

"Good for you," the policeman says. "So many animals without homes. Anyway," he continues, rubbing his head, "I'm here as part of the investigation into the disappearance of Eli Macgregor. And today Eli's family isn't, I assure you, celebrating Thanksgiving. Those poor folks don't have much to be thankful for." Mrs. Morgan blanches.

"I'm not sure how we can help you," says Bryan, leaning his back on the sink. "None of us were friends with Eli."

"You're sure?" says Officer Spaulding slowly. "Not even you, Kailey?" He turns to me, and I'm overwhelmed with the smell of his spearmint gum. I hate how it invades the kitchen, overpowering even the strong scent of onion and sage from Mrs. Morgan's cooking.

"I liked his music," I say softly. "But Bryan's right. We weren't close. I wish I'd known him better."

"What can we do to help, Officer?" Mrs. Morgan wipes her hands on her apron, and I sense her guard going up, like a mama bear who will do anything to protect her cubs.

"Oh, no, you don't have to *do* anything. I just wanted to check in. And Kailey and Bryan—you know we have a counselor on staff down at the station, in case either of you wants to talk about anything."

"I'm fine," I answer quickly. "Sad, but fine."

"Me too," says Bryan.

Officer Spaulding stares at each of us, then nods his head. "Well, I'll let you *fine* folks get back to your holiday. If any of you start to feel depressed, please don't hesitate to call up the station. Especially the girls—much more prone to emotional distress."

Bryan nods, earning a jab in the ribs from Leyla.

"Aren't you going to open that?" Leyla asks, turning to me and eyeing the yellow envelope in my hands. I notice that Officer Spaulding pauses halfway to the door.

When I make no move to open it, she plucks it from my hand. "May I?" she entreats, looking to me for permission.

"Go for it," I reply, and she gleefully rips into the envelope, removing a thick, ivory card with a deckle edge. "Oh my god!" she squeals, reading to herself.

"You want to share with the rest of the class?" asks Bryan with a wry grin.

"Sorry, yes. It says we're all invited to Reed and Rebecca's family's winery this weekend—for an overnight trip." Leyla's eyes sparkle—she's clearly elated at the prospect of a weekend away with her idol Rebecca. But the idea of spending a night on Cyrus's turf fills me with dread.

"Let me see that," I say, pulling the card from her hands.

Sure enough, in the same fine handwriting as the front of the envelope, it reads: "To: Bryan and Kailey. CC: Leyla, Chantal, Nicole, Noah, Madison. The Sawyer family requests the pleasure of your delightful company this long weekend at the Looking Glass Winery."

I set the card down. "Why couldn't they just invite us over e-mail, like normal people? Or ask us in person?"

"I think it's cool to send a paper letter," counters Leyla, her cheeks rosy. "No one does that anymore. Totally classy."

"Yeah, but then they had to write 'CC' on it and ruin the illusion. That's an e-mail thing." I know I sound petulant, some irritating combination of a whining student and her schoolmarmish teacher.

"Fine by me," Leyla answers. "'Cause now I know I'm invited, too."

"Sounds like fun," Officer Spaulding says, one hand on the door. "I could use a vacation myself." He nods and walks out. Everyone's posture relaxes slightly at the sound of the front door slamming shut.

"Strange guy," remarks Mr. Morgan, returning to his pistachios.

"Strange?" echoes Mrs. Morgan. "More like sexist. That crap about girls being so fragile. Good lord—what year is it?"

"C'mon, Lisa, I think it's great that the police are checking on the kids. Better safe than sorry, no?" He pops another nut in his mouth, oblivious to the glare that his wife is aiming in his direction.

I'm barely listening. All I can think about is the terrifying prospect of the weekend ahead. Cyrus must have invited everyone he thinks of as a suspect. He's narrowed me down to this group, but he doesn't know who I am, and he must think that a weekend away from the outside world will help him figure it out.

I excuse myself to the bathroom, where I hurriedly check my e-mail on Kailey's phone. Another bidder has put an offer in for the book, and the price is already up to $75,000. I'll call Lucia as soon as I have a chance and give her the details. Hopefully her computer guy can track the e-mail addresses.

I need to prove that Reed is Cyrus, and quickly. Before the trip to the Looking Glass Winery. If I know Cyrus's identity for sure before we go, I might be able to use the overnight trip to my advantage. We'll be in a remote location, far from the coven.

Far from anyone Cyrus can call for help.

It's only later, as we're eating apple pie together, that I realize there was no stamp on the envelope, no address. It must have been hand-delivered.

My greatest enemy was standing on the Morgans' porch earlier today, mere feet away from the people I love and care about.

The thought sends a shiver of anger up my spine.

TWENTY-NINE

Nicole's laughter is the first thing I hear as Echo and I walk into Madison's house for our Friday afternoon dance committee meeting. Somehow I know what I'm going to see even before I walk into the wood-paneled dining room.

Nicole is sitting inches away from Noah, her torso turned toward him, leaning forward and hugging her chest to maximize her impressive cleavage. Of course, her shirt is low-cut and fitted, and I see his eyes flit to the view she offers before he glances up to see me. I don't miss the blush that creeps up his neck. *Traitor*, I think, knowing I am being unreasonable.

"Kailey, good. We can finally get started." Madison shuffles the papers in front of her.

I clear my throat. "I invited Echo to join our committee," I tell her. "She's very excited about the mural."

I can't read the stare Madison shoots at me. Is she angry that I took it upon myself to recruit Echo? But it only lasts a moment before she smiles broadly. "Of course. Welcome, Echo. Please, take a seat."

The only two spots are sandwiched between Reed and Rebecca. I feel Reed's eyes on us as we make our way to the chairs, and send Echo a silent thanks as she sinks into the seat next to Reed. I concentrate on the comforting weight of my knife, tucked as usual, into the knee-high boots that I've been wearing for a week straight, since the ill-fated concert on Treasure Island.

Across the table, Leyla watches me, then Noah, then me again, like she's at a tennis match. *Real subtle, Leyla*, I think, but I'm touched by her concern, and force my smile to open even wider, like I don't have a care in the whole damn world.

But it's hard to remain composed this close to Noah. I try to look anywhere else, but my eyes keep drifting to him, my true north.

"I'm delighted to begin our meeting with an announcement," Madison speaks softly, but all conversation instantly ceases as everyone shifts the attention to her. I have to give her credit—she possesses a confidence now that she didn't have when she first took charge of the dance committee.

"Rebecca has proven extremely helpful to me. She used to throw parties at her old school in Sonoma. I'm happy to announce that from now on, she will be cochair of this committee. My second-in-command, so to speak." Madison shoots Rebecca a radiant smile.

Rebecca, for her part, positively glows under Madison's attention. She holds her willowy frame straight in her chair, arching her back slightly like a ballerina or a cat that wants to be petted.

"Doesn't cochair mean she's your partner?" asks Nicole. "Not second-in-command." I suppress a smile.

Rebecca smoothes her blond hair, bowing her elegant neck slightly. "Either way, it's fine with me," she says quietly. "Whatever Maddy needs." *Maddy, huh?*

Madison clasps her hands together. "First things first. I've secured a venue. Quite a coup, actually."

Leyla blinks. "We're not having the dance in the gym? That's where it usually is."

"Please," sniffs Madison. "We're not throwing the usual party. And I refuse to ask couples to slow dance in the same room that the basketball team plays in. That's disgusting."

"Hey," Bryan protests. "I'll have you know that I shower after every practice."

Madison ignores him and continues. "The dance is going to be held in the ballroom of the Claremont Hotel. I just got confirmation this morning. And they'll even let us in to start the decorations on Sunday, so we'll have the rest of the week to make it look perfect."

I'm surrounded by a chorus of oohs and ahs. I have to admit, it's a great choice of venue. The Claremont Hotel, built almost a hundred years ago, is nestled in the foothills on the border of Oakland and Berkeley. It's a gorgeous old resort with beautiful views of San Francisco. Too bad I have no intention of attending the dance after my breakup with Noah. Especially if he takes Nicole. I shudder, picturing them in my mind: Noah in his suit jacket, arms around Nicole, holding her close . . .

Stop it, Sera.

Madison leans back, obviously soaking in the attention. "I have news on the music front as well. Several DJs have agreed to play."

Chantal looks confused. "DJs, huh? I thought you were adamant about having live music?"

"I *was*," Madison answers, "until I realized that no one wants to hear morose indie rock all night."

"Are you serious? That's your favorite music." Chantal is incredulous.

"I know, I know. It's *my* favorite. But if we want actual

dancing, we're going to have to give the people what they want."

"I agree," Rebecca says.

"Of course you do," Nicole quips.

Madison sets down her clipboard. "Let's go around the room," she says. "Everyone can give me—I mean *us*," she corrects herself, winking at Rebecca, "an update. Nicole, take notes."

Nicole sighs, pulling out a pen from her purse, but does as she's told.

Leyla and Bryan fill us in on the artisan grilled-cheese truck that will be catering the event. "We're also considering an heirloom donut vendor for dessert," Leyla adds, licking her lips. I note with satisfaction that she's dressed like her old self again: a yellow-and-black striped sweater that makes her look like a bumblebee, the insect theme continued with the butterfly barrettes she wears in her magenta-streaked hair. I like it better when her fashion choices are influenced by Bryan's poetry rather than Rebecca's vintage posings.

"Sounds like a gluten-fest," Rebecca mumbles.

Noah's eyes light up as he tells us about the photographer he found. "He's a great guy. A real up-and-coming photographer. His portraits are amazingly surreal. These won't be your usual awkwardly posed couple shots." I smile, even though my heart aches. I love when Noah talks about photography.

"Sounds fantastic," Nicole purrs, putting her hand on his arm. "I can't wait to get my picture taken." I quickly look away.

Madison nods at me. "What's happening with the mural?"

"Actually, um, Echo's taking it over."

Madison raises an eyebrow. "So you found a way to get out of it after all. I suppose you deserve points for resourcefulness." She smiles, but I wonder if she's annoyed with me.

Echo pulls her initial sketches from her black portfolio, spreading them out on the table. "Kailey told me about the solstice theme," she begins, "so I started the design with winter constellations." The drawings are beautiful, a large circular compass rose over a swirling backdrop of shimmery stars. "Here's Andromeda," she continues, pointing out the constellations with her slender finger, "Cassiopeia, and my favorite: Orion, the hunter."

Woven in the celestial tapestry are astrological signs, their familiar symbols rendered in a graceful script. At either side of the main circular shape are two women in an art nouveau style, draped in flowing robes. They each wear a circlet around their head made of stars.

"Very cool," Reed says, and the approving murmur

from the group tells me they agree. Even Madison looks impressed, and I gratefully sink back into my chair as everyone praises Echo's work.

"Great. I think that's it. Next time we meet will be Sunday at the Claremont. Bring your work clothes." Madison pushes her chair back.

"That's not *quite* it," Reed interjects, and Madison raises her eyebrows, no doubt shocked that he would have the temerity to contradict her. "You'll all be joining us at the winery during the break, yes? My sister and I are so looking forward to hosting you."

Echo drops her gaze shyly. "I don't know what you're talking about," she admits.

"What? No, you were on the list." Reed snaps his head to his sister.

"I must have accidentally forgotten your invitation, Echo," she says, frowning. "How incredibly rude of me."

"You *have* to come," Reed tells Echo. "You'll love the winery."

"Thanks, but I can't. My family's harvest feast is this weekend. New moon in Cancer." She seems pleased to have been invited, but my blood runs cold. If Reed wants Echo at the winery, it must be because he thinks she could be me. I shiver at the thought of what he has planned. It's much better that Echo will be here, safe in Berkeley.

The rest of us confirm that we're going, except for Noah. Nicole's face falls. "You have to come," she whines.

"Come on, Noah, don't you think a night away will do you good?" Madison chimes in, and I see his resolve weakening. She's unknowingly spoken the magic words. He'll do anything to avoid his father.

"You're right," he says. "I'll go." My heart starts to thud. As much as I want to spend time with him, I don't want him anywhere near Cyrus.

On the way out the door, Nicole asks Noah for a ride home, saying that there's something she wants to talk to him about. My body goes rigid—I'm sure she's going to ask him to be her date for the dance.

It makes me want to die. It makes me want to disappear.

I can't afford to think about them right now, though. I need to worry about keeping everyone alive. So I force myself not to care as they walk away together into the frigid air, their arms brushing. I force myself to laugh at whatever Chantal just said, even as I see Noah open the passenger side door of his car for Nicole, just like he used to do for me. And I keep a ridiculous smile on my face as his taillights disappear into the night, even though I want to scream.

THIRTY

I lean my head back, looking upward. Through the red-wood tree's lacy boughs the moon plays hide-and-seek, its champagne-colored light made dim by its shape. It's neatly sliced in half—I feel the same way.

I came to the tree house directly after dinner with the Morgan family, needing to be in a place where I can be entirely alone, entirely safe. I turn my face away from the fickle moon and bury my head in my bent knees, denim scratching my cheeks.

I miss Noah. Seeing him tonight was even more painful than I expected. I wrap my hands around the birdcage necklace that he gave me—I put it on before slipping outside, needing something to hold that connects me with him, however tenuous that connection has become. He could be kissing Nicole, right now. He could be forgetting I exist. And it's all because of Cyrus.

The breeze shifts, bringing with it the earthy scent of the Morgans' garden, a neighbor's seasonal wood smoke, and memories. This isn't the first time Cyrus has sabotaged a love affair.

I will always remember how hot it was that night in March, Charlotte's birthday, when we went out to the local bar to celebrate. We were living in Mexico at the time, laying low while Cyrus worked out some complicated business dealings involving, I think, shipments of cocaine to the States. It was hot and sultry, the temperature soaring well past 80 degrees even at night. I was slick with sweat, standing at the bar with Cyrus as he downed tequila like it was water, watching Charlotte dance with Sébastien on the bougainvillea-drenched patio, the brilliant purple flowers forming a dramatic backdrop for her scarlet hair. Neither Cyrus nor I missed Charlotte's rosy cheeks, echoing the color of the rose she had tucked behind her ear. Sébastien grinned as he twirled her around and around till she collapsed dizzily into his chest. And then they danced some more.

"Do I detect a blossoming romance?" Cyrus asked over

the blare of the mariachi musicians. I knew him well enough to sense there was a threat hiding behind his question. Cyrus hated Charlotte, regretted bringing her into the coven. He wanted to be the only person I confided in, the only person who cared about me. Once Charlotte joined us, he wasn't, for the first time in four hundred years.

Cyrus was supposed to be the center of our world, the sun that we all orbited. If Sébastien and Charlotte fell in love, they would care about each other more than they relied on him. And *that* he could never allow.

"I think they're just having fun," I replied, sweat dripping into my eyes. On the patio, the song slowed down as the musicians launched into a traditional rendition of "Amor Eterno"—"Eternal Love." Sébastien drew Charlotte close, his hand wrapped around her waist and tangling in her black lace shawl.

"That had better be true," Cyrus said icily. "Sébastien is one of my soldiers, and your bodyguard. I can't have him getting distracted by your dear friend's . . . *charms.*" The way he said "charms" suggested he thought Charlotte was an evil seductress out to ruin Cyrus's life. I wouldn't be surprised if he thought exactly that. "I'd hate to have to remove such a *distraction.*" I shivered, despite the night's heat.

I found Sébastien later that night on the beach when Charlotte slipped away to use the bathroom. "Cyrus is watching you and Charlotte," I breathed over the crashing waves. "He doesn't like it."

Sébastien's face darkened. "Why should he care?"

"Cyrus is in charge of us. We don't get to ask what he cares about." I scrunched up my toes in the sand, defeated.

"But . . . I think I love her," he said softly, his eyes searching mine. I shook my head. I couldn't risk Charlotte's life. And I had no illusions that if Cyrus had to choose between her and Sébastien, she'd lose in a heartbeat.

"If you love her," I said sadly, "you'll stay far away from her."

He stared at me. "It's not right," he said finally.

"Please," I begged, grabbing his hands. "I need to know she's safe. That's the most important thing." After a beat, he nodded.

He snubbed Charlotte after that. She was heartbroken. She didn't understand. And though I held her as she cried, though I let her talk about it for hours, analyzing what she did wrong, how she lost his affections, I never admitted that I knew the reason.

Sébastien did the right thing—he put Charlotte's well-being over his own happiness. And that's what I need to do with Noah. That's what I need to remember, when I'm tortured by thoughts of him kissing Nicole, of his crow-black hair falling over hers.

I can only hope that now, with Cyrus in Berkeley, Sébastien and Charlotte are finally together. If only they'd known the truth about the other Incarnates, I think bitterly, they could have escaped Cyrus's control years ago. Joined another coven. I could have gone with them. . . .

A door slams nearby, making me jump.

"Your mother had the right idea!" a man's voice shouts, a familiar voice. "I'd leave here too, if I could! If I didn't have to worry about *you*. Waste of fucking time. Waste of a life." It's Noah's father, and the venom of his words carries clearly to where I sit on weary boards, shrouded by leaves.

Just a few moments later, I hear footfalls growing near. I hear someone walking through the Morgans' backyard, padding softly across the spongy carpet of redwood needles that covers the grass.

My fingers move inside my coat, wrap themselves around the birdcage necklace that hangs over my heart. A few seconds later, Noah's face appears. His eyes meet mine in a beam of champagne moonlight. "Sorry," he mutters. "I didn't think you'd be here."

"It's okay," I tell him, making no move to leave. He hesitates, looking up at me, his eyes full of questions that I am incapable of answering. "Come on up," I say.

He launches his body the rest of the way into the tree

house and sits in the corner opposite me. He bends his head into his lap.

"He's horrible. I would do anything to get out of here."

"I'm sorry," I whisper. The words sound hollow, even to me.

"Kailey," he says, but it sounds like a question. I turn my head toward his.

And then he's next to me, his muscled arms holding me, his hands wrapping around me. My birdcage necklace glints in the half-full moon. He touches it with one finger. "Why?" he asks. I have no answer.

His lips are on mine, searing me. I wasn't aware of how cold it was up here until he appeared, until he tangled himself up in me. My own lips must be freezing. It must be like kissing a dead girl. *Borrowed time,* I think. *A borrowed kiss. A debt I will certainly have to pay.*

He holds me tight, tighter, like the secrets I keep. Finally, I pull away, touching my fingers to my lips.

"Let's try again, Kailey," he says.

"No," I whisper. "This was a mistake."

I want so badly to cross the tree house to where he sits, to pull him into my arms. The gulf between us shatters me. His pain shatters me. Thoughts of Nicole are nothing compared with this. I don't care about other girls. I just want him to be okay.

"You should go," I say sharply, and he flinches.

He stands up and I'm immediately freezing. He reaches into his pocket, pulls out a piece of paper, thrusts it into my hands.

I look down and my breath catches in my throat.

It's a photo of Kailey. No—not Kailey—*me*. The photo he took of me last Friday, only a week ago, before my world fell apart, before Cyrus destroyed it with a song. My eyes look into the camera, full of love, the golden setting sun changing their color, an abandoned fountain behind me.

"Keep it," Noah says, as I hear him leaving. "I don't want it anymore."

THIRTY-ONE

Sunday afternoon has been torturous. I stole away from the Morgans' house earlier to call the hospital from a pay phone. Taryn is still in a coma, and the nurse didn't sound optimistic. And then I had to come here to help set up for the dance, where I've been forced to work alongside Noah for hours.

He flicks a switch, and my back is flooded with heat from the photographic lights he's arranging around Echo's mural backdrop, diffused with white umbrellas.

"Damn," I mutter, as my hammer hits the nail off-center, bending it in half. "Echo, can you give me another nail?" I ask.

"Here you go." She pulls one from the front pocket of her overalls and hands it to me.

I'm acutely conscious of Noah's nearby presence, awash in longing that's tainted by awkwardness. We haven't spoken the entire afternoon—no small feat when we're both wedged in the same small corner of the Claremont's ballroom, the makeshift photo studio that just needs Echo's mural to be complete.

On top of that, I'm anxiously waiting to hear back from Lucia. She's had the details on both bidders for days, but she hasn't called me back yet. I've been checking my phone compulsively all day. She must not have heard back from her computer guy yet, the guy who should be tracing the identities of the bidders. And until she does, I'm in a state of suspended animation. I can't do anything about Reed until I know for sure that he's Cyrus, and it's driving me mad. I'm worried I won't have my proof before the auction is over tomorrow, while we're at the winery. Time is running out.

"Echo, it's beautiful." I stiffen at the sound of Reed's voice behind me.

"Thank you," she replies. I glance at her face and am surprised to see her blushing, her brown cheeks rosier than I've ever seen them, nearly matching the cinnamon-hued scarf that she's wrapped around her mass of yarn-and-ribbon hair.

Reed's right—her mural *is* beautiful. The ten-foot-wide

finished canvas is absolutely stunning, the celestial star map shimmering with metallic paint and exquisitely rendered detail.

"Hey, Noah, Kailey."

"Hi," I answer Reed coolly, not turning around, and raising my hammer for another whack at the nail that my fingers somehow manage to hold perfectly straight.

"Hey," Noah tosses back with genuine friendliness.

"You'll definitely want to bring your camera tomorrow," Reed tells Noah. "The winery is quite picturesque."

"Don't worry," Noah replies. "I never leave home without it."

I hate this—Noah and Reed bantering like the best of friends. My stomach starts to ache.

"We're going to have a fantastic time," Reed declares. I aim my hammer. With a satisfying *thunk*, I hit the nail right in its center, driving it deep into the wall with one bang. I kneel down to the box of nails and grab another handful, dropping them into the pocket of my baggy cargo pants, before whirling around to face Reed.

"What are we going to do up there, anyway?" I ask.

He appraises me. "You think you can make me show my hand so easily? Nice try, Kailey."

"So you're going to surprise us?" Noah grins at Reed, careful to avoid looking at me.

Reed chuckles softly. "It wouldn't be a surprise if I answered that, would it?" His face turns serious. "I'm just looking forward to getting to know you all."

Looking forward to knowing who Seraphina is, you mean. And then punishing her. I turn around to the mural, pulling the canvas taut and moving several feet down, readying myself for the next nail.

"You two won't mind if I borrow Echo for a minute? There are some glitter-covered stars that require her artistic direction," Reed says.

"Go ahead," I say listlessly. I sense Reed and Echo walking away, leaving me alone with Noah, but I keep focused on my task, holding the next nail in my lips as I pull the canvas into place. *Please*, I plead silently to the phone in my pocket, *ring. Please call me, Lucia.*

I can feel Noah's eyes on my back. I wish he weren't coming tomorrow, that he would stay home where he's safe. Even verbal abuse from his father is preferable to whatever Cyrus has planned.

"Noah?" I ask.

"What?" he says flatly.

"Maybe you shouldn't come tomorrow."

He sucks in his breath. "Seriously? You hate me so much you can't even stand to be near me for a night?"

Against my better instincts, I shove the hammer in the

loop of my cargo pants and turn around. His sweatshirt sleeves are pushed up to his elbows, revealing his well-muscled forearms and large, long-fingered hands. One of the photo lights is shining on his face, illuminating the hurt in his blue eyes. They remind me of a mountain lake, high in the Sierras, treacherous and deep. "I think we need some space. Some time apart," I say quietly.

He folds his arms across his chest. "Can't we even be friends? The way we used to be, before . . . this? Before your car accident. We used to have so much fun together."

"Things change," I say coldly. "And I'd rather you just stay away from me." His eyes flash with pain. I don't know who my words hurt more, him or me.

I look behind him, on the ballroom's antique floral carpet, the crystal-dripping chandeliers, the straight white columns that flank the parquet dance floor. Out of the corner of my eye, I see a girl approaching, a vision of shiny brown hair and a clingy tank top. Nicole.

"If that's really how you feel, maybe I'll stay home tomorrow," he says sadly, raking his hands through his hair.

"What are you talking about?" Nicole cries, hurrying to his side. "You have to come. I was going to ask you for a ride. You wouldn't let me down, would you?" She pouts, jutting out her glossy lower lip even as she gazes hopefully into his eyes. I shove my hands inside my pockets and clench them into fists.

"Well, if you need a ride . . ." Noah smiles at her, and I want to die.

"Thank you!" She beams. "I never got to ask you that question I had the other night. We can talk about it in the car." She puts her hand on his arm. "Plus, I make a *very* good road trip partner."

I press my lips together tightly. Regret curls around my heart. I struggle to breathe.

"Noah, there you are!" Madison is positively cooing. Nicole's eyes dart in Madison's direction, taking in the high-waisted skinny jeans that cling to her curves, her slim legs emphasized by brown ankle boots. Rebecca follows a few steps behind, holding the clipboard. Nicole lets her hand fall away.

I suddenly feel like I'm watching vultures sweep in to pick at the carcass of my relationship.

Noah takes a step backward. "What's up, Maddy?" he asks, shifting uncomfortably.

"I need some help moving those tables around," Madison says sweetly. "And you're done here, right?" She gestures toward the photography setup. I want to punch her in the stomach when he nods. Judging from Nicole's poisonous expression, she feels the same way.

"Sure," he says. "Show me the tables."

"Thank you," Madison replies with a wide smile, a dimple

appearing in her chin below her jeweled stud. "After that, I think it's quitting time."

She leads him away, her arm looped through his, and I turn on my heel toward the mural. I make quick work hanging the rest of it, putting nail after nail through the canvas, punching each one deep into the plaster with a swift *thwack*. I don't miss once.

My task complete, I stash my hammer in the janitor's closet in the hallway, then wander around the ballroom, feeling disconcertingly like a ghost among my friends. Reed and Echo are perched atop matching ladders, draping the chandeliers with snowflakes. Bryan and Leyla are decorating the buffet tables with antique telescopes that we borrowed from the shop where I work. Chantal and Nicole are on stage, doing complicated things with the soundboard and moving speakers around.

A peal of bright laughter comes from Madison's direction, and I see her throw back her head at something Noah said. He's smiling too. Everyone's laughing, I realize. Everyone's having a great time as I slink around in the shadows.

My phone rings, the sound muffled from the folds of my deep cargo pockets, though I feel its vibration against my knee. I fish it out—an unknown 510 area-code number flashes insistently on the screen.

"Hello?"

"Is this Jane Smith?" asks a throaty voice that I immediately recognize. My pulse begins to race, and I hurry out to the hallway so no one will hear me.

"Lucia! I'm so glad you called," I say, trying to keep my voice down but unable to muffle the joy I feel. "How are you?" I fish a pen out of my pocket as I speak, ready to take notes.

"Your words ask Lucia how she's doing, but your tone says you need this info quickly. So I'm not going to do the small-talk thing, okay?"

"Okay," I reply, a grin stealing across my face.

"I have good news and bad news. Which one do you want first?"

"I could definitely use some good news right now."

"One of the e-mail addresses came from a book dealer in the UK. Sterling Books in London. Does that mean anything to you?"

My heart sinks. It sounds like a run-of-the-mill dealer. Cyrus is definitely in Berkeley, however much I wish he were overseas. "No. What's the bad news?"

"The other e-mail address was untraceable."

Damn it. "Untraceable? How?"

"I don't know the technical details, sweetie. Sorry. But clearly the person at that address doesn't want to be found."

It's Cyrus. It has to be. "Can you ask your guy to keep trying?"

She sighs heavily. "I thought you might ask that. He's already working on it. It's possible, he told me, but no guarantees."

There's still a chance. "Thank you, Lucia. Thank you so, so much."

"Don't mention it, sweetie. I'll call you when I know more. Take care," she says, and hangs up.

I briefly tuck my hand inside my boot, verifying that my knife is inside, before striding back into the ballroom. Echo is nowhere to be seen, but Reed stands at the base of the ladder she was on earlier, one hand draped across its rungs.

In his other hand he holds his phone, tapping away on the keys. I watch as he presses a button, then drops it into his pocket.

Just then, my iPhone vibrates to announce a new e-mail has come in. The movement reverberates through my whole body. I break out in a cold sweat, my breath coming faster as I open the e-mail. Somehow I know what it's going to be before I read it, but the confirmation brings a riot of goose bumps to my arms.

It's a new bid, from the same untraceable address and beating the offer from Sterling Books in London. It was submitted only moments before, at the same time I saw Reed typing on his phone.

Reed glances up and catches my eye. The smile he shoots me is laced with evil.

And tomorrow, I'll be staying at his winery. His turf. Where he could have god-knows-what kinds of traps laid for me to walk into.

One of us will win. Right now, I am not certain it will be me.

THIRTY-TWO

Leyla spends the entire car ride to the Looking Glass Winery extolling the epic coolness of Reed and Rebecca to Bryan, who's not so easily convinced.

"They both seem to me like kids who are trying to pretend they're someone else. What's with the weird clothes?" he says.

"What's wrong with expressing yourself through fashion?" she retorts, tossing her magenta-streaked hair. "I *like* it when people do something different. Otherwise—how boring would life be?"

"My life is perfectly complete without suspenders and bowties and that stupid hat Reed wears."

I silently cheer Bryan on from the back seat, my eyes trained out the window to hide my amusement, pretending to be absorbed in the sun-soaked late-autumn landscape.

"It's a bowler," Leyla explains. "It's quirky."

"It's lame," he retorts.

She turns to look at him for a moment, and I want to gently turn her attention back to the winding road.

"What?" Bryan asks. "Would you like me better if I wore a stupid hat?" He flips down the mirror, regarding himself in it. "Perhaps a top hat? Perhaps I should wear a tuxedo to school?" He catches my eye in the mirror and winks.

Leyla tries and fails to keep a straight face. Her laughter is contagious. "I'm trying to picture you in a top hat," she sputters.

"What?" Bryan complains. "If Reed can pull it off, so can I."

"Leyla, the road? Perhaps look at it?" I say, from the backseat.

We almost drive past the sign for the Looking Glass Winery, the letters barely legible in sun-faded paint.

The road turns to gravel, marred with deep ruts that make Leyla's Honda shudder alarmingly. Bryan grabs the handle above the passenger-side window, earning him a challenging glare from his girlfriend. "You don't trust my driving?" she asks, jerking the wheel hard to avoid a large rock in the middle of the road.

"I totally do," he says.

"Then stop grabbing the 'Oh shit' handle," she orders, pointing to his hand.

"Yes'm."

When we finally reach the main house, I see only two other cars: Noah's VW and Reed's candy-apple red SUV.

"Chantal's mother wouldn't let her come," Leyla explains, putting the beleaguered Honda in park and applying a fresh coat of lip gloss in the rearview mirror.

"Are Reed and Rebecca's parents here?" I ask. It was the one condition the Morgans had required. They weren't too thrilled about their underage children spending the night at a winery, but a quick phone call to Mrs. Sawyer seemed to assuage their fears. Reed's mother assured her that there would be no underage drinking, that the bed-and-breakfast was nothing but wholesome, and that the vineyards were a perfect excuse to teach us about local agriculture. By the end of the phone call, Mrs. Morgan had even made reservations for herself and her husband to visit Looking Glass this coming June.

"I don't think so," Leyla says, opening the door. "Not

that it would matter to Chantal's mom. That girl's going to go crazy one day, mark my words. Shaved head, punk band. The works."

I contain the smile that curls the corner of my mouth. I have to admit that the idea of preppy, dignified Chantal screaming in front of a throbbing mosh pit is kind of appealing, if only for the comic value.

"Finally," says Reed, his arms held open in an expansive gesture as he walks up to the car, feet crunching on the gravel path. "You're the last to arrive." He's wearing a pair of fitted tan riding breeches tucked into leather boots similar to my own. I just hope he's not also concealing a knife in his. *Cyrus hasn't armed himself in years*, I remind myself. *Although that's because he always had Jared to protect him.*

We retrieve our overnight bags from the trunk of Leyla's car and follow Reed toward the rambling farmhouse that looks out over the rolling vineyards. The grapevines are a riot of late autumn color, scarlet and gold and orange, making it seem like the hills are in flames.

"Welcome to the Looking Glass Inn," Reed says, pointing to the house. "Built in 1892." The house is admittedly incredible, a three-story Victorian with a wraparound porch, its white siding brilliant in the late afternoon sun. A weather vane tops its ornate peaked roof, lazily spinning back and forth in the gentle breeze.

"You grew up here?" Leyla asks. "Lucky."

"Yeah," he replies. "Though we gutted the whole thing a few years ago. Completely modernized."

We ascend the tall wooden staircase leading to the covered porch, and Reed opens the door. He's right: The inside is nothing I would have expected from the historic exterior. It's stark and modern—Cyrus's style. A stainless steel reception desk stands to the right, its shiny surface reflecting the chocolate-colored wide-planked wood floors. A placard sits atop it with the name of the inn's open wireless network spelled out in a sans-serif font. Thick rugs in geometric patterns cover the wood, and the walls of the lobby are lined with many framed mirrors. Everywhere I look, I see my own face reflected in them. The effect is unsettling.

"What's with all the mirrors?" asks Leyla, regarding herself in one of them and patting her hair.

"Well, it's called the Looking Glass Inn, genius," Bryan answers with an amused tone.

"Duh. Got it."

"Are there any other guests staying here?" I ask, wandering over to a tall window that overlooks the vineyards, feeling the weight of the inn's remote location settle over me.

"It's just us." Reed smiles, his teeth very white. "We always close the inn for the winter. We have the whole place to ourselves."

"I thought your parents were here too?" I ask, my voice faint.

"They're in Berkeley. My dad agreed to speak at a wine-makers' conference tonight. I think we'll have a *lot* more fun without them." He winks, and I shiver. Just what does he have planned?

"Come on," he says, "everyone else is in the great room." Reed leads us down a short hallway, the bright white walls covered with more mirrors. Even without the lights on, the space feels startlingly bright.

We emerge in a large, open room with high ceilings and a slate-tiled fireplace that's large enough to walk into. One whole wall is made of glass, revealing a terraced garden dotted with iron tables and furled umbrellas. Stretching away from the house is another gravel path leading down the hill.

Noah looks up from the coffee table book he's reading when we enter, giving a stiff wave and managing to avoid my gaze. Madison sits closely next to him, her feet splayed on the matching ottoman in front of her, seemingly oblivious to the scuff marks she's making with her dusty Doc Martens. Rebecca is sharing the ottoman with Madison's feet, looking elegant, as usual, wearing a beaded black drop-waist dress and a long, embroidered sweater.

At the other end of the backless couch, Nicole and

Chantal are sitting very close together. I'm surprised to see Chantal and even more surprised that Nicole's not cozying up with Noah. Looks like Madison beat her to the punch.

"Chantal!" Leyla squeals, rushing in front of me and plopping onto the couch next to them. "I thought you couldn't come?"

Chantal smiles angelically. "I wasn't supposed to," she replies. "But Rebecca convinced me to lie to my mother. Supposedly I'm staying at a friend's house in Oakland tonight. If I go to hell for this, I blame the Sawyer family."

My stomach twists. Her presence must mean she's still on Cyrus's list of suspects.

"Hell is more fun anyway," Reed replies. "All those sinful rock stars are down there having a party."

"Now that everyone's here," Madison interjects, "maybe we can take that tour you mentioned?"

"Definitely," Reed agrees. "Although first we'll show everyone where they're sleeping. There are only four guest rooms, so we'll be sharing."

"I'm with Madison," Rebecca chirps quickly, and I notice Chantal's face fall slightly. Madison and Chantal have always been close—but it seems like Rebecca's moving in on Chantal's best-friend status lately.

"We can share, Chantal," says Nicole. I'm sure she'd do

anything to avoid sleeping in the same room as me.

Leyla points at my chest. "You and me, Kailey."

"Looks like we gentlemen will share the last room," says Reed, gesturing to Noah and Bryan. I shiver at the thought of Noah and Bryan sleeping in the same room as Cyrus, utterly defenseless. Is Noah here because Cyrus wants to make him an Incarnate?

"Sounds good," says Noah, with a genuine smile on his face. "Man cave."

Bryan pounds his chest. "Man cave good."

Reed and Rebecca lead us up the stairs to the second story. I follow the group in a confused fog, seeing myself out of the corner of my eye in one of the hallway's mirrors. *Through the looking glass,* I think, remembering the story about Alice in Wonderland that bears the same name.

Leyla immediately flings herself onto the king-sized bed in our shared room. The hot pink bedspread is the only spot of color in the room's palette of muted whites and grays. "Mmm, thread count," she murmurs into a pillow.

I wish I could be so carefree. But I've been dying to check my messages since we arrived, to see if there are any more bids on the book or a missed call from Lucia. "Going to hit up the bathroom," I tell her and dart out to the hallway, nearly colliding with Reed. He's on his phone, tapping away on the screen.

"Excuse me," I mutter, and shove past him into the bathroom's door, which is slightly ajar.

And run straight into Nicole, who's leaning over the sink, touching up her lipstick.

"Oh, sorry," I say, turning to leave.

"It's okay," she tells me. "Stay. I wanted to talk to you, anyway."

"About what?" I ask warily, bracing myself for one of her trademark bitchy remarks.

"Noah," she answers, pulling a tube of mascara out of her unbleached cotton makeup bag.

My stomach sinks. I feel like I know what she's going to say—she's going to brag about being his date for the dance. I feel ill. "About how you're going to the dance with him?" I ask matter-of-factly.

She opens her mouth and eyes wide as she recoats her already coal-black lashes. "Actually, he turned me down." She laughs bitterly. "He wouldn't say why, but I think I know." She puts the tube back in her bag and faces me. "He's obviously still in love with you."

Even though my heart beats faster at the news, I make my face a mask. A cool, haughty façade. "Too bad for him, then. Because I don't feel the same way."

She appraises me. "Right," she says, turning back to the mirror. "Well, then this won't matter to you, but I'd watch

out for Madison. She was all over Noah before you got here."
I suspected as much, but it hurts to have confirmation.

I have a memory of Madison in our art class, pressing me on the subject of Noah. *So you wouldn't care if he went out with another girl? Hypothetically speaking, of course.* She must have been referring to herself. I feel betrayed, somehow, even though I know I have no right to be.

"We're broken up," I answer stiffly. "He can go out with anyone he wants."

"All's fair in love and war," Nicole agrees. "Though I have to say it's completely *unfair* that the only guy left on this trip for me to flirt with is Reed—and he's been on his phone all day."

As if on cue, my own phone buzzes in my sweatshirt pocket. I whip it out—"new e-mail." My heart starts to pound.

"Anyway, I'll let you do your business," Nicole says. "I'm happy we got to talk."

I don't even stop to process how strange Nicole's acting. I lock the bathroom door behind her and quickly pull up the e-mail screen on Kailey's iPhone.

The bidding war has continued between my two buyers—Sterling Books and the untraceable one. There's a new offer from the latter, for $80,000.

As I read the message, I picture Reed out in the hallway,

typing a message on his own phone only minutes before. Could it be a coincidence? *Hell to the no*, I think, to borrow Echo's phrase. Strike two.

If I can only get a look at his phone, I'll know for sure if he's Cyrus. I take a determined breath as I step into the hallway.

THIRTY-THREE

"Just take them off, Kailey," says Leyla, nodding toward my mud-covered boots. The familiar weight of Mr. Morgan's sheathed fishing knife reminds me why that's not an option.

"They're almost clean," I protest, wiping at the soles with the rag that Rebecca gave me. *They're so* not *almost clean*, I realize ruefully.

The mud is caked on, gathered from the hours-long tour we took of the property. We tromped through the vineyards where hawks swooped overhead, through the temperature-controlled barn where the barrels of wine are aged, through the woods that cover the nearby hills. I didn't miss Reed subtly pulling out his phone on our hike, the way he glanced at it when he thought no one else was looking.

The highlight of the tour was a beautiful Victorian greenhouse made entirely of panels of leaded glass. Rebecca explained that it had long since been converted to a lounge for guests. The air inside was heady with flowers, which bloomed in colored glass pots next to the overstuffed couches and reading chairs. Old-fashioned hurricane lamps adorned the side tables. Ornate mirrors—the trademark Looking Glass touch—were hung on each of the four walls, spreading the afternoon light over our faces like honey.

Rebecca told us that the previous owners thought the greenhouse was good luck, having survived several earthquakes with no damage to its glass walls. Despite the danger that taints this whole trip, I felt like it was true. The greenhouse radiated good energy. I was gripped with the desire to stay there, to let the rest of the group continue on without me while I curled up on one of the couches, safe in a pool of sun.

I have to hand it to Nicole. Her intuition was right on about Madison—the way she walked closely to Noah, talking to him more than anyone else, tells me she's definitely interested in him.

Strange that I've started thinking of Nicole as an ally. Through the looking glass, indeed.

"Don't worry about your boots, Kailey," says Rebecca. "We're staying out anyway. Time for a bonfire to warm us up."

I nod, gratefully abandoning the mud-streaked towel.

Reed appears from the darkness, his arms full of kindling and newspaper. "If you're not going in, want to help me get the fire started?" I look at his eyes—they appear black in the shadow of the newsboy cap he wears pulled low over his forehead.

"Sure," I reply. "I love flammable objects." This might be my chance to look at his phone, to prove that he's the one who's been bidding on my book.

I follow him down the gravel path. My right leg stings from where the knife's been rubbing against my calf, but I don't mind. I watch his back, taking in every movement like the hawks we saw earlier.

"Noah's cool," says Reed when we reach the fire pit, dropping the pile of kindling and paper to the ground and selecting several large oak logs from a nearby stack. I sit in one of the gathered chairs, watching him. "I have to admit, he didn't make the best first impression on me, but he's been a lot friendlier since then. It's too bad you guys broke up." He leans the logs together in a teepee shape, stuffing newspaper into the triangles between them. I'm reminded suddenly of the fires Cyrus used to build for us, back in the early years before we had money and security. I shiver, and not just from the cold.

"Too bad for who?" I ask warily. Is this a test?

He pulls a book of matches from his pocket and strikes one, shielding it from the bracing wind. Since the sun set, it's dropped many degrees.

"For both of you," he answers, cupping his hands around the tiny flame he's managed to coax from the paper and blowing on it gently.

He stands up, and the wind finishes the work of his breath, feeding oxygen to the fledgling fire. Soon our faces are lit orange and hot, and flames leap around the oak.

I pull my phone from my pocket, tapping at the screen with a frown. "Shoot," I say, with exaggerated disappointment. "I need to call my parents, and my phone doesn't get reception over here. Can I use yours?"

He watches me for a moment. "Sure," he says hesitantly. "Of course." He pats the pockets of his blazer, of his breeches. "Sorry, I must have left it in the house," he says.

"Left what?" says Bryan, from the path, followed by Rebecca and Leyla.

"Kailey's phone doesn't work. I was going to let her use mine . . ." Reed's smile deepens in the firelight, shadows lining his cheekbones, the dimple in his chin.

"Just use mine," says Bryan, stepping into the light and thrusting his phone into my hands.

Heart sinking, I dutifully compose a text message to Mr. and Mrs. Morgan, informing them that Bryan and I are having an educational and wholesome visit. I lean back in my chair, watching as the rest of our group joins us at the fire.

Rebecca passes out glasses of wine to everyone, and I take a deep swallow. I hadn't realized how thirsty I was, but the day's walk must have dehydrated me. Almost immediately, I feel a warm burn in my stomach.

"You might want to slow down there, Kailey." Leyla's voice is gentle as she points to my half-empty cup of wine. "Reed suggested a game of 'Never Have I Ever' when we were inside."

"Never have . . . what?" I repeat, confused. I can't for the life of me parse the sentence she just spoke, and I wonder if the wine has already gone to my head.

"At our old school, we just called it 'I Never,'" says Reed. "But I'm sure the rules are the same."

"I'm in," says Chantal.

"Bring it," echoes Nicole.

It slowly dawns on me that they're talking about a game, one that everyone appears to know the rules for. Everyone but me. I need to tread carefully.

"How did you play it at your old school?" I ask.

Reed stands up and selects a couple of logs that he tucks into the fire, releasing a billow of fragrant oak-scented smoke. "We go around the circle and take turns saying something we've never done. Whoever *has* done it has to drink." The flames leap up, accepting the new wood, and I feel my face grow hot.

This game could be very bad for me. What if Kailey's friends realize I'm not who I say I am? Or more to the point, *Cyrus* realizes? This must be his plan—the reason for getting us out here. This game is a perfect way to reveal who I am.

I pretend to take another drink of wine, tipping the cup to my closed lips so that I don't actually swallow. If I get a question wrong, I'll blame it on the alcohol.

"Same as how we play," says Bryan. "Kailey, I think the last time we played this you puked in the bushes."

"Charming," remarks Madison.

"Yeah, that was a crazy night," I agree vaguely.

"I'll start," says Nicole, with a wicked gleam in her eyes. "Never have I ever kissed a girl."

Reed, Bryan, and Noah take a drink. I don't move. I'm certain Kailey *has* kissed a girl—Taryn—but as far as I know, that was a secret that she withheld from her school friends.

Nicole stares at me. "You sure about that, Kailey?" I

282

hold her gaze, nodding slowly. "Hmm, I must be mistaken, then," she says.

"Never have I ever told a lie," says Chantal, looking downcast as she takes a sip herself. Everyone else joins her in taking a drink, except Madison.

"Come on, Maddy, everyone's lied at some point," says Noah.

"I haven't," she protests. "Though it's good to know I'm surrounded by a pack of liars. Better watch my back." She grins, sitting up straighter. "My turn. Okay. Um. Never have I ever been in love."

Everyone groans. "Too easy," says Leyla. "Everyone's been in love."

"Fine," says Madison. "Never have I ever been in love more than once."

No one drinks, especially not me, even though I suppose I qualify. I did love Cyrus once, though to use the same word for my relationship with him as the one I had with Noah feels like a betrayal.

"That sentence makes no grammatical sense," Chantal informs Madison, poking her in the arm.

Rebecca is next. "Never have I ever had sex." She immediately takes a gulp of wine, and everyone laughs.

"TMI," says Reed, covering his ears. "I don't want to know that about my sister." He does, I notice, take a drink as well.

So do Nicole, Leyla, and Bryan. Madison, Noah, and Chantal don't drink. Neither do I. I look down at my lap where I'm gripping my glass, my fingers white against its surface. I assume Kailey was a virgin, at least as far as this group knows. I look around slowly. No one calls me out for not drinking, and my fingers finally relax.

"Maddy, that is a damn lie," says Chantal. "I think you owe us two drinks now. For lying about sex, and for lying about lying."

"No retroactive penalties," Madison says, her face reddening as she takes a drink.

Reed rubs his hands together. "This is getting good," he says. "My turn. Never have I ever . . ."—he pauses, locking eyes with me across the circle—"betrayed the trust of someone in this circle."

Across the fire, Bryan takes a drink. Leyla whips her head in his direction, a shocked expression on her face. "What did you do?" she demands.

"Remember that time you made me watch the *Harry Potter* movies? And I said I liked them? I was lying," he admits.

Leyla relaxes. "Oh. Well, that's not so bad."

"I mean—wizards? So cheesy."

"I get it," she snaps. But I can tell she's not really mad.

Reed is still staring at me. "Kailey?" he presses. I'm

284

flustered. What exactly does he mean? Rather than call more attention to myself, I take a swallow. Next to me, Noah coughs, spilling wine on his jeans. I can only imagine what he suspects me of doing.

Reed swivels his head toward Rebecca. "Sis, did I miss you taking a drink?" he asks. She shakes her head, looking confused.

"That time you ratted me out to Mom and Dad, when you were mad at me for taking the car?"

"Oh!" Rebecca reddens, taking a drink. "Sorry about that one." She's pissed, I can tell.

"Awkward!" Leyla declares. "This is getting a little personal, don't you think?"

"That's the whole point," Reed snarls, and I start to panic. What else will he ask me?

I stand up, and the movement makes me immediately dizzy. "I have to go to the bathroom," I say weakly, and begin to walk away from the fire.

"I'll come with you," says Rebecca. "It's so dark outside. I'd hate for you to wander off the path and get lost."

"Thanks," I say, since I can't think of any polite way to refuse.

Rebecca's right about the dark night. As soon as we step away from the fire, I'm effectively blind. I pause for a moment while my eyes adjust. She leads me to the gravel path, and

I find myself staring up at the sky. I can see so many stars. It's been a long time since I've been out in the countryside. The sky reminds me of Echo's mural, its glittering swirl of celestial light.

"You don't see that in Berkeley," says Rebecca, following my gaze.

"No," I agree.

"But it won't be clear for long," she observes, gesturing west. "Storm's coming."

She's right. A pile of clouds looms over the distant hills. As if on cue, the wind picks up, trying to push us from the path.

"Thanks for inviting me up here," I say, teeth chattering. "I'm having a great time."

"We're glad you came. Reed and I are so lucky to have found such cool friends already," she replies.

"How's Reed doing, anyway?" I make my voice casual. "I know moving can be hard. Has he been upset at all?"

A moment passes before she responds, and I hope that my question didn't sound weird. "Maybe a little bit," she finally says. "But if anything, he seems happier in Berkeley. My brother is a bit . . . eccentric. I think he fits in better in Berkeley than he ever did in Sonoma." So she does notice *something* different about Reed, though I'm not sure it sounds like Cyrus.

"I know if my parents moved me away from my friends, I'd be *furious*. Does he seem . . . angry?" I press. It wouldn't be like Cyrus to conceal his violent side for long.

"He *does* have a temper," she admits.

"And it's worse since you moved?" I press, walking slowly. I need more than this.

"No, I wouldn't say so," she answers. "He's always had a bit of a short fuse."

We've reached the back deck of the house, and we step into the pale circle of light from the wall-mounted lantern near the door.

"Do you want me to wait while you use the bathroom?" she asks.

"Oh, no, that's okay, I think I can find my way back," I answer confidently.

From my jacket pocket comes a jangling ring, extremely loud in the quiet rural night. Startled, I whip it out and regard the screen—it's Lucia.

Rebecca cocks her head slightly, narrowing her eyes. "I'll let you get that," she says curtly. "See you back at the fire," she adds, striding away toward the dark path.

I quickly throw the door open as I answer the call, closing it firmly behind me so she won't hear my conversation.

"I have good news," Lucia chirps.

"And bad news, too, right?" I brace myself.

287

She laughs. "Not this time. All good in the 'hood, as they say. We got it."

"Tell me."

Lucia begins to speak, but a wave of static crashes into her voice. I run to the window. "Sorry," I interrupt her. "Can you say that again? I couldn't hear you. The reception's terrible up here."

"Where are you?" Her tone is urgent.

"Sonoma."

Silence on the line.

"Lucia?"

"I'm here," she says finally. "Sonoma is where we traced the address to. Whoever sent you that e-mail, they're at 4570 Cavedale Road."

My heart bangs into my chest. That's the address of the Looking Glass Winery.

"You there?" Lucia prods.

"Yes," I whisper.

"Are you in trouble?" she asks.

"No, I'm totally fine," I lie. "Really."

"Okay," she says uncertainly. "But call me if you—"

Her voice dissolves once more into static before the call goes dead.

THIRTY-FOUR

I stare upward, where the ceiling should be, but all I see is blackness. I am wide awake, alert; every muscle in my body is rigid. My right hand clenches the knife under the suffocating weight of the pink bedspread. The nightgown I'm wearing is damp with sweat.

Next to me, Leyla snores softly, deeply asleep.

Reed's room is down the hall. I want nothing more than to creep in there right now, while he's vulnerable, and kill him. But Noah and Bryan are sleeping there, too.

The wind has picked up outside. It shakes the house, rattles the old windows in their wooden frames. From over my head I hear the incessant squeal of the rusty weather vane.

Suddenly, I hear another sound coming from down the hall. Is that a door opening? I lift my head from the pillow, straining to hear. It's silent. Nothing but the wind outside.

I lean back, relaxing my neck. And then I hear it again. Footsteps pad down the hall, pausing outside our room, and my pulse goes wild. My palms grow slick. The knife handle is slippery when I tighten my grip.

It takes an eternity for me to peel back the bedspread and inch into an upright position. Beneath me, the mattress springs squeak, and I freeze, waiting for the door to burst open, to see Reed's face twisted with malice.

But then I hear the footsteps move on, past our door and down the hall. A minute later, a door slams downstairs.

I slip from the bed and crouch on the carpet, tugging on my boots without a sound, stuffing my knife in its usual spot. Leyla shifts on the bed, turning to her side and kicking a leg out from under the covers, and mumbles something that I can't understand. I freeze, hoping she won't wake up.

She doesn't. I dart soundlessly to the window and peer out.

Everything is gray and shapeless. The approaching storm has filled the sky with clouds, covering up the moon, the stars. I can barely make out the shape of the concrete patio below and the dark sea of the vineyards beyond.

But then a powerful gust of wind coaxes the storm clouds

to part briefly, and I see something moving in the resulting flash of moonlight. No, not something—*someone*. It's
definitely a man, but I can't tell who. The clouds shift again,
and he vanishes in the darkness.

Cyrus. It has to be.

I hurry to the door and slip out, wearing only my nightgown and my boots. In the countless mirrors lining the hall,
I see my reflection, pale and fleeting. With my white, long-
sleeved nightgown, I could be the ghost of a girl who used
to live here.

Outside, the storm trails icy fingers along my face. I
take off running down the path, the sound of my footfalls
obscured by the wind, which tears, howling, through the
vines and tosses leaves up to the sky. I pass the fire pit, a
pile of ash whirling in its center, and continue on. I don't see
anyone in the darkness.

The path forks. To the left it runs straight into the forest,
where the jagged tops of pine trees jut toward the sky like
teeth. To the right I know it heads deeper into the grape-
vines, where it eventually stops at the glass house. I cock my
head, but there's nothing to hear.

On impulse, I decide to go left, toward the woods.
I'm rewarded a few minutes later when another brief burst
of moonlight illuminates the path. There's a messy scuffle
of footprints from the group hike earlier. But on top of

these, etched into the packed sandy soil, is another, sharper set of tracks.

I glance toward the forest and freeze. The figure is standing in front of a copse of trees. It's too far to tell if he's facing me, but I throw myself to the ground anyway, sand digging into my chin.

When I look up a moment later, he's gone.

I take off in his direction at a faster pace, breath ragged. It's even darker in the forest. The wind tears through the trees, swaying in unison over my head. My footsteps fall in rhythm with my thundering heart.

And then I see him. I skid to a noiseless stop, watching as he steps into a clearing up ahead, the moonlight illuminating him for a fraction of a second. But it's enough to reveal his powerful shoulders, his navy uniform, the handcuffs tucked in his belt.

It's Officer Spaulding.

I'm too terrified to be confused, to even worry or consider why he's here. I just know that I'm in danger and have to act now. I reach down and grab my knife, gripping it as I dart from tree to tree, keeping to the shadows.

But when I reach it, the clearing is empty.

I slump against the trunk of a redwood tree, its ridged surface digging into my shoulders. I close my eyes in disappointment. I lost him.

Suddenly, a meaty hand lands on my left shoulder and pulls me away from the tree. I stumble forward. My right arm is yanked painfully upward behind my back, my knife pried from my fingers.

"Seraphina Ames," Officer Spaulding growls. "I've been looking for you."

THIRTY-FIVE

I scream, or try to, but his left arm wraps around my throat and the small, pitiful sound is cut off, tossed away on the wind like a bird's lost feather.

"Don't bother," he snarls.

The wind howls in response.

He lets go of my wrist and yanks me closer, pinning my arm between my body and his. I try to bend at the waist, to throw my torso forward and free my arm, but I may as well try to overpower a column of marble. He outweighs me by a hundred pounds at least.

I hear a small, metallic sound, a clicking. Oh, god.

He's reaching for his handcuffs. If he gets them on me, I'm screwed. I relax every muscle in my body, and his grip reflexively loosens. Not much, but enough. I yank my chin down, into his elbow, then whip my head back. Hard.

"Bitch!" he yells, as my skull connects with his jaw. But before I can struggle any more, he shoves his elbow against my throat again and wraps his left leg around mine, planting it firmly in front of me in the earth between my feet.

I feel his hot, minty breath against my left ear, the side of my neck. Is he . . . *sniffing* me? "Your hair smells good," he murmurs. "Vanilla and roses." My skin crawls.

"I like this body you picked out," he goes on. "It's different. So . . . young."

I hate you, I want to say, but I can't even breathe. Dots appear in my vision, red and purple and black, swimming through the air like undersea creatures. Every cell in my body aches for air. I think of Cyrus grasping his hunting falcons. They'd flap their wings in vain, trapped, an impressive display of powerful muscles that went nowhere.

"Oh dear, you're turning blue," he whispers in my ear, and somehow he makes the words sound disturbingly tender. He's enjoying this. "I'm going to let you breathe. But you'd better not scream again, Sera." I try to nod.

He lets go of my neck, swiftly moving his hand up above my eyes, pinning my head back against his massive chest.

I inhale greedily, oxygen clearing my vision, my mind.

"Here's what's going to happen," he says against my cheek. "I'm going to put the handcuffs on you. You're going to come with me. And then you're going to tell me where you hid the book."

"I threw it in the bay," I gasp, my voice gravelly, sharp notes of pain in my throat. It's actually safe in Berkeley, behind the painting of Taryn on Kailey's wall.

He jerks his hand against my stomach. A threat. A warning. "Don't lie to me. I know you beat me to the punch, finding that junkie girl before me. She told me that she saw you. Told me about the car crash and the girl named Kailey. She called you an angel, which is laughable at best. And she said that she had 'your' book. Though I think we both know whose book it is."

Taryn. I say a quick prayer of thanks that she's woken up. I picture Officer Spaulding—that is, *Cyrus*—running up the stairs to her apartment when she ODed.

"But it wasn't at her apartment. And you know how much I hate being bested," he continues. "Especially by you. So don't lie. It makes me *very angry*."

"Taryn's awake," I say, ignoring his question.

He chuckles. "She was, earlier today. But she's gone back to sleep, poor thing. For good."

"You're a *monster*." I spit out the words.

"So are you!" His voice rises. "We're both monsters. We're exactly the same. You always seem to forget that."

"But she didn't do anything! She was innocent!" Rage, blood-red rage, ascends through my body. Another innocent, another life, tossed away like garbage.

"I had no choice. She had read the book. No human can have that knowledge. Her blood is on your hands, too—if you hadn't stolen the book in the first place, she might still be alive." He talks about violence the way a normal person would describe a trip to the grocery store. It makes me sick. "Doubt it, though, considering the size of the heroin stash she had in her bedroom."

He moves his arm away from my middle, and I feel him fumbling for his handcuffs.

"Tell me where the book is, Sera."

I grit my teeth. "I. Don't. Have. It."

He laughs again, the sound chilling. "Maybe you'll change your tune after I kill that nice family you're living with."

No. Not them. Not the Morgans.

"Or that boy next door. Noah. I might enjoy that."

Something snaps inside me, giving me a surge of power I didn't know I had. In one wrenching motion, I bend my knees, slipping out of his grip. I coil my leg muscles and throw the weight of my body against him, my shoulder slamming into his kneecaps.

With a clang, the handcuffs slip from my hand and hit the dirt. And with a grunt—of pain or surprise, or both— he does, too, crumpling to the ground, holding his knees, moaning.

My knife. Where is it? My eyes sweep the ground, frantic, till I spot its silver blade a few feet away. He seems to see it at the same time I do, using his arms to heave himself toward it. I dive, scooping up the knife before hitting the ground with my shoulder and falling into a tumbling roll.

I pop back up to my feet, brandishing the knife in front of me. He flips on his side and sweeps his leg out. His boot hits my ankle, knocking me off my feet. I fall flat on my back, the wind knocked out of me, struggling to breathe.

And then he's on top of me, straddling my chest, pinning my arms above my head, rendering my knife once again useless. His fingernails dig into my wrists.

"You're going to regret that!" His face is twisted with rage. I notice his lower lip is cut from when I slammed my head into his face.

Only my legs are free. I whip my feet upward, toward his head, the momentum lifting my hips briefly from the ground. Then I slam them down, using the force as leverage to wrench my chest upward, sideways, slipping my hands out from his as he falls to the side.

I spring to my feet and take off running, my knife firmly

in my right hand as I find the path and follow it through the clearing, to the thick forest beyond.

I hear heavy footsteps behind me, and I look back, briefly. He's running after me, awkwardly, favoring his right knee. But he's gaining.

I run faster, fear giving me a burst of speed, yet his footfalls grow nearer. The path turns sharply, into a grove of oaks. A gust of wind sends a shower of leaves over my head.

I round the corner and skid to a stop, panic knifing through my heart.

The path ends abruptly at a concrete driveway that leads to a weathered barn. Old stone walls extend out from the barn on both sides, at least eight feet high. The only way out is the way I came in.

I run to the barn and slam my palms against the door. It's wreathed with a thick steel chain and a padlock the size of my fist. I'm trapped.

My terror takes over. My rational brain turns off. I whip around to face him, dropping my knife onto the pavement where it bounces away from my reach. It's useless to me now. A knife won't do anything if he slams into me with all his force.

I don't think. I let my body do the driving. I take a wide stance and bend my knees, my elbows. He's running straight at me in a flat-out sprint.

Right before he slams into me, I whip my left hand out, high, to the inside of his upper right arm, grabbing onto his police uniform. In a smooth motion, I step into him, sweeping my right arm up into his left armpit, pivoting on my foot and heaving him over my head.

His own force is his undoing. I barely have to exert any strength. His body rolls over my shoulder, momentarily in the air, then slams down to the concrete, hard. His head hits a second later with a sickening wet thud.

I back away slowly, breathing hard, and retrieve my knife. My hand shakes.

He blinks once, twice. Opens his mouth. "You ruined everything," he says, with effort, a shudder wracking his body. His chest rises, falls, rises, falls.

"I just wanted to be free," I whisper.

Then he stops moving.

For a long, horrible moment, his body lies motionless, whole. The only sound is my raspy breathing and the incessant wind.

And then it begins. His feet, his hands, his head are covered by a wave of gray, the human coloring washed out. It travels down his face, up his arms, his legs, leaving an ashy, crumbled surface in its wake. It takes his clothes, his belt, his handcuffs—everything he's wearing disintegrates with his flesh.

The wind has paused, leaving his body undisturbed, a photographic negative of what it was, all gray.

I hear the wind approaching through the trees, the leaves quivering in a dry death rattle as they float to the ground. The breeze approaches the barn like a wave swallowing the beach, the air beating with invisible wings. It covers the pile of dust that was his body and throws it upward in spiraling currents.

Another gust, and another, and another. Moments later, the dust is carried into the air, carried into forever.

And a few moments after that, it begins to rain.

THIRTY-SIX

Tears of relief mingle with the rain, streaming down my face as I run back toward the house. I can't believe it's all over. For the first time since Cyrus appeared in my biology class on the first of November, I'm free.

I burst through the trees, past the sea of swaying grape-vines, past the drenched fire pit, past the clapboard Victorian inn till I reach the small parking lot where we parked our cars. There's no police cruiser there, but Cyrus must have driven here somehow. He probably hid the car somewhere up the road.

I take off again, jogging slower as I circle the property,

retracing the tour I took earlier with Reed and the rest. Reed. A bolt of remorse hits me as I realize how wrong I was about him, how close I was to killing him. Just like I was wrong with Noah.

I'm about to turn back when I scan the vineyard one more time. In the east the path curls toward the one place I haven't checked: the glass greenhouse. Even though my nightgown is plastered to my body and my fingers throb with cold, I decide to go check it out, just to be sure Cyrus came alone.

I walk more slowly now, listening to the percussion of the rain as it pelts the vines, pelts my face. I don't even mind. Cyrus is dead. Finally, truly dead. I saw it with my own eyes. I did it. I should feel triumphant, I should be rising to the sky. But as long as I'm apart from Noah, there's no victory.

Noah. I'm consumed by the sound of his name. Each footfall on wet earth sounds like "Noah" to me. I quicken my pace, pushed along by the wind at my back. The sooner I make sure the glass house is secure, the sooner I can go back to where Noah sleeps. I can wake him up right now, apologize, try to make things right. Nothing can keep me from him anymore. Cyrus is gone.

I stop cold when I crest the small hill. The glass house lies below me, brilliantly lit in a flickering orange glow that I suspect comes from the many candles within.

Someone's in there.

I dart through the storm like a phantom, sweeping my gaze left, then right as I approach the house's glass walls. I cup my hand around my eyes and look inside. It's Noah.

He sits on a faded blue couch in the center of the green-house, his knees drawn up to his chest, a blanket over his shoulders. My breath catches at how beautiful he looks. And so sad, like the storm that rages outside is nothing compared to what's inside of him. I bite my lip and tap my finger on the glass. He doesn't respond—the rain swallows all sound. I tap again, harder.

His head jerks up. He looks around, then sees me. I press my hand against the glass. He rises to his feet, his expression unreadable, then nods toward the door, inviting me in.

The greenhouse is flickering with fire. Noah has lit a couple of the candles, and their light dances off the glass walls, the antique mirrors, reflecting over and over into infinity. The heat amplifies the scent of flowers that spill out of their pots: jasmine and roses and lilies.

Noah's eyes are red, wary. He's wearing jeans that sag around his narrow hips, a gray T-shirt with a hole near the neck. It's fitted, revealing the line of his body. His defined arms are sinuous in the candlelight.

"What are you doing here?" I ask. He shouldn't be in a glass house in this kind of weather.

"I could ask you the same question." There's a sharp, bitter edge to his voice.

"I need to talk to you," I say, shivering. Water drips from my hair, my sodden nightgown. "Please?"

"Come on in," he says, but it doesn't feel welcoming.

I walk uncertainly to the couch he was on. His stony expression tells me I haven't earned the right to sit next to him, so I huddle in a nearby armchair. I can't stop shivering. I wrap my arms around myself, but it does no good. I let my chin drop toward my chest, and am surprised when I feel Noah gently placing his blanket around my shoulders.

"Thank you," I whisper hoarsely. He just nods and returns to the couch.

I notice that he's barefoot; and for some reason this fills me with tenderness. We sit in silence for a while. I struggle to find the right words, not sure how to begin. "What do you want?" he asks finally.

I look up toward the glass roof. Rain streams across it in sheets. It's like being inside a waterfall.

"I made a mistake," I manage to whisper. "I'm sorry, Noah. I'm so sorry."

"You destroyed me, Kailey. You ripped my heart out, over and over." He stands and begins to pace through the greenhouse, orange light illuminating his shoulder bones, jutting against his T-shirt. "Why should I let you hurt me again?"

I stand up too. I approach him, reaching my hand out to his shoulder. The heat from his skin sears me, sends an electrical jolt through my body.

"Don't touch me!" he says roughly, throwing my hand off. I sink to my knees, praying to stay strong. A sob erupts from my throat. I was just trying to keep him safe. I never thought I'd actually lose him.

For the first time, the cold hard truth comes into gut-wrenching focus. He may never forgive me. He doesn't have to forgive me. Our relationship wasn't ironclad, wasn't immune. It could crumble into dust.

I wrap my arms around myself and cry. I don't care how stupid I look, how foolish, how desperate.

"I love you, Noah," I sob, my voice ragged. "I messed up. But I refuse to believe we end here. We were supposed to be forever."

The couch's springs creak as he sits. "Forever, huh? I'm not sure I know what that means."

"I do."

I stand. I walk toward him again, to where he sits on the couch, his face in his hands. All I have to give is my heart, my scarred heart. My ancient soul.

The air is charged. It's a battery to power a thousand

cities, a thousand lives. I reach across the space between us toward his face. He needs a shave. I tentatively stroke his rough cheek.

"You don't have to believe me." My voice is stronger now. "But Noah Vander, I love you. And my love lasts a long time." My voice cracks, my heart cracks wide open. "Goodbye," I say. He's trembling, too. I kiss his forehead and turn to leave.

I go to the door. Behind me, I hear a sound.

"Wait."

One word. One little word. I turn around.

"Do you mean it? Please don't lie to me."

"I mean it," I whisper.

We collide in the center of the greenhouse. Our souls collide. Outside, wind destroys the grapevines. Water courses down walls of leaded glass. Inside, it is safe, it is warm, it is orange. We are a chemical reaction. Our souls are quicksilver, water, entangling, magnetic. I reach my hand to his face again, I plunge it into his crow-black hair. I pull his lips to mine. His hands are around my waist.

I need him like oxygen, like sunlight. We stumble over to the faded blue couch. He tugs off his T-shirt and it's him everywhere, his skin, his arms around me.

"I love you," he murmurs. I answer him with a kiss.

And for the first time in forever, I forget about forever. I am just here. He is just here. Our breath becomes one thing, a shuddering, hungry gust of wind. My compass heart stops spinning. This is the direction it wants me to take.

"Look," he says, putting a finger to my lips. I follow his gaze upward to the glass roof. "The rain stopped."

It did. Though the room is bright with candles, I can make out stars through the glass. Noah gets up, moves about the greenhouse blowing out candles. With each one he extinguishes, the stars grow brighter. I think of the stars in Echo's mural, the stars in Kailey's room.

"Wait," I tell him. "Leave one lit." He doesn't ask why, and I don't offer. I want to do something for Taryn. To give her small flame in the world after her own has gone out.

Noah returns to me in the dark. We lie on our sides, facing each other. "This feels like a dream," he murmurs. "I wanted this to happen for so long. I'd better not be sleeping. It had better be real."

"It's real," I answer.

"Don't ever hide yourself from me," he says softly. "I love you. I love the parts I know and the parts I don't."

I snuggle close to him, burying my face in his warm chest. His words mean more to me than he can know. I want to tell him everything. About who I am, where I come from.

But instead my lips find his jaw, kissing his rough skin. "So . . . I hear there's a dance this week," I murmur.

"Right, that hippie solstice party at the Claremont hotel."
He grins.

"That's the one."

He reaches down, finds my hand. "Will you go with me?"

"I thought you'd never ask."

His arms wrap around me, our limbs entangled as we sink deeper into the couch. I feel his body everywhere, his pounding heart, his muscled shoulders, the warmth of his skin. At some point, we fall asleep. I wake, hours later, but I don't move. How could I? I never want to leave this moment. I'm tucked away with the boy I love in a glass house full of flowers, with silver starlight falling on our hair.

THIRTY-SEVEN

"Oh. My. God." Leyla triumphantly yanks the dress from the rack and holds it against her body. "This is the most amazing dress I have ever seen."

Chantal pales. "It's grotesque."

Leyla hugs the dress. "I know," she says happily.

Nicole claps. "Bravo, Leyla. You managed to find the weirdest dress possible in downtown San Francisco."

"I think I just won shopping. Like, if it were a sport. I'm so glad I let you guys talk me into coming here. Oh, god, I hope it fits." She holds it up again, nervously inspecting herself in a full-length mirror.

The dress has a fitted, boned bodice and a sweetheart neckline. Its full skirt suggests a 1950s prom gown. But it's the printed pattern that delights Leyla and grosses everyone else out.

It's covered in bacon, tiny red-and-white slices on a light brown background.

"Bryan will love it," I say.

Rebecca wrinkles her nose. "Maybe he could bring you a little sausage. For a corsage."

"Or a sau*sage*," Echo declares, making the word rhyme with *corsage*.

Madison smiles wickedly. "I don't think Bryan would appreciate his sausage being described as little."

"Ew!" I yell, clapping my hands over my ears. "Don't ever talk about Bryan's sausage to me again."

"I'm going to try it on," Leyla says. "Anyone want to come with me?"

Nicole and Chantal, carrying armfuls of dresses, follow her to the dressing room.

I haven't found anything yet, but I'm not bothered. Now that I know I'll be going to the dance with Noah, I could be wearing a bathrobe for all I care. Noah. Just the thought of his name makes me smile. I've been engulfed in a joyful fog ever since I woke up in his arms on Tuesday morning in the greenhouse, dawn's rosy light lighting his face. The storm from the night before proved brief, mere bluster with no staying power. And today, Wednesday, I floated through our first day back at school on a ray of happiness.

My girlfriends were unanimously delighted to hear that Noah and I were back together. Even Nicole winked as she shook her head in mock sadness. "Another one off the market," she sighed. "But I'm happy for you two. Seriously. Of course, I don't have a date. I guess that means I'll get to dance with tons of boys while you're stuck with the same one all night!" I laughed at this. Nicole has always been good at the chase.

Only Madison's words of encouragement felt hollow somehow, like she didn't quite approve. She's probably jealous, but at least she has the manners not to say anything mean.

Echo fingers a floor-length dress in pale lavender, its empire waist encircled with a sunset-yellow ribbon that ties in the back. "What do you think?" she asks us.

"I like it," I say. It suits her boho style.

Rebecca cocks her head and turns to the rack. "Pretty, but I think you should try something like this," she says, handing Echo a short, off-the-shoulder dress in a glittery dark blue.

Echo regards the hemline with suspicion. "It's a bit . . . *short*, isn't it?"

Rebecca laughs. "That's the idea. You've got those crazy long legs. You should show them off."

"I don't know," Echo murmurs. "I *do* like the fabric." So do I—it reminds me of her mural.

"Reed'll like it. Trust me, I'm his sister." Rebecca grins as a flush appears on Echo's cheeks.

I'm confused. "Reed? What does he have to do with it?"

"Reed's taking Echo to the dance," Rebecca says.

I whip my head toward Echo. She nods. "I didn't get a chance to tell you, Kailey," she says shyly.

I give her a hug. "That's great," I say. Her smile is radiant. "When did he ask you?"

"Yesterday," Echo says. "As soon as you came back from Sonoma. But we were texting the whole time he was there."

"The whole time?" I repeat. I think of Reed at the winery, the way he kept pulling his phone from his pocket, the way he wouldn't let me borrow it.

"Look," Echo says, tapping on her phone's screen and handing it to me. I quickly scroll through their conversation, noting the messages' times; they're all from Monday afternoon. I feel a flush of shame at how certain I was that he was Cyrus, bidding on my book auction, when it was Cyrus all along, piggybacking off the inn's open wireless network.

"Young love," says Madison drily. "Isn't it precious?" I wonder again if she's bitter about Noah and me.

I decide to ignore her tone. "It *is* precious," I say. "I'm so happy for you, Echo."

She nods sagely. "Well, he's a Libra, and they *do* appreciate fashion. Okay, I'll try it on." She smiles, accepting the dress from Rebecca and draping it over her arm.

The three of them drift away to another display, and I trail behind, lost in thought.

"How about this one for you, Maddy?" Rebecca holds up a short, silver tunic with a high neck and bell sleeves.

Madison shrugs her shoulders. "Sure, if you say so. I don't know what looks good on me."

"I *am* your date, after all," Rebecca smiles. "You should trust me."

Echo raises her eyebrows. "You guys are going together? That's cool, I didn't realize . . ."

Madison throws her head back and laughs. "We're not *dating*," she explains. "We're just going together since we're both date*less*. We're basically going to be working the entire night."

Rebecca blushes and looks down at the floor. I wonder if there's more to this exchange—if Rebecca really does want to date Madison. She's certainly got a gigantic girl-crush on her. But Madison likes guys—that much was clear from the way she flirted with Noah.

"What about you, Rebecca?" asks Echo. "We need to

find you a dress, and you've been so busy helping the rest of us."

"Oh, I have one already," Rebecca says. "It's vintage Dior." Of course it is. "Silver satin." She throws an arm around Madison's shoulder. "I'll match with Maddy. We'll look great in pictures, especially with Echo's mural as the backdrop."

"Mmm-hmm" is Madison's reply. She sounds bored.

"I guess that just leaves me," I say with a sigh, approaching the racks of dresses.

"Commence Operation Find Kailey a Dress," Echo declares. She and Rebecca begin to dig through the racks while Madison and I follow.

Echo holds up a turquoise-blue shift. "How about this?"

I nod, taking it from her. "I'll try it."

"Or this?" she says, handing me a lacy black strapless dress. "I bet black looks good with your blond hair. Plus, you're a goddess of war *and* an international woman of mystery."

"I am neither international nor mysterious," I lie, arching my eyebrow.

"Put those down," Rebecca pronounces somberly. "This is the one." I smile—I can tell she's enjoying this. At least she's using her powers of fashion for good.

I catch my breath when I see the dress she's holding. It's

a deep, emerald green, with pin-tucked cap sleeves and a low, square neckline. Gathered panels of raw silk fall from the high waist. It's beautiful, but that's not why I gasp. Everything about it reminds me of Charlotte. It's exactly the color she would pick—she loved to wear green, the dramatic contrast it made against her fiery red hair, her milky skin. This dress is short, but if it were floor-length, I'd swear it was a replica of a gown I've seen Charlotte wearing before. I can picture it sweeping the cobblestones in 1880s Manhattan as we hurried through the streets together, Charlotte always turning back to make sure I was following.

I miss her. I miss her so much.

"You're right," says Echo, watching me. "Look at Kailey's face. She loves it."

"I do," I admit, reaching out to touch the dress. It's just as soft as I knew it would be.

"You should try it on," Echo says gently, putting her hand on my arm.

I nod and follow her to the dressing room, blinking back tears. Suddenly, I'm overwhelmed with memories of Charlotte: the two of us eating ice cream on San Francisco rooftops, scouring the flea markets in Paris, running through the streets of Morocco.

I slide the dress over my head, the silk cool against my skin. It feels light as air. And suddenly, I do too. There's no reason for me to be sad—nothing is keeping me from Charlotte anymore. Worrying about Cyrus has become so ingrained in me, I need to learn how to stop.

When I get home, I hang the green dress in my armoire, sit at the desk, and flip open the laptop. Then I do what I haven't dared since I became Kailey Morgan: I log on to Gmail with my own e-mail address. The inbox is full to bursting, message after message from Cyrus, concerned and angry and threatening. I'll delete them later. But for now I just click the COMPOSE button and enter Charlotte's address in the TO field. I hold my hands over the keys, take a deep breath, and type.

THIRTY-EIGHT

"Eureka!" Echo emerges from my armoire, where's she's been digging around for the perfect pair of shoes to match my dress.

Leyla nods, satisfied with the sparkly burgundy platform pumps Echo's selected. "Perfect. Red shoes, green dress, like a Christmas tree. Put 'em on, Cinderella."

I laugh, sitting on the bed to unzip the boots I was wearing earlier, more out of habit than anything else. "More like Dorothy Gale than Cinderella, no? They're ruby, not glass." Luna tries to climb into my lap as soon as I sit.

"There's no place like home," Echo agrees. "Just don't

click them together three times and disappear."

"But this *is* my home," I protest. "I wouldn't go any-where."

"You never know," says Leyla. "You might end up in Oz. Don't risk it."

"Noted," I say, slipping the ruby pumps on my feet and standing up, ignoring Luna's meows of protest at the loss of a warm lap. I approach the mirror again and smile—Echo did my hair, fluttering around me like an ethereal fairy god-mother, and I love the result.

My hair is gathered at the crown of my head, secured with a generous handful of light gold bobby pins that Echo expertly tucked away, leaving just a few tendrils to fall around my face. She added a few tiny braids at each of my temples that are swept up with the rest of my hair. The only jewelry I'm wearing is the birdcage necklace that Noah gave me.

"Thank you both, so much," I say softly, feeling sud-denly wistful and overwhelmed at how lucky I am to have such good friends. But it's bittersweet, because getting ready for the dance with them makes me think of Charlotte. She hasn't responded to my e-mail yet, and I'm starting to worry. Then again, she was never one for checking her e-mail very often. I tell myself she just hasn't gotten around to reading it yet.

There's a soft knock at the door. "Come in," I call, and Mrs. Morgan's face appears.

"You girls look beautiful," she says. "Although in Leyla's case, perhaps I should say you look beautifully carnivorous."

"Thank you, Mrs. Morgan," says Leyla, smiling radiantly. "That's what I was going for." She's wearing red fishnet stockings underneath her bacon dress, and dangly earrings in the shape of T-bone steaks. When I told her how impressed I was that she found the meat earrings between our shopping trip and tonight, she scoffed. "These aren't *new*, Kailey. I've had them for a while—I just never had anything to wear them with."

She never fails to crack me up.

"And Echo, you are quite the moon goddess," Mrs. Morgan tells her.

"Thank you," Echo replies. "I take goddess references very seriously." We all laugh, and I have to admire Mrs. Morgan's choice of words. Echo's hair is woven with silver ribbon and pulled up in twin high buns. A silver rose is pinned at each temple, giving her glittery, space-age outfit an art nouveau flavor. Opal earrings drip from her ears ("Reed's birthstone," she informed me), and she's wearing a necklace that she made herself: a cross-section of a large blue geode, strung on a midnight-blue ribbon that matches her sparkly sapphire dress. Its hem floats several inches above her knees, revealing, as Rebecca promised, her mile-long legs.

"Anyway, I thought you girls should know that Reed and Noah are here. They're in the living room being cross-examined by my dear husband. So you might want to come out and rescue them." Mrs. Morgan delivers this news with a wink.

Bryan appears behind Mrs. Morgan. "I don't mean to crash this girl-power party," he says, "but, Ley? I think I need help with this tie." He holds out the aforementioned tie, a gift from Leyla. Of course its design is a single wide strip of bacon.

"There's my hunk of beef," she says fondly. "Come here, I'll do it."

"My little filet mignon," he replies, plopping heavily down on the bed as she approaches. Luna leaps up and scampers through the open door, apparently offended by Bryan's invasion of her space. "Did you know 'mignon' means cute? In French? I googled it." He smiles proudly.

"Truly, your research capabilities are stunning," Leyla replies, making short work of the tie. "There," she says. "Are we ready?"

In the living room, Reed and Noah are seated on the sofa, Mr. Morgan looming over them. "I'm only going to ask this once. There aren't any plans for after-parties in hotel rooms, right? No staying out all night?"

I clear my throat. "Dad, no. I'll be sleeping in my own bed, safe and sound."

He whirls around, catches his breath. "Kailey, you look beautiful. So much like your mother when she was in college."

Noah rises. "I'll second that," he says. "I mean—not the part about Mrs. Morgan. I wasn't born yet. But you look gorgeous, Kailey." He grins.

Mr. Morgan grabs the camera that's resting on the coffee table. "Photos! Gather around the fireplace."

He starts snapping away, Mrs. Morgan standing behind him with a wide smile on her face. He takes picture after picture: group shots, couple shots, individual portraits. He only pauses once, briefly, when Noah suggests a different setting for the camera's flash.

"Just one more," Mr. Morgan says.

Bryan adjusts his meat tie. "Dad? We're not getting married. I think you've got enough."

"Seconded," I add. "We should be going."

Noah leans over me, whispers in my ear. "Let him have his fun. You're lucky that your dad cares."

"Or, keep taking photos if you want," I tell Mr. Morgan, but he shakes his head.

"I'm good. You kids have fun tonight." He sets the camera on the table.

Mrs. Morgan hugs me tightly. "I'm so glad you decided to go," she whispers. "Have the best time ever."

"I will," I promise.

Luna darts out from behind the couch and plants herself in front of the front door, holding her ground even as our large, noisy group approaches. I kneel in front of her. She meows, plaintively, like she doesn't want me to leave.

"I'll be home before you know it, little kitty," I say, stroking her fur and noting happily how much she's filled out in the last few days. I couldn't save Kailey, and I couldn't save Taryn. But at least I saved Luna.

THIRTY-NINE

Noah's hand closes tightly around mine as we approach the entrance to the Claremont hotel. "Madison's really outdone herself," he observes.

"She'll go down in winter dance committee history, which I guess was the point," I agree, taking in the spectacle that lies before us.

Bryan and Leyla's grilled-cheese truck is parked on the circular drive, a long line of formally dressed Berkeley High students extending from its service window, all in search of melted cheesy fare. Fire breathers roam the area, and a troupe of acrobats wearing crowns of holly handspring around the lawn.

Noah places his hand on my lower back to guide me forward into the ballroom. I can't believe that only last weekend that we were both here setting up the decorations, so far apart from each other, on opposite sides of the vast gulf that Cyrus created.

The ballroom has been utterly transformed. I had a part in it, but I'm still impressed at how everything came together. The ceiling drips with thousands of tiny white lights among the glittering snowflakes. In the center of the room is a spinning globe in place of a disco ball, casting a soft, feathery glow on the dancing couples below. Flanking the dance floor are buffet tables laden with tiered trays of cupcakes and tacos, punctuated by blue bowls of punch.

A hand falls on my shoulder, and I whirl around to see Madison and Rebecca, each wearing a silver dress. Rebecca's is more muted compared to Madison's highly reflective material, making them look like a lopsided star system.

"Well, don't you two make a lovely couple," says Madison, her tone sounding just the smallest bit insincere.

"Any loveliness is because of Kailey," Noah grins. "I take no responsibility."

"I agree," says Madison with a wink. "Kailey, you *are*

beautiful tonight. That dress is perfect for you."

"Actually, I bought it because it reminds me of an old friend. She has a dress just like this."

"Who?" asks Madison. "Anyone I know?"

I shake my head. "She doesn't live here. Her name's Char—" I pause. "Charlene." I clap my mouth shut, momentarily horrified that I almost just blurted out Charlotte's name.

It doesn't matter anymore. When will you stop acting like prey? When are you going to get used to Cyrus being gone?

"I can't imagine anyone else wearing that dress as well." She smiles. "You're very lucky," she adds, turning to Noah.

"Thanks?" I say, not quite sure if I should take her at face value. The way she interacts with Noah feels fake, an act she's putting on for my benefit to show she's not attracted to him anymore. And if she ever did like him, the way he looks tonight would make her weak in the knees.

He's wearing a dark suit with no tie and a charcoal dress shirt that clings to his chest. His hair, as usual, is haphazardly parted in the middle and hanging to his chin in tangled black waves. I love the combination of his messy hair falling around his crisp collar, tousled above his immaculate suit.

None of us speaks, and the moment stretches out, edging into awkward silence. I wish Leyla were here. She'd have some witty quip to make us laugh. But no—I crane my neck and see that she and Bryan are already on the dance floor. And I'd have to be color-blind to miss Nicole shimmying through the crowd, dressed to kill in a skin-tight cherry-red sheath dress that earns her appreciative glances from more than a few male students.

Madison follows my gaze. "Well," she says haltingly, "don't let me stop you two from dancing. That's what you're here for, isn't it? You don't want to lose your chance."

I frown at her strange phrasing, glancing at her face. Her mascara is smudged, and even in the dim light I can see her eyes are red. *She's probably exhausted*, I think. *Planning this party has taken a lot out of her.*

"Good idea," says Noah, holding out his hand to me. "Shall we?"

I nod, taking his hand and following him into the crowd. My hips unconsciously begin to sway as we walk toward our friends, matching the bass line of the song that the DJ is playing. I am caught in the music as Noah and I finally reach the middle of the crowd, our friends closing around us in a tight circle. I watch their faces—Leyla, Bryan, Chantal, Nicole, Echo, and Reed—as I listen to the words, indescribable happiness floating over me like a fallen star.

I've been on this earth for more than six hundred years, yet I just learned what love is really like. It's not a handful of powder thrown hastily on a fire, a combustible display of fierce color, a possessive arm thrown around my shoulders, a prison that I entered at the age of fourteen.

It's this, it's now. I close my eyes. It's as though the whole terrifying stretch between the night on Treasure Island and now has been erased. No breakup, no Cyrus, no choking elbow against my throat in the forest. I'm with my friends, with Noah. I'm six hundred and sixteen at once, old and new. Everything I've been through has led me to this moment.

Noah reaches for my hand and I take it, sliding my other arm up over his shoulder. He pulls me close, till our bodies are pressed together, till we're one. I turn my head to the side and rest it on his chest as we sway.

We dance for a long time, songs melting into one another like candle wax in a house made of glass. I lean my head on his chest and listen to the sound of his human heart beating. How is it possible, I wonder, that it took me more than six hundred years to find Noah? And then I realize that if Cyrus had never placed that drop of elixir on my lips, I would have died in the fourteenth century. Not even a footnote to history. I never would have met Noah. I never would have known the greatest love of my life. And now that Cyrus is dead, I can almost, in a strange way, be grateful to him.

For song after song, we stay like this. Finally I pull away. "I need to go to the bathroom," I whisper to Noah.

"Okay," he says. "Come back."

"I will," I say, turning on my heel to fight my way out of the crowd.

I run into Echo at the edge of the dance floor. "Where are you going?" she asks, putting a protective hand on my shoulder.

"Bathroom," I answer. "Back in a sec."

She doesn't reply, just blinks at me with big brown eyes rimmed in silver pencil.

"You shouldn't go," she says at last. I wonder if I heard her right—the music is so loud.

"When Mother Nature calls, I answer," I retort with a smile that she doesn't return.

"You shouldn't go alone. I'll come with you."

"It's okay," I say quickly. "I don't need an escort." Echo's long-distance stare and slow speech are creeping me out.

"Okay," she answers, nodding, as though unseen forces are telling her to back off. "You're right. Good-bye, Kailey." There's a strange finality in the way she says it.

I slip past her into the hallway that leads to the women's restroom. Something feels . . . *off.* I can't put my finger on it. I open the door to the bathroom and hear muffled sobs. I pause, surprised. It's Madison.

She's leaning on the counter, staring at herself in the

mirror, fumbling in the silver clutch that sits on the counter in front of her.

"Maddy, what's wrong?" I ask, quickly traversing the space between us. She looks so distraught. Her shaggy hair's a mess, like she's been raking her hands through it over and over. "Are you okay?"

She shakes her head, sniffing. "I have something to tell you," she says.

I brace myself, hoping that it's not something to do with Noah. Did something happen between them while we were broken up? "What is it?" I ask.

"Seraphina," she whispers. "It's me. Charlotte."

My eyes widen. My heart pounds against the walls of my chest.

My ears hear her words, but it takes a minute for my brain to catch up. My first instinct is to lie, to stay in hiding, where it's safe. To say "Seraphina? I have no idea who you're talking about." But it's *Charlotte*.

"Char?" I ask slowly.

"That's what I said, dummy." She smiles, reaches out to stroke my hair. "I've missed you, Sera."

"Me, too," I reply. Tears sting my eyes.

"Listen," she says. "We don't have much time. You're in danger. Terrible danger."

"What are you talking about?" I ask.

330

"Cyrus," she whispers, glancing around as if to confirm that the bathroom is, indeed, empty. "He's here."

"Impossible," I breathe. "I killed him. Three nights ago."

Her brow furrows. "Are you sure?"

"I'm sure. He followed me to Sonoma, pretending to be a police officer. But I—I took care of him."

Charlotte swallows hard, her gaze darting upward as her eyes fill with tears. "Oh, Sera. I'm so sorry," she says sadly, taking my hands in hers, gripping them so tightly the bones scrape together. "That was *Jared*."

My mind reels, and I stagger backward. Officer Spaulding was Jared? I thought Jared was in San Francisco, working with the police to keep them occupied in the investigation of Mr. Shaw's supposed death. If Jared was the police officer, then who is Cyrus?

"Noah," she whispers, as though she can hear my thoughts. "Noah is Cyrus."

"You're wrong," I say immediately. The idea is ridiculous. "Noah is *Noah*. I would know if he were Cyrus."

"Sera," she says gently. "Why do you think he forgave you so easily after the breakup? Why do you think he was standing right next to you when Eli's band played that song on Treasure Island?"

"No," I whisper. I am falling apart. My world is shattering

like glass into a million tiny pieces that can never be put together again. "No. Noah isn't dead."

"I'm sorry," she answers. "But the boy you think you're in love with isn't even Noah. He's Cyrus—he's been Cyrus ever since Eli disappeared. Noah died two weeks ago. I wanted to tell you sooner, but I didn't know if you were Seraphina."

I stare at the walls. I wait for the tears, sobs. I will break. But I don't. I can't. All I can think of is Noah's hands running across my body three nights ago, of kissing him deeply, of being so deliriously in love with him that I nearly lost control of myself.

But it wasn't Noah. It was Cyrus.

I feel like I'm going to be sick.

This, this is betrayal. This is pain. This is what he wanted me to feel.

"Sera, I'm so sorry," she whispers again.

I look up. I meet her eyes. "How *dare* he?" I ask. I'm shaking with rage.

"You know what you need to do," she says.

She's right. I do.

I whirl around and tear out of the bathroom.

FORTY

There are no tears, not yet. I have forever to mourn. Right now I want revenge.

I have enough presence of mind to run to the janitor's closet and throw open the door. My hammer is there, right where I left it.

I tear into the ballroom and scan the crowd. I don't see Noah anywhere. I push my way through the dance floor, dodging boys in suits and girls in gowns, holding the hammer low at my side.

"Sera!" Charlotte hisses, and I spin around. "He's

outside. In the back, by the kitchen loading dock."

"Show me," I say firmly.

I follow Charlotte's silver dress down a shadowy hallway, so grateful that she's here with me. I just can't believe I didn't realize it sooner. I should have known.

She points to a steel door, holds a finger to her lips. I push it open.

I think, suddenly, that my life has been made of nothing but doorways, a whole house full of doors. Some I walk through many times, back and forth. And some I only walk through once. They lock behind me. They are doors made of consequences that cannot be undone.

Noah—Cyrus—stands under a bare bulb at the bottom of the sloped driveway. The night has filled with dense fog, and the light he stands under makes the surrounding mist glow like a halo. The air hums with air conditioners and generators. Behind my back, I slip my hammer into my other hand, so he won't see it as I hurry down the stairs, my footsteps slowing as I meet him.

"Are you okay?" he asks, his brow wrinkled in the perfect imitation of concern, of love.

"I'm fine," I say, my voice shaking with anger. I can't bear to look at his face, the face that Cyrus ruined. The soul that Cyrus evicted.

"Maddy texted me that you were sick, that you were out here all alone."

Thank you, Charlotte, I think.

"I *am* sick," I answer, taking a step toward him. My fingers curl around the hammer, so solid and deadly in my grasp.

"What's wrong?" he asks. "Is it your stomach?"

"No," I answer. I take another step. "Not my stomach."

"What, then? A migraine? I'm worried. Should I take you home?" He holds out his arms. I take another step. I'm close enough now. Within striking distance, as they say.

"I don't have a home," I say softly. "Not anymore."

"Kailey?" His eyes are so blue.

I let my eyes drift past him to the top of the driveway. "What the hell is *that*?" I gasp, pointing theatrically. He turns to look in the direction I pointed. I say a prayer of thanks that I won't have to see his face when I kill him.

"It's so foggy," he says. "I can't see anything."

In answer, I raise the hammer. I grasp it with both hands and aim at his black hair.

And just as I'm about to slam it down, I hear a voice, a voice I know too well. A voice that's never lost the soft brogue that she inherited from her Irish-born parents no matter how many new bodies she occupies.

"Stop! Sera, *stop!*" the voice yells.

I freeze.

She comes running down the hill toward us, red hair streaming behind her.

I drop the hammer.

It's Charlotte, in the body I last saw her in.

And if Charlotte is here, who the hell is Madison?

FORTY-ONE

Charlotte skids down the hill. Through the fog, I see a figure behind her—Sébastien, his dreadlocks tied back in a low ponytail. He starts to run after Charlotte.

I steal a glance at Noah's face—he's utterly, painfully confused. "Kailey?" he asks, but I just shake my head. I don't know how to begin to explain.

"Charlotte! Sébastien! Freeze. Don't take one more step." The familiar female voice comes from behind them, at the top of the driveway. "I've got a gun, and I *will* use it."

Charlotte and Sébastien stop in their tracks, raising their hands slowly and turning around to see who it is. But I already know. I should have known when she told me Noah was Cyrus. I should have asked her a question that only Charlotte knew the answer to. But I was hurting too much to think clearly.

She walks forward slowly, like she has all the time in the world, pausing to open the silver clutch purse that was tucked under her arm. She pulls out a small pistol. Its shiny metal matches her glittery silver dress.

She aims it at Charlotte and Sébastien, who are halfway up the slope. Noah and I stand at the bottom. The four of us are surrounded by loading dock walls. The only way out is up the wooden steps to the walkway above, the door I came out of.

"Madison?" The first touch of fear has scarred Noah's voice. "Is that a gun?"

She laughs, pivoting her torso and her outstretched arms toward Noah, pointing the pistol at him. "First of all, my name isn't Madison."

Oh, god. My blood turns to ice, and my body erupts in cold sweat.

"What are you talking about?" Noah asks. "Please, put that down and we can talk."

"Not going to happen," she says. I still think of her as a *she*, even though I know who it really is. I calculate the distance from us to the stairs. Perhaps twenty feet. She stands at least twice that distance away at the top of the hill. We *might* be able to make it, if we run, fast. It's difficult to hit a moving target.

But if we try, someone might very well get shot. I glance at Noah, Charlotte, Sébastien. I can't. I can't risk them getting hurt.

I hear a scraping sound from above and whip my head around. Rebecca slips through the door and hurries onto the wooden walkway. I can see from here that she's carrying a knife.

"Stay there, Amelia," says Madison. My mind spins.

"Shit," whispers Sébastien.

We're trapped. And if Rebecca is Amelia, that means I'm right, that Madison is—

"Cyrus," Amelia says calmly. "Just let them go. Like we discussed."

I whip my head toward Madison—toward *Cyrus*. "It was you?" I ask him, already knowing the answer. "All this time?"

He smiles. "Of course it was. My one regret is that you didn't figure it out sooner. Before it came to this."

To my right, I hear the gritty sound of shoes on asphalt. Cyrus hears it at the same time and whips around, aiming the pistol at Sébastien, who quickly skids to a stop. "No heroics, Sébastien," Cyrus says with a sigh. "I don't want to have to kill you."

"Will someone tell me what the hell is going on?" demands Noah. "Madison, why are you doing this?"

"For the last goddamned time, my name is not Madison!" Cyrus's face twists with rage.

"It's Cyrus," I say sadly. Cyrus nods approvingly, like I'm his devoted pupil.

"Are you guys playing a joke on me?" Noah's face is shiny with perspiration, or mist, or both.

"He's kind of slow, isn't he, Sera?" Cyrus gestures at Noah with the barrel of the gun. "I'm surprised you never told him the truth about you. About us. But then again, that would have taken guts, wouldn't it? Which you clearly don't have."

Anger rises in me like a high tide, sweeping away everything before it. "I escaped from you, didn't I?"

"Running away is an act of cowardice." Cyrus spits out the words. "And you couldn't even do it right. If you really didn't want to be found, you would have ditched that body and taken another one. You would have fled the country."

Everyone is staring at us, listening. Even Noah, who seems to have temporarily accepted that the world has gone utterly insane, that his friends have lost their minds.

"Oh, I'm a coward, am I? Just because I refuse to be a killer? Just because I don't want to end human lives for my own benefit?" My tone is dangerously approaching hysterical. "You killed Eli. You killed Madison. You're a monster."

"You killed Jared," he points out.

"He was going to kill *me*."

"A finite distinction," Cyrus declares. "And anyway, I doubt Jared would have killed you. If I had known he was trying to find you"—he pauses, seemingly irritated, and I wonder if there was some sort of falling-out between Jared and Cyrus—"I would have ordered him to bring you back to me. Where you belong, I might add."

"I do *not*," I say fiercely. "I hate you."

Cyrus meets my gaze, chuckles softly. "No you don't, Sera. If you hated me as much as you pretend to, you would have left—really left. Lost Kailey's body and disappeared into thin air. You try to act so high-and-mighty, but we're the same. We're killers. The real reason you stayed in Berkeley is because deep down, you *wanted* me to find you. I know you better than you know yourself. Always have."

I glance at Charlotte and Sébastien. Charlotte's green eyes meet mine, brimming with helplessness. But Sébastien never turns away from Cyrus. He's watching, I realize, waiting for an opening.

Cyrus smiles. "I'm right, and you know it. You love me."

Noah flinches. This small gesture hurts me. "Cyrus, I

don't love you anymore. Once upon a time, yes, I did. But I haven't loved you for hundreds of years."

Amelia interrupts from the walkway above. "Cyrus— you heard her. *She doesn't love you.* Let's go. You promised."

Cyrus shakes his head. "I can't," he says sadly. "You know I can't. She's everything to me. I'd rather die than live without her. I love her. I'll always love her."

"Shut up!"

I glance up when Amelia yells. She has her knife tucked into the sash of her vintage Dior gown, both hands over her ears. "I am so fucking sick of hearing about perfect Sera! Who came to Berkeley with you? Who has been here for you this entire time? Who's been loyal? Who *loves* you? Not her! It's me!"

Cyrus shifts uncomfortably. "Amelia, my dear, I never said your service was unappreciated. You *have* been loyal. And that loyalty will be rewarded."

"I don't want be *rewarded*, like some pathetic dog that gets a bone. I want you to *love* me. That's all I ever wanted." Her voice cracks. She's crying now, softly, tears slipping down her face like falling stars. I almost feel bad for her. "You said you just needed to know if she loved you," Amelia continues. "That if she didn't, you would let her go. You *promised*."

Cyrus shakes his head. "You heard what you wanted to hear."

"Bullshit." And in one smooth silver streak, she's kicked off her shoes and leapt gracefully to the top of the railing, clinging to it with her trained acrobat's feet. She pulls the knife from her belt, stretching both arms out for balance.

"Get down, Amelia." Cyrus's voice is firm.

"No." She sounds like a petulant child. "She needs to go."

Amelia kneels, coiling the powerful muscles in her legs, then jumps straight up like a gymnast flipping off the balance beam. She twists in the air, sinuous and graceful, heading straight toward me.

I remember when I first saw her perform with the circus, Cyrus at my side. Brooklyn, 1933. Lady Amelia, the bird without wings, they called her. The little blond aerialist who could defy gravity. But I've always thought of her as more like a cat—purring, unreadable. And she always landed on her feet.

As she does now.

She brandishes her knife, just a few feet away. Noah takes a protective step toward me. I see a red blur out of the corner of my eye—Charlotte, hurrying to close the gap between us.

"Amelia," I say, putting my hands up in surrender, "you can have him."

"Oh," she says with a laugh, "I will."

And she leaps forward again, knife held out toward my heart.

A gunshot splits the night. A bird falls from the air. Amelia's body crumples at my feet, her back facing the sky. A red flower of blood blooms in the center of her silver dress.

Noah's head swivels toward Cyrus, who's still holding the gun outstretched, arms shaking. "Are you *insane?*" he yells.

The gun goes off again. I tear my eyes from Amelia to see Sébastien stopped short, his eyes closed. There's a hole in the asphalt at his feet, like a tiny pothole. Wisps of smoke rise from the rubble.

"Oh my god," Noah whispers. "What the hell is happening?"

I follow his gaze to Amelia's crumpled form as it dissolves, loses color, as the silver sparkle of her gown fades into a dull gray pile of dust.

"You see, Sera?" Cyrus's voice chokes. "You see what I would do for you? I will kill *anyone* who comes between us."

I wonder, briefly, if the sound of the gunshots will summon help from inside. But I think about how loud the DJ is—the DJ that Cyrus hired—and the hope dies in my chest.

Noah kneels next to the ashes that were Amelia. "I don't understand," he says, letting his fingers drift toward the pile. "Look what you did!" he yells at Cyrus, standing up. "You killed Rebecca."

Cyrus laughs. "Don't be such an idiot, Noah. I thought you were smarter than that. I thought you were worthy of my secrets, my knowledge."

Noah pales. "I don't understand," he says for the second time.

"Come on, boy! Don't tell me you forgot our conversations after school. About science. About alchemy. About the physical properties of the human soul—"

"Mr. Shaw?" Noah furrows his brow.

"—about immortality," Cyrus finishes.

Noah's eyes fly open. I see in them the first dim glimmer of understanding. He doesn't speak.

"You could have been one of us," Cyrus says sadly. "You could have lived forever. But unfortunately, you fell in love with the wrong girl." He waves the gun in my direction and cocks the trigger. The small clicking sound sends fingers of dread through my cold heart.

He aims at Noah's chest. "I'm sorry," says Cyrus. "Believe it or not, I am. You had such promise, more than I've seen in hundreds of years."

I start to shake. "Cyrus, don't. Leave him alone. I'll go with you right now. We can take new bodies and move on, just like you wanted. Just please, don't do this." I silently curse the pleading note in my voice.

Cyrus shakes his head. "Nice try, Sera. But Noah has to

go. Once he's gone, you'll remember how you really feel. How much you love me." His voice softens. "But just to prove I'm not as cruel as you think I am, I'll let you say good-bye. Go ahead." He gestures toward me with the gun. I take a tentative step toward Noah, and when he doesn't shoot, I take another.

Out of the corner of my eye, I see movement. I don't turn my head. Sébastien is moving slowly, carefully, toward Cyrus. But Cyrus is concentrating hard on Noah and me and doesn't see him yet.

"Cyrus is right, Noah," I say flatly. "You're just a human distraction. You were fun while you lasted." He's bewildered, scared, angry. It breaks my heart. I look up toward Cyrus for confirmation, then risk pulling Noah close, into a quick hug. "Noah," I breathe into his ear. "Whatever happens next, I need you to do exactly what I say. Even if I tell you to run. Especially then. Please trust me."

"What *are* you?" he whispers.

I shake my head, ignoring his question. "And I want you to know that I love you. I haven't always been honest—I *couldn't* be. But I love you, so much."

Cyrus laughs from above, bitterly. "He's a boy, Sera. He doesn't even know your *name*. He hasn't been by your side for six hundred years. He could never know you like I know you. And now he'll never get the chance." He raises the gun—

Sébastien leaps toward Cyrus, throwing him to the ground—
And at the same instant, I step in front of Noah.

Another gunshot splits the night into halves: *before* and *after*.

Sébastien was a second too late.

The pain is brilliant. It rips through me in every color, like a palette where Kailey might dip her brush to make magical creatures come to life: angels, fairies, dragons. Tongues of fire lick the side of my body. Fire and water, dripping to the rough asphalt ground.

Except it's not water; it's blood. My blood, Kailey's blood. It doesn't make any difference; they are the same.

"Noah, run!" I yell. Or I think I do. Is that my voice?

The pain takes shape. It stands up. It walks toward me. It lifts its boot above my ribs and stomps. I cry out.

Dimly, the sounds of struggle. Blows landing on flesh. Somewhere, Charlotte screaming.

The pain must have a conscience. It must have decided I've had enough. It strokes my face, it presses itself to my broken side, nuzzles me like a cat, like Luna.

Noah is staring at my face. He's terribly pale. "Kailey?" he asks. "Or are they telling the truth? You have a different name?" His voice sounds thick and slow.

Why is he still here? Sirens, blood-red sirens snake through the misty night. Coming closer.

"I said to leave," I whisper, as the pain changes its mind, knifes through my lungs. I arch my back.

"I can't," he swears.

"Noah. Listen to her." Charlotte's brogue. Oh, how I've missed it.

"She needs to go to the hospital." Noah's voice cracks.

"We'll take care of her."

"But what if she dies?" he pleads. The sirens grow louder.

"She won't. I'll make sure of that."

"You can't. She's been *shot*."

"If this body fails, I'll find her another. Now *go*."

With great effort, I open my eyes. Noah is staring at me. With—what? Love? Horror? I'll never know. He turns away from me, a sob wracking his body, and stumbles into the mist. The mist that weaves around me, that puts out fire, that lifts me up to a raw silk meadow, and it's green, but more than green. It's a color I've never seen before with any human eyes I've possessed.

Footsteps, sirens, shouts. Nothing is the right color.

The gun goes off again.

Fire and ice twist inside me, and the sound of their struggle is the sound of my blood, pumping to the ground.

My eyes close, and I know no more.

FORTY-TWO

The girl is painting my portrait.

She dips her brush in water, then holds it poised over a tray of paints, biting her lip in indecision. Her hair is dark blond, grazing her chin in waves. Her gray-green eyes flick to me, then back to the canvas.

"You know," she says, "this would be a lot easier if you took off your mask."

I hurry to untie the satin ribbons that hold the mask to my face. I had forgotten I was wearing it. "Of course, sorry." I set the mask in my lap, admiring the molded leather, the way it curls out in a brilliant golden spray at the forehead.

"I wanted to be Athena. The warrior goddess," I explain somewhat lamely. How long have I been wasting her time, trying to have my portrait painted with a mask on?

She doesn't seem annoyed, though. "Much better," she murmurs. "It's really coming together now. You can move around, if you want. I know it's hard to hold the same position for so long."

"Thank you." I stretch gratefully, noting the ache in my ribs and taking a deep breath. It smells like jasmine for some reason. A thought occurs to me. "Who hired you to do my portrait?"

She waves her hand in the air. "This one's on the house. I need the practice. I'm still learning."

I relax. "You must be pretty good, though."

"I'm all right," she smiles. "Getting better all the time."

"Forgive me," I say. "I'm not sure what's wrong with me, but I seem to have forgotten your name."

"You'll remember it soon enough," she replies cryptically, chewing on the edge of her paintbrush. I feel myself blushing—she's so kind, and despite what she says, I have no idea what to call her. How inconsiderate I am.

The door to the studio opens, bringing with it a floral breeze, heady and sweet. A thin girl with shaggy brown hair walks in, a guitar strapped to her back. Her piercing green eyes blink at me in confusion.

350

"Oh," the brunette says. "I didn't realize you were busy. I didn't expect her to be here."

The artist chuckles. "She's not staying," she answers from where she sits on a weathered redwood bench.

"I see." The brunette moves to stand behind the artist's back, looking at the canvas. "Lovely work, as always."

"Thank you," the artist replies, smiling. "I'm not quite done."

"Can I see?" I ask.

The artist frowns, tucking her blond bangs behind one ear. "I'm not sure." She cocks her head, listening, then sighs. "All right. I suppose it's time, after all."

I stand, a wave of pain crossing the cramped muscles in my right side. I wonder how long I've been sitting here. How did I even get here?

The artist turns the canvas toward me.

She's painted a girl with short, dark blond hair and gray-green eyes, hovering in the sky at sunset over the bare roof of a cathedral. Wings sprout from her back in shimmering hues, in almost every color I can think of.

I whip my head to the artist. "You made a mistake," I say, feeling rude but determined to point it out. "You painted yourself."

She arches an eyebrow, amused. "Did I?" she asks, gray-green eyes sparkling. The other girl seems to find this funny, too. She wraps her arms around the artist's waist, chuckling softly.

"Yes," I insist.

With a dramatic sigh, she reaches underneath the easel and pulls out a mirror. "Okay, so how would you have done it?" she asks.

I decide to humor her, bringing the mirror to my eyes.

And in an instant, I remember.

"Kailey," I whisper.

"I'm kind of beyond names now," she answers, holding her hands wide.

My throat constricts. Suddenly I am in her arms, smelling her jasmine perfume. "I'm sorry, Kailey. So sorry."

"Don't be," she says. "This is how it was meant to be, Sera."

I pull back, looking again at her painting. "Why did you give *me* wings?" I ask, upset. "*You* deserve them. You always wanted them."

"I have them, silly." And for a split-second, she does: great, snowy white wings, gone so quickly I wonder if I imagined them. "Besides," she adds, "yours are *bird* wings." She sounds offended that I couldn't tell the difference.

"Because I'm no angel," I say bitterly.

"No," she answers, putting her hands on my face—on *her* face. "Because you were caged, and now you can fly."

Taryn nods. "Kailey," she says, and they both look upward, as though they hear voices that are silent to me. "It's time for her to go."

"But I have so much to ask you, so many questions—"

"Shh," Kailey murmurs. "You need to go back. To Noah, to Leyla, to everyone."

"But your family . . ."

"I know." She nods sadly. "They don't know that I'm gone. But the thing is, I'm not. Not really. It's no use worrying them. They'll be here soon enough."

"How soon?" I must look concerned, because she puts her hand on my shoulder.

"Time moves differently for me now. Don't worry about them. They're fine. Years, hours, whatever. It's all the same." She smiles.

I feel a tug at my navel and look down, expecting to see the ghost of my silver cord. But there's nothing.

"Now go," Kailey murmurs.

"Take care of Luna," Taryn asks. "By the way, her original name was *so* much more bad-ass. But Luna will do just fine."

"Oh, and tell Bryan to keep writing," Kailey adds. "I was such a jackass about that. He wrote this one poem— I can't remember the name . . ." She pauses, tapping her paintbrush against her coral mouth. "Oh! I've got it. It was called 'So-Called Yellow Laboratory.' It was pretty good. I was *really* mean about it, though."

"I'll tell him," I promise. I feel dizzy, like I'm in a deep cavern, their voices echoing back and forth.

"Sera," Kailey's voice turns serious. "You have my body. You have my name. You have my life. *Don't waste it.*"

And then she reaches out and pushes me.

I blink. A curtain of red hair falls over my face.

"Careful!" Charlotte gasps, over the squeal of car tires. I'm thrown to the side again, my face pressed against slick leather.

"We don't have much time," Sébastien says from the driver's seat.

"I know. We'll take the first human we see." Wetness falls on my face, and I realize Charlotte is crying. "Sera! You're awake? Hang in there, we're about to get you a new body."

I open my mouth, lick my lips. "Hospital," I manage to say. "Please."

"It's too late for that," Charlotte whispers. She takes my hands.

You have my body.

"It's not too late," I choke, my voice growing stronger. "Sébastien, please. This is my choice."

"Don't listen to her." Charlotte's voice shakes. *You have my name.*

"Don't be like Cyrus. Let me choose," I say, weeping. I think of my mortal self, a fourteen-year-old girl on an ancient bridge over the Thames, a girl who would have died if not for Cyrus's burning elixir. A girl who never got to choose her destiny but had it forced upon her.

You have my life.

"Damn it, Sera. Damn you." Charlotte's voice is quiet. "You win." And then, louder, stronger, for Sébastien to hear: "The hospital. Hurry!"

The car accelerates as Sébastien changes course, screeching and flying through the streets of Berkeley. I close my eyes. The next thing I know, we've skidded to a stop outside the hospital's emergency entrance.

"You're sure, Sera?" Sébastien asks, his voice calm, as Charlotte continues to cry.

I nod once, barely.

Charlotte takes a deep breath, then throws open the car door.

"Gunshot victim!" I hear her yell. *"Help!"*

Don't waste it.

FORTY-THREE

The voice breaks through the fog surrounding me.

"Please, let me see her."

Noah, I try to say. But I have no mouth. I'm made of mist. On weakened wings I drift.

"Kailey, can you hear me?"

I try to move, to throw my spirit fists against the window that keeps him from me. I can see him, his crow-black hair and blue eyes, on the other side.

"Seraphina," he says softly, almost like a question, like a palm held to the window on a rainy night. And the glass breaks.

"You called me by my real name." My voice sounds strange, raspy.

"Thank god, you're awake," Noah exclaims. "Nurse—"

I reach out and take his hand. "Wait," I murmur. "You know my name. I've wanted you to say it for so long."

His face comes into focus with the rest of the room. It's dark outside; rain lashes at the hospital windows. I look down at the plastic bracelet encircling my wrist, nearly identical to the one I was wearing just over a month ago. *Kailey Morgan. F. Age 16.*

"None of this seems real," Noah murmurs. His hand feels so warm in mine.

"How much do you know?" I ask. "Did Sébastien and Charlotte—"

"They wouldn't tell me anything, except not to talk to the police. Not to talk to anyone." He pauses, choosing his words carefully. "Who *are* they? I keep replaying it in my mind. That girl with the red hair—Charlotte?"

I nod.

"She said she'd get you a new body." It's a question, not a statement.

"Yes," I answer. We've come too far for me to lie now. He saw Amelia crumble to dust in Rebecca's body. But I've never done this before, and I'm afraid—*terrified*—that when Noah knows what I am, he'll run from me.

357

He lets go of my hand, and my fingers instinctively grasp the cotton blanket at my side. I need to hold onto something. "What did she mean?" he asks.

I'm at one of those doorways through which there is no going back. Time will forever be divided into two halves: into a before and after. Before and after I shattered Noah's innocence, before I laid my secrets bare before his judgment.

"I'm going to tell you everything," I say, "if you'll promise to hear me out. Because it's crazy and you probably won't believe it. But it's all true." I pause and take a shuddering breath. He stands and moves over to the window. I note the distance he's put between us—but at least he's listening.

"The night I was shot, you saw unbelievable things. You saw Rebecca's body turn to dust. But it wasn't Rebecca—it was another soul living inside her. Just like . . . just like I'm living inside Kailey." My voice grows thick. I swallow hard and continue. "I was born in the year 1334, in London. When I was fourteen, I met a boy named Cyrus at a masquerade ball. He was an alchemist. He's the same person you knew as Mr. Shaw. The same person who put his soul inside Madison. You heard him say as much."

"He said he was in love with you." Noah's voice is barely audible.

"Not long after we met," I continue, choosing not to answer his remark, "I was stabbed on a bridge and left for dead. Cyrus saved me. He gave me the elixir that made me immortal. He freed my soul from my dying body, and I took another."

"The silver cord," Noah whispers, "that connects the soul to the body. It's real? Mr. Shaw told me about it."

"Yes," I say. "Yes. Mr. Shaw was Cyrus. He's been alive this whole time. As have I."

"But Kailey—"

I forge ahead. "Two months ago, I ran away from Cyrus. He's damaged. He's cruel. He hurt me, many times." Noah's arms are crossed across his chest. His hands clench into fists. "I saw a car accident in Jack London Square. A sixteen-year-old girl driving her brother's car. She was broken, Noah. Bleeding. She was about to die."

"Kailey," he whispers.

"Kailey," I agree. "I tried to save her, I really did. But I ended up accidentally taking her body instead. I didn't mean to, and when I woke up in her body, in her *life*, I thought this was the end of the road for me. Until I met you." The ghosts of jasmine perfume and gasoline rise around me now, the ghost of lost girls painting portraits in a dream.

"Stop." His voice is harsh. "Don't say anything else." I think suddenly of my mortal father—how he cursed me and spat on me when I tried to tell him what I was. As far as he was concerned, I was already dead.

"Do you believe me?" I ask, my words laced with sorrow. I'm not even sure I want to know the answer. I wonder if it would have been better to take another body and try to make Noah fall in love with me again as someone else. But then I think of Kailey—*Don't waste it*—and know that I owe her this.

"I shouldn't believe you," he answers finally, stepping toward me in the dim orange light. He sits heavily next to me on the narrow hospital bed, the movement sending a rip of pain through my side. But that's not why tears squeeze out from my eyes.

"But you do anyway?" I ask.

He doesn't answer me, just reaches out to take my head in his hands and presses his forehead to my own. He breathes in, out. We breathe the same breath.

"Just give me some time," he says finally, his words stabbing into my heart like hundreds of miniature daggers.

"I love you," I answer, and his hands clutch me harder.

But he doesn't say it back. He pulls away and stands up. "Some time," he repeats, moving toward the door. And then he's gone.

Charlotte bursts in. "Thank god you're awake, Sera." She's followed closely by Sébastien.

"Quickly," he murmurs. "Before the parents come in. We need to get you out of here."

"I'm not leaving," I say.

"Cyrus was shot," Charlotte tells me. I know what's coming next before she even says it.

"He's not dead, is he?" Trust Cyrus to be indestructible.

"Very much alive," she agrees. "And he knows who you are."

"Is he here?" I ask, my heart racing in sudden panic.

"No," she replies. "Sera, he was taken into custody."

FORTY-FOUR

"Madison Cortez," I tell the security guard at Napa State Hospital, previously known as Napa State Asylum for the Insane. He shudders.

"Unit T-Fourteen?" He gestures me toward a waiting area, and I nod, wincing at the pain that blossoms on my right side. Apparently, the bullet wound was "clean," a funny term for its destructive path through my body, shattering two ribs and grazing my right lung.

I nearly died, they say. I was lucky.

The weary guard leads me beyond the razor wire that rings the hospital's secure unit, reserved for the most dangerous patients: the criminals who are mentally unfit to stand trial for their crimes.

Charlotte and Sébastien—in their guise as the "concerned passersby" who had the quick wits to take me to the hospital—have continued to visit, bringing me what news of Cyrus they could. Apparently "Madison" was caught the night of the dance in the middle of Garber Park, bleeding from a gunshot wound that was determined to be self-inflicted. She didn't come quietly, though. She managed to empty her gun's clip at the arresting officers before she was taken, and continued to struggle even once handcuffed.

"It was the strangest thing," said one of the officers in a news report. "She kept trying to *kiss* me. But it wasn't deranged so much as, well, *terrifying*." He added that Madison burst out laughing when asked about the whereabouts of Rebecca Sawyer, insisting she'd been dead for weeks.

The guard escorts me through security and down the hall, past a row of closed, windowless doors. "She's being kept in solitary," the guard tosses over his shoulder by way of explanation. "She wouldn't stop talking about something—Astronomy? Algorithms?"

"Alchemy," I offer.

"That's it. Strange stuff, very disturbing to the other patients. Plus we have to keep her restrained. She keeps trying to kiss everyone."

I keep my mouth shut as he punches a code into a keypad and opens another door. The room that I step into is stark and bright, walled in white brick and containing a single visiting station. Several cameras are trained on the plastic chair where the guard tells me to sit in front of a thick pane of glass. "Wait here," he instructs me, then departs. And I'm alone.

I hear a muffled click as a door opens on the other side of the glass. My breath quickens. The ache in my ribs becomes an insistent shriek.

Two orderlies appear, holding the slender frame that would appear to anyone else as an average eighteen-year-old girl, her skin as dull as the white cinder blocks behind her.

Cyrus.

His arm is in a cast—the aftermath of the second gunshot, the one I heard right before I passed out. Apparently Cyrus had aimed at Noah again, but Sébastien managed to tackle him in time, and he shot his own elbow instead. Even with the cast, he's handcuffed.

Sébastien and Charlotte had both begged me not to come. But I had to see him for myself: the man who kept me in his cage for hundreds of years, now trapped in his own glass-walled prison. Shackled inside a secure room, inside a secure building, on a property lined with guards and barbed wire.

Cyrus takes his seat on the other side of the glass and stares at me. His eyes—usually ice-blue, now warm brown and flecked with hazel—flash in anger.

I pick up the waxy black telephone receiver and hold it to my ear. He does the same. For a long time we don't speak.

"You're hurt," he says finally. "I never wanted you to be hurt."

"You shouldn't have shot me, then," I say, my words laced with anger.

"I didn't," he whispers. "I was aiming for someone else, if you recall."

I glance upward, at the cameras recording this entire conversation. Then again, I don't suppose it matters what Cyrus says. He's been declared criminally insane.

"Why couldn't you just let me go?" I say, instead of arguing.

He sighs, scratching his forehead with his palm. His wrists are bruised and raw from the handcuffs. "I've asked myself that same question, many times."

"Don't say it's because you love me," I interrupt. "Because you don't even know what that means."

"Loving you is *all* I know, Sera. It's the only thing I've ever been certain of." His voice cracks. Suddenly, he's not my captor anymore, not the man who's been hurting me for hundreds of years—he's my young scientist, broken and scared, stroking my hair on a bridge. A boy who loved a girl once upon a time, who would have done anything to keep her safe.

I'm surprised to feel a single tear sliding down my cheek.

"Everything I did, every person I hurt, it was all for you," Cyrus tells me.

I pity him. "We're broken, Cyrus. It will never be how it was."

"Never say never," he argues, with what could almost pass for a smile. "You know better than anyone that life isn't short."

"It's been too long," I answer.

"Sometimes it feels like this whole awful life is just a dream. A chemical reaction in my head. That I'll wake up, and we'll be together at that masquerade ball. We'll dance the whole night, and I'll ask your father for your hand." He cocks his head. "Do you know what I mean?"

"You can't undo what's happened," I answer. "I should go."

"Wait," he says, as I turn to go. "Please, Sera. Don't leave me."

"This is good-bye, Cyrus."

"Maybe," he says affably, "maybe not. But the moment I get out, I'll come looking for you."

Suddenly, I'm so angry I want to reach out and smack him all the way back to solitary. "I'll be long gone by then," I say, but he persists.

"Where are you headed?"

"I know there are others out there, Cyrus. I read your book."

He nods. "I will always find you," he promises. "You can't escape destiny."

"Destiny? As if there is such a thing." When I laugh in his face, he smiles at me in pride.

"That's my girl," he says delightedly.

"Good-*bye*, Cyrus."

I hang up the phone and stand as the orderlies start to pull Cyrus away. He doesn't break eye contact with me until he's literally dragged through the door. "Good-bye," I whisper even though I know he can't hear it.

FORTY-FIVE

Luna crouches in the grass, tail switching as she watches the nonchalant butterfly. Finally, with a great burst of speed, she pounces, but the winged insect has already fluttered maddeningly out of her reach. Charlotte and Sébastien explode in laughter, delighted by the novelty of a cat that doesn't hate them. Luna is not impressed. She stares at them balefully, her dignity wounded, before licking her silky gray paw as if to say, "That butterfly? I didn't want it, anyway. I meant to let it escape."

"There's nothing we can say to make you come with us?" Charlotte tries again, but I shake my head. My place is here in Berkeley, in this verdant backyard with its stately redwood tree, this dilapidated tree house where a certain mortal boy kissed me for the first time.

"I can't wait to hear what you find," I answer.

"Or *who* we find, Sébastien corrects me with a grin, his teeth very white against his chocolate skin. The two of them were as stunned as I had been to see the hidden page in Cyrus's book. Their sense of betrayal was quickly overcome by their thirst for adventure, and they made plans to set off at once in search of the lost Incarnate covens. Sébastien's already hired a swarm of private investigators to convert the seven-hundred-year-old list of names into viable leads.

"And you have the phone, right? You have to always keep it with you, Sera." He nods, satisfied, when I dig the tiny cell phone out of my pocket and show it to him.

"The batphone shall always be charged," I vow.

Posing as concerned relatives, Sébastien and Charlotte have bribed a guard at the hospital to call this number if there's ever an incident with "Madison." Cyrus will have close to ten years in Madison's body before it begins to fail. If in that time he ever manages to kiss one of the guards, if anything happens to him, they'll call and alert me within minutes. If that phone rings, I need to leave, no matter what, no matter where I am.

"And *you* promise you'll keep in touch," I say.

I know they think I'm crazy not to go with them. They don't understand why I would choose to be a high school student over traveling the world with my own kind. But they haven't lived as Kailey, here in Berkeley, so they can never really understand. *You have my life. Don't waste it.*

"What are you going to do about Noah?" Sébastien asks gently.

I bite my lip and look down at the yellow sour-grass blossoms that carpet the Morgans' lawn. Noah never came back to see me at the hospital, and some instinct prevents me from contacting him. Is he afraid of me now? "He won't say anything," I tell Sébastien. "We can trust him."

"That's not what I meant," he replies. "We thought you were going to make him one of us. Why else would you tell a human the truth?"

"I don't even have the elixir," I protest. "And as for making it myself, well . . ." I'm distracted by the pointed stare Sébastien shoots Charlotte. They're communicating without words. Even in my bewilderment, I'm happy to see that they've grown so close.

"Sera," Charlotte says at last. "I have something for you." She pulls her black backpack into her lap and rummages inside, finally unearthing the very last thing I would have expected: a silver clutch purse marred with streaks of dried blood. The bag that Cyrus was carrying the night of the dance.

Charlotte opens the clasp with milk-white fingers and pulls out the small glass vial. The vial that Cyrus had worn around his neck for the last six centuries.

"It's yours now," she murmurs, pressing it into my palm. "To use . . . or not. Keep it safe."

"I won't be like him," I promise. "We can share it. Char, if you ever need it—"

"I know where to find you," she finishes for me. "And I plan on visiting often."

I stare wonderingly at the tiny silver object in my palm. So much death from one small vial. So much life, too. The Morgans' back door opens with a creak, and I quickly stuff the elixir in my pocket.

Luna prances beside Bryan as he strides across the grass. "I have been instructed by our dear mother to invite the heroes to stay for dinner," he announces gallantly, referring to Charlotte and Sébastien. I smile. Mr. and Mrs. Morgan adore my rescuers. *So cultured,* they say. *So full of stories.*

"Heroes, huh?" repeats Sébastien, amused. "I feel like I should have an epic poem written about me. All I did was drive Kailey to the hospital." Hearing Kailey's name on Sébastien's lips is almost as strange as when Noah called me Seraphina, but I like it. My two worlds are merging together.

"I know who could write that poem," I add, grinning

wickedly. A thought occurs to me. "Hey, Bryan, didn't you write one called . . ." I search my memory, conjuring the words back through the fog, fully prepared for him to laugh at me or give me his trademark *my-sister-has-totally-lost-it* eye roll. "'So-Called Yellow . . .'" I wrinkle my nose, trying to remember the rest.

"'So-Called Yellow *Laboratory*,'" he quips, his face appearing at the edge of the tree house. "See, it's a play on words. A yellow Lab is a dog, right? Anyway, you already dissed it plenty. You don't need to embarrass me in front of your hero friends."

A chill runs up my spine and crowns me with ice.

"What's the matter, Kailey?" Bryan asks, worried. "You look like you saw a ghost. Are you feeling okay?"

"I'm fine," I manage to say. I look up at the redwood branches. A gust of wind disturbs the calm dusk, showering me with spent, fragrant needles. *You have my body. You have my name.* I shiver, tilting my head back again. The last honeyed drops of sunlight cover the branches.

Thank you, Kailey, I say silently.

The sound of wood scraping gravel drags across the dusk. I whip my head toward the gate, where a tall, dark-haired boy is stepping into the yard.

"That's definitely our cue to go," Charlotte announces, stepping neatly over the side of the rough platform. "To *dinner,*" she clarifies to my fallen face. "We'll be waiting for you."

They depart. I wait in the tree house, in the now-calm twilight, as Noah crosses the yard.

"I missed you," I greet him when he climbs up over the ladder to join me in the tree house.

"I believe you," he says at the same time.

In the yard below, the wind chimes stir. I look down and see Luna precariously perched on the eave above them, batting the metal cylinders with her paw.

"I was afraid," he whispers.

"Of me?" I ask. I'm a little sad but not surprised.

"Of *losing* you," he corrects me.

"Oh, Noah," I say, reaching for his face.

"You don't understand, Kailey." He hesitates. "*Seraphina.* One day you were the girl I'd known my whole life, who I used to play hide-and-seek with. Who forced her way into the forts I built with Bryan."

I smile. Impetuous, temperamental Kailey.

He rakes his hair. "And then one day, without warning, I was in love with you. It was like magic."

My heart flutters. "I'm not magic," I say. "You should know that. I'm a creature of science."

"That's what Mr. Shaw would say."

"What *Cyrus* would say," I amend. "But he's right. You're

the magical one." And he is. Noah was made by the stars, his newly minted soul in its intended body. To me, this is a miracle. This is more amazing than a ghost that takes human form.

"It doesn't matter what you say. Your world is so . . . *big*. And what am I compared to that? How could my tiny existence be enough for you?" The redwood boughs cast shadows on his cheeks, making him look older than he really is.

"I know what you are, Noah. Don't tell me what you're not."

"I know what you are, too."

"Yes," I answer softly. "You do."

The wind stirs. The chimes ring. The night's first beams of starlight make their way to us, glance across his jaw. I wait. He doesn't break his gaze.

"I love you," he says finally.

I find his arms. We find each other. He holds me close, in the tree house that holds us both.

"I want to be like you," he murmurs against my ear. "I want you to change me the way that Cyrus changed you."

I pull back, appraise his face. "But I *like* your body," I protest.

He throws his head back and laughs. "Are you hitting on me? Why, thank you, Kailey. I mean Seraphina."

"You can still call me Kailey, if you want," I offer.

He cups my jaw, his face serious once again. "I mean it, though. I want to go with you, wherever it is. I know what I'm asking. You know I do."

"I'm not going anywhere," I answer. "Not anytime soon, and not without you." I take his hands in mine. "Let me tell you this. The answer to your question is *yes*. Of course I want to spend forever with you. But you have to do one thing for me in return: You have to wait. There's no rush."

He nods.

"The next time you ask me this, I'll honor your request. So I want you to be sure—be *very* sure—before you ask. Promise me." It has to be his choice. I am not Cyrus. I won't decide for him.

"I promise," he repeats, his lips moving closer. And then we kiss under sighing stars, under ghostly skies.

The back door slams open. "Noah!" Bryan calls. "Kailey! Seriously, guys. I'm *hungry*. You have the rest of your lives to kiss."

He's right. We do.

  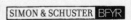

Some loves
are worth dying for.

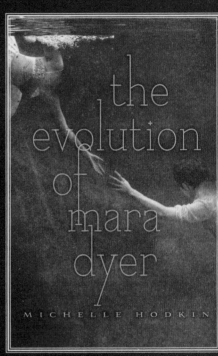

Others are worth
killing for.